The Orchid Mystery

The Cambridge Mysteries Book One

NANCY L. MANGAN

CAVEL PRESS

KENMORE, WA

A Camel Press book published by Epicenter Press

Epicenter Press
6524 NE 181st St.
Suite 2
Kenmore, WA 98028

For more information go to:
www.Camelpress.com
www.cambridgecoffeeandcrime.co.uk

All rights reserved. No part of this book may be reproduced or transmitted in any form or by any means, electronic or mechanical, including photocopying, recording, or any information storage and retrieval system, without permission in writing from the publisher.

No generative AI was used in the conceptualization, planning, drafting, or creative writing of this work. No permission is given for the use of this material for AI training purposes.

This is a work of fiction. Names, characters, places, brands, media, and incidents are either the product of the author's imagination or are used fictitiously.

Cover design by Scott Book
Design by Melissa Vail Coffman

The Orchid Mystery
Copyright © 2026 by Nancy L. Mangan

Library of Congress Control Number: 2025942367

ISBN: 978-1-68492-279-6 (Trade Paper)
ISBN: 978-1-68492-280-2 (eBook)

For my parents, who, though sadly no longer here, instilled in me an enduring love of reading.

Acknowledgments

I would like to thank all my friends who have supported me on this journey. My deepest gratitude goes to my family, Tess, James, and little William, for their love, patience, and gift of a laptop.

Special thanks must go to my dear friend Marie, whose unwavering positivity has sustained me over many years. Marie listened patiently and offered invaluable encouragement as I explored countless plots and characters, always believing in my work even when I had doubts.

My heartfelt appreciation also goes to my friend, Caroline Biggs, whose resilience and determination have inspired me profoundly. Caroline's wonderful work, The Spinning House, introduced me to the intriguing possibility of delving into Cambridge's darker histories, albeit fictionalized in my own narrative.

To everyone who has supported me in this endeavour, my sincerest thanks.

Prologue

THE NIGHT AIR WAS THICK, THE kind that made you question if the seasons had shifted when you weren't looking. Cambridge had a way of holding onto the mist, clutching it like an old miser hoarding coins, and tonight was no exception. It pooled in corners, blurred the edges of buildings, and softened the city's ancient stone into something dreamlike. The early summer air carried the deceptive tranquility of Easter Full Term; an illusion, for Cambridge never truly slept.

For now, the city rested. The usual symphony, bicycle wheels skittering over cobblestones, the clipped voices of students convinced of their own brilliance, was absent, replaced by an eerie hush. Occasionally, a distant footstep or muffled conversation would emerge from the mist, only to be swallowed back into silence. Yet there was always the chance of a lingering figure in the shadows—a student who had overstayed their welcome in the buttery or one sneaking back through a side gate after an illicit night out, hoping the porters were feeling charitable.

In the heart of the city, where narrow alleys twisted like an old tapestry's threads, a lone individual moved with quiet certainty. Their long coat billowed slightly as they slipped into the ancient walls of St Michael's College, one of those institutions that relished being described as "hallowed" as much as it did "exclusive." The College, older than most could trace its lineage, loomed through the mist, its heavy stone facades watching in silent judgment.

The newcomer hesitated at the entrance, casting a glance over their shoulder. Cambridge was a city of secrets. They whispered in the ivy clinging to walls and lay buried beneath the weight of centuries. Satisfied they were unobserved, or that any onlooker would have the courtesy to pretend otherwise, the figure passed through the gates with practiced ease.

Beyond the cloisters, the path led through a succession of courtyards, each more austere than the last, before opening onto a hidden garden. St Michael's Garden was one of those concealed spaces known only to those who understood its worth. By day, it offered quiet reflection; by night, under moonlight and shadow, it transformed into something else entirely. The hedges thickened, the trees loomed, and what was familiar became something more uncertain.

The visitor entered through a narrow gate, its hinges groaning softly in protest. For a moment, they stood still, absorbing the night's sounds: an owl's distant call, the wind stirring leaves with a curiously deliberate touch. No other presence revealed itself. Moving with the deliberation of someone carrying out a plan, they crossed to the center of the garden, where an aged stone bench stood beneath a gnarled oak. Countless students had perched there over the years, some lost in thought, others feigning productivity. Tonight, however, it served another purpose.

From within their coat, the individual withdrew an orchid, a pale bloom that appeared to hold its own faint glow in the darkness. With precise care, they set it upon the bench, its fragile petals stark against the cold stone. A silent offering. A message. They regarded it for a lingering moment before turning on their heel and vanishing into the night, the garden gate whispering shut behind them.

The city remained oblivious to what had just transpired. The orchid, left in solitude, was the only witness to whatever intent had placed it there. Secrets, as any scholar worth their salt would attest, have a habit of revealing themselves at the most inconvenient moments.

As the night deepened, the mist thickened, wrapping Cambridge in an almost possessive embrace. Familiar landmarks—the spires, the bridges, the venerable Colleges—dissolved into ghostly outlines. Somewhere beyond, the bells of Great St Mary's tolled the hour, their resonance swallowed by the heavy air.

The lone visitor wove through the empty city with the same quiet purpose, steps unwavering. They passed the market square, where shuttered stalls stood like silent sentinels, and crossed the bridges where the Cam's dark waters reflected the waning moonlight. The city fell away behind them, its historic weight giving way to the open countryside beyond. Here, the mist was thinner, the air lighter, and for the first time, they paused. The task was complete. Whatever it had been, it was finished.

Yet even as they stood on the outskirts of Cambridge, a trace of hesitation remained. The orchid was no ordinary gesture. It was a message, carefully placed for someone who would understand its significance. A reminder of a past that had refused to be buried.

A faint smile touched their lips, the kind that never quite reached the eyes, before they turned and disappeared into the darkness. The city, in its oblivious rhythm, would soon wake. The mist would lift, and Cambridge would resume its careful order, but that orchid, waiting in the garden's hush, was about to stir the waters of a place that prided itself on stillness.

In the coming days, life within St Michael's College would carry on, breakfasts taken, debates waged, lectures attended with varying degrees of enthusiasm. The storm, though, long dormant beneath layers of tradition and propriety, was about to break. The secrets held so carefully within these ancient walls were about to come to light, whether Cambridge was ready or not.

As dawn began its slow unveiling of the city, one thing was certain: nothing would be quite the same again.

Chapter 1

THE FIRST LIGHT OF DAWN EDGED its way over the rooftops of Cambridge, painting the university town in a soft, golden hue. The River Cam, still partially shrouded in mist, wound its way through the city like a ribbon of silver, offering a quiet contrast to the awakening day. The streets, normally bustling with life, were mostly silent, disturbed only by the distant hum of a milk float, the soft click of bicycle wheels on cobblestones, and the gentle rustle of leaves stirred by a tentative breeze. It looked set to be a warm summer in 1977—though, with any luck, not quite the furnace of the previous year. The summer of '76 had been a scorcher, the hottest since 1911, and no one was in a hurry to relive that particular ordeal.

St Michael's College, one of Cambridge's oldest and most venerable institutions, stood proudly amidst this scene of early morning tranquility. Its stone walls, weathered by centuries of wind and rain, bore the marks of history with a dignified grace. The towering gatehouse, crowned with crenellations, cast a long shadow across the meticulously manicured lawns of the quadrangle. For now, the College appeared peaceful, untouched by the world beyond its gates.

As day began to break, emerging from one of the College buildings was George Henson, the gardener. An older man with a weather-beaten face and a slight stoop, George had been tending to the grounds of St Michael's for as long as anyone could remember. His hands, calloused from years of toil, and his deep-set eyes, rich with the wisdom of experience, spoke of a life spent in the service of the College's gardens. Every morning, without fail, he would take a solitary walk through the grounds, ensuring that everything was in order before the students and fellows began their day.

Today, as George walked through the quadrangle, his footsteps barely audible on the stone paths, he felt an unusual stillness, a sense of unease that gnawed at him. The mist, instead of dissipating with the dawn, clung stubbornly to the walls, and an unnatural silence hung over the College like an unwelcome guest. Come on, George, it's just another morning, he told himself, but the knot in his stomach only tightened.

He quickened his pace, his keen eyes scanning the familiar surroundings for anything amiss. The ancient stone buildings, the neatly trimmed hedges, the well-tended flowerbeds, all appeared as they should.

It wasn't long before he found the source of his unease.

At the far end of the quadrangle, nestled against the College's ancient walls, lay St. Michael's Garden. This garden was George's pride and joy, a place of quiet beauty where he had spent countless hours tending to the flowers, shrubs, and trees. As he approached the entrance, he noticed something that made his heart skip a beat: the gate, usually kept securely locked, was slightly ajar.

Odd, George thought, frowning as he gently pushed the gate open. The hinges creaked softly in the still morning air. He stepped into the garden; his eyes immediately drawn to the stone bench beneath the spreading branches of the old oak tree. There, on the bench, was a sight that made his blood run cold.

A man lay motionless on the bench, his head resting awkwardly against the stone. His eyes were closed, his face pale and still, and he was dressed in the somber black gown of an academic, the long folds of fabric draped over the bench like a shroud. Beside him, placed with unsettling care, was a single flower, a pale orchid, its delicate petals stark against the cold, grey stone.

No . . . it can't be . . . George's mind struggled to make sense of what he was seeing. The man on the bench wasn't just any academic; it was Dr. Charles Atherton, one of the College's most respected fellows and a renowned botanical historian. George had seen him countless times, striding through the College with a confidence that bordered on arrogance. Now he was so still, so unnaturally still.

A wave of panic surged through George. This wasn't right. This wasn't how the day was supposed to begin. He had only intended to check the gardens, make sure everything was in order, and go on with his day. However, this . . . this was something from a nightmare.

He took a tentative step closer, his heart pounding in his chest. "Dr. Atherton . . . ?" The words escaped in a whisper, as though speaking to them any louder might make the scene before him more real. There was no response, no movement. Atherton's skin was as pale as the orchid beside him.

For a moment, George stood frozen, his mind reeling with shock. What do I do? What do I do? The question echoed in his head, but he couldn't find an answer. He knew he had to get help, to tell someone, but his legs felt like they were anchored to the ground.

With a sudden burst of clarity, he remembered the whistle in his pocket. His hands shook as he reached for it, pulling it out and blowing with all his might. The shrill sound cut through the stillness of the morning, sending echoes bouncing off the stone walls. Almost immediately, doors began to open, and figures emerged from the surrounding buildings, their faces etched with confusion and concern.

Among the first to arrive was the College's Master, an elderly man with a stern countenance and an air of authority. He hurried towards George, his eyes widening as he took in the scene.

"What's happened here, George?" he demanded, his voice tight with a mixture of shock and disbelief.

George could only shake his head, his voice trembling as he forced out the words. "It's Dr. Atherton, sir . . . He's . . . he's dead." The words felt foreign on his tongue, as though saying them aloud might somehow make them less true.

The Master's face drained of color as he turned his gaze to the lifeless figure on the bench. For a long moment, he stood in stunned silence, trying to process what he was seeing. This can't be real . . . but no matter how hard he tried, the scene refused to disappear.

Finally, with a deep breath, he straightened, his voice regaining some of its usual authority. "We must notify the authorities at once. This is a matter for the police."

As the College descended into chaos, with students and staff gathering in hushed, anxious groups, George felt a heavy weight settle on his chest. The peaceful world of St Michael's had been irrevocably shattered, and a shadow had fallen over its ancient halls.

Please, let this be a bad dream, George thought desperately, even as he knew, deep down, that it was all too real.

CAMBRIDGE, THAT ELUSIVE JEWEL OF ACADEMIC grandeur, stirred from its nocturnal slumber, draped in a delicate grey mist.

Detective Chief Inspector Jonathan Rievaulx, whose surname, pronounced "ree-voh," was a point of frequent correction—often to his quiet irritation—pedaled through the mist on his well-worn Raleigh bicycle. In his early forties, tall and lean, with dark hair just beginning to show streaks of grey, Rievaulx cut a striking figure against the foggy backdrop. His blue eyes, sharp and observant, mirrored the reflective calm of the morning. Clad in a well-kept, though modestly worn, outfit that hinted at his academic background, he moved with the ease of a man who belonged as much to the university's hallowed halls as he did to the world of criminal investigation.

The soft click of his bicycle wheels against the cobblestones was his only companion in these early hours. This quiet ritual, this communion with a city not yet fully awake, offered Rievaulx a rare moment of peace. In these tranquil interludes, he found the mental clarity needed to untangle the knotted threads of unresolved cases. Today, though, an uneasy premonition gnawed at him, and Rievaulx couldn't shake the feeling that he was on the brink of uncovering something profoundly significant.

His intuition was proven right when a shrill whistle, slicing through the morning's stillness like a knife through silk, abruptly interrupted his reverie. Rievaulx's heart quickened. Without hesitation, he steered his bicycle towards the source of the commotion. The piercing cry had emanated from the direction of St Michael's College, that venerable bastion of academia where tradition held sway like a monarch on its throne.

As Rievaulx approached the College gates, the fog began to lift slightly, revealing a gathering crowd; students in their academic regalia, huddled like anxious birds, their faces pale with a mix of fear and confusion. The cold morning air amplified their distress, their breaths forming frosty tendrils that mingled with the mist. The atmosphere was thick with a palpable, suppressed panic; the kind that follows an unspeakable tragedy when no one quite knows how to react.

Dismounting his bicycle with the practiced ease of a seasoned cyclist, Rievaulx threaded his way through the crowd, his manner outwardly calm, yet his mind was already racing. The onlookers parted reluctantly, their whispered conjectures trailing behind him. The serene garden of St Michael's had been transformed into a grim tableau of horror.

There, on a stone bench, lay the lifeless body of Dr. Charles Atherton, a respected professor of botany. Rievaulx knew Atherton, not personally, but through their shared interest in orchids. Atherton's body was sprawled in an awkward, almost unnatural pose, his eyes wide open and fixed on the drifting mist, as if searching the heavens for answers. Beside him, placed with deliberate care, was a rare orchid, its pale petals glowing with an eerie vibrancy against the pallid morning light. The flower's presence, so out of place amidst the death, spoke volumes, there was clearly a message here, though its meaning remained a mystery.

Rievaulx knelt beside the body, his gaze sweeping over the scene with his practiced detachment. There were no visible signs of violence, no blood, no wounds, no indication of a struggle. Yet the orchid placed there suggested a more elaborate narrative, someone had left behind a cryptic clue rather than merely committing an act of murder.

"Clear the area," he instructed, his voice cutting through the murmur of the crowd with an authoritative edge. "This is now a crime scene."

A gardener, who had been standing nearby, clutching his cap in a state of shock, finally found his voice. "I . . . I found him like this," he stammered, his hands trembling. "I was just doing my rounds, and . . . and there he was. The Master called for the . . . the police."

Rievaulx regarded him with a sharp, assessing gaze. "You did the right thing by alerting us," he said briskly, with a hint of reassurance. "Now, step back and let us take over."

As he spoke, the distant rumble of an approaching car engine intruded upon the scene. A small, boxy red Mini Cooper's headlights piercing the mist like twin blades. The car came to a stop, and Detective Constable Emily Carter stepped out, her face a picture of resolve, tempered by barely concealed anxiety. She was something of an anomaly in the force; a young woman, bright and ambitious, navigating her way in a profession where the old guard still held sway.

She stepped out of her car and stood for several seconds surveying the scene. She wore high-waisted, emerald green flared trousers, a nod to the fashion of the moment, and her blouse, with its vibrant hues and intricate patterns, added a splash of color. Her chestnut brown hair was styled in a sleek bob, framing her face with a modern, sophisticated touch. Her bright, inquisitive brown eyes reflected her eagerness to prove herself in her role as a detective constable.

Her car radio had been blaring ABBA's *Dancing Queen*, the upbeat tempo a jarring contrast to the grim scene she now faced. The cheerful strains of the song lingered in the air, an oddly surreal backdrop to the serious business of murder. As Carter reached in and switched off the engine, the song's infectious rhythm, so at odds with the morning's dark discovery, played on in her mind as she approached the scene. There had been recent legislative changes, the 1976 Police Act, that had officially placed women on an equal footing that hadn't entirely shifted the deeply ingrained attitudes that permeated the police force.

Her role in the force was a testament to the modernity of the 1970s and the evolving landscape of law enforcement, yet the challenge of balancing her new responsibilities with the lingering biases of the old guard was a daily task. Carter knew this all too well, and every step she took was scrutinized, every decision weighed. Whenever she felt herself faltering, Carter would think back to her quiet admiration for that remarkable woman who navigated a male-dominated world with such grace, never disturbing a single masculine ego. Queen Elizabeth II. This year, 1977, was her twenty-fifth on the throne, a milestone being celebrated with great enthusiasm across the country and indeed throughout the Commonwealth.

"Morning, sir," Carter greeted, her voice steady. "What's the situation?"

Rievaulx looked up, his expression grim but not displeased. Carter had answered the call, and that was something. He trusted her instincts, sharp, unflinching, and rarely wrong. She'd earned her place, despite her youth, cutting her teeth in a Midlands city where petty crime had a habit of turning nasty. She had a knack for reading people, picking out the truth from a tangle of half-lies and dodges. Her blunt manner didn't always make her popular, but those who knew her understood the loyalty behind it. Once she had a lead, she was a terrier: determined, relentless, and impossible to shake off.

He gestured towards the body and the orchid. "Dr. Charles Atherton was found dead on that bench. No visible wounds or signs of a struggle. But look at this", he indicated the orchid, its delicate beauty stark against the somber scene.

Carter leaned in to examine the flower, her frown deepening. "An orchid? That's certainly unusual. Any idea what it means?"

Rievaulx's gaze remained fixed on the flower. "It's a rare variety, not easily recognized. Whoever placed it here knew exactly what they were doing."

Carter's unease grew. Though not her first encounter with a murder case—it was her second—she felt an unsettling churn in her stomach, the remnants of breakfast threatening to make an unwelcome reappearance. Why, she wondered, hadn't someone at least closed the professor's eyes? They stared upwards with a glassy intensity that sent a shiver down her spine.

"Shall I start interviewing witnesses?" Carter suggested, eager to begin, partly to distance herself from the unnerving proximity of the body.

Rievaulx nodded. "Yes, but take your time. There's more here than meets the eye. Observe everything carefully."

Carter suppressed a sigh, knowing that Rievaulx's meticulous nature often clashed with her own sense of urgency.

As Carter began her interviews, Rievaulx's attention remained focused on the scene before him. The rare orchid, the positioning of the body, and the reactions of those present all hinted at a deeper mystery. The investigation had only just begun, but with Carter's fresh perspective alongside Rievaulx's seasoned approach, they would be well-equipped to unravel the truth.

THE GARDEN OF ST MICHAEL'S COLLEGE now thrummed with the unwelcome energy of a crime scene. The morning's serene stillness had been shattered by the arrival of uniformed officers, their sharp whistles slicing through the crisp air as they moved purposefully to cordon off the area and disperse the curious onlookers. Even here, in the heart of Cambridge's hallowed academic precincts, the grim reality of the outside world had forcefully intruded, turning the tranquil setting into a tableau of investigation and unease.

Detective Constable Emily Carter moved through the scene with a focused efficiency that belied the turmoil of thoughts beneath her composed exterior. She oversaw the initial procedures with the practiced confidence of someone who had earned her place in a world still adjusting to her presence.

As Carter coordinated with the scene-of-crime officers, Rievaulx stood a short distance away, contemplating the stone bench where Dr. Charles Atherton's body lay, his eyes still open, staring sightlessly at the sky. Clad in his characteristic tweed coat, a sartorial relic that felt as enduring as the very stones of the College, Rievaulx moved with a deliberation that suggested a man deeply attuned to both his surroundings and the significance of the moment. His presence, rooted in the traditions of the past yet keenly aware of the demands of the present, lent the scene a peculiar gravitas. He was a figure straddling two worlds—the storied history of Cambridge and the stark reality of the crime at hand.

A failed academic—at least in his parents' eyes. He was the only child, and something of a late and unexpected addition to the household, born to a pair of revered classical scholars who'd long since assumed their legacy would be passed on to dusty volumes rather than offspring. They had never quite forgiven his defection to Oxford, nor understood why he abandoned their world of dusty texts and theoretical debates. But for Rievaulx, the choice had been clear. Classicism was a life lived at a distance, dissecting the past while the present slipped by. The police force offered the opposite: immediacy, unpredictability, a world where instinct mattered as much as intellect. Here, truth wasn't confined to footnotes but revealed in a suspect's hesitation or a witness's nervous glance.

His parents saw it as a waste of his mind. He saw it as the only way to truly use it.

"Sir," Carter called out, her voice carrying a professional crispness, yet with a hint of impatience. "Shall we start canvassing the area to see if anyone witnessed or heard anything unusual last night?"

Rievaulx lifted his gaze from the scene, his expression thoughtful, almost meditative.

"In due course, Carter. First, we need to fully comprehend the scene itself. There's a deeper story at play here."

Carter's tension in her shoulders betraying her frustration. Rievaulx's meticulous approach, though undeniably thorough, often felt like a restraint on her own sense of urgency. She had entered the force with a drive to make a meaningful impact, and every delay felt like a missed opportunity to advance the investigation. The shift from segregated duties to integrated roles had not only altered her job but also heightened the expectations placed upon her. Each decision, each action, was scrutinized not just for its efficacy but for what it signaled in a changing world.

Their exchange was interrupted by the arrival of Dr. Sylvia Harper, a senior academic at St Michael's. She approached with a brisk, authoritative stride, her tall frame and severe bun giving her an imposing presence. Her gaze, as cool and assessing as the morning air, swept over the scene with barely concealed disdain.

"What is the meaning of this?" she demanded, her voice sharp and unyielding. "This spectacle is entirely inappropriate."

Rievaulx met her gaze with the calm authority of a man well-versed in handling difficult situations. "And your name, madam?"

"Dr. Sylvia Harper," she replied, her tone clipped, her eyes narrowing slightly as she assessed him in return.

"Well, Dr. Harper," Rievaulx continued, his voice a model of gentlemanly politeness, "we're investigating a murder on College grounds. We require your full cooperation."

Harper's expression tightened, her mouth pressing into a thin line. "This matter must be handled with the utmost discretion. The reputation of St Michael's is at stake."

"We'll do our best to maintain discretion," Carter interjected, her tone professional but tinged with impatience. "However, we need to gather information about Dr. Atherton, his work, personal life, and any recent conflicts."

Harper hesitated, a flicker of something, perhaps reluctance, perhaps something deeper, crossing her face. Her gaze drifted to the spot where Atherton's body lay, and for a brief moment, a shadow of genuine sorrow softened her features.

"Dr. Atherton was . . . a controversial figure. His research often challenged established theories, which did not endear him to everyone within the academic community. But I find it hard to believe anyone would resort to . . . this."

"Enemies?" Rievaulx's interest sharpened, his blue eyes locking onto hers with renewed focus. "Can you think of anyone who might have had a motive to harm him?"

Harper's lips pursed, and she weighed her words carefully. "There were disagreements, certainly. You might want to speak with Professor Lang and Dr. Forsyth. They were both closely connected to Atherton, though in different ways."

Rievaulx made a mental note of the names, his mind already beginning to piece together the threads of potential motives. "We'll follow up on that. In the meantime, we'll need access to Dr. Atherton's office and personal papers."

Harper's face hardened, the momentary softness vanishing as she resumed her steely manner. "I'll arrange for the keys to be brought to you. But please, be mindful of the sensitive nature of his work."

Rievaulx nodded, watching as Harper turned and walked away, her stride brisk, her back rigid with the effort of maintaining composure. There was something about her; it was an air of guarded secrecy, a sense that she was holding back more than she had revealed. For now, there were more immediate concerns that demanded their attention.

As the crime scene continued to buzz with activity, Rievaulx and Carter exchanged a glance, a silent understanding passing between them. The rare orchid, the peculiar positioning of the body, and Harper's guarded responses all suggested that this case would be anything but straightforward. The investigation had only just begun, but with Carter's fresh, determined perspective and Rievaulx's seasoned, methodical approach, they were ready to delve into the tangled web of secrets that lay hidden beneath the surface of this already puzzling murder.

BY THE TIME RIEVAULX AND CARTER emerged from the garden, the serene atmosphere of St Michael's College had been thoroughly upended. Word of Dr. Atherton's death had spread with the speed of an unchecked rumor, igniting the College with a mix of shock, curiosity, and underlying fear. Clusters of fellows, students, and staff had gathered in the quadrangle, their usual morning routines abandoned in the wake of the grim discovery. The air was thick with unease, the usual calm replaced by a palpable tension that clung to the ancient walls.

Sir Geoffrey Howard, the Master of St Michael's, stood near the entrance to the main building, his stern visage dominating a small assembly of senior fellows. Like a general attempting to maintain order in the face of an unexpected ambush, he commanded the attention of those around him, his authoritative voice cutting through the hushed whispers that swirled like smoke. Despite his attempts to project calm and control, the strain of leadership in such a crisis was evident in the furrow of his brow and the tightness around his mouth. His annoyance, or perhaps even irritation, was clear, a subtle indication that this situation was far more troublesome than anyone had anticipated.

As Rievaulx and Carter approached, Sir Geoffrey's sharp eyes homed in on them with intensity. With an impatient gesture, he excused himself from the gathering of fellows, striding towards the police officers with a briskness that belied his age. His expression, though controlled, betrayed the tension simmering beneath the surface. The way his hands clenched and unclenched at his sides reminded Rievaulx of a dog barely restrained by its leash, eager to spring into action but held back by an invisible force.

"Good morning, Master," Rievaulx said, introducing himself and Carter with a nod.

"Chief Inspector," Sir Geoffrey responded, his voice steady yet tinged with irritation. "I presume you've taken the liberty of inspecting the scene?"

"We have, Sir," Rievaulx replied, maintaining a respectful but businesslike tone. "It's too early to draw firm conclusions, but I can confirm that Dr. Atherton's death was not natural."

Sir Geoffrey's expression darkened, his composure cracking. "Not natural, you say? How dreadfully quaint." His gaze darted around, as if expecting the very walls to whisper scandal. "You can't sugar-coat a statement like that, Chief Inspector. We're not in the realm of academic debate here; we're dealing with a tragedy."

Rievaulx felt a twinge of sympathy for the man. Individuals like Sir Geoffrey, steeped in the rarefied atmosphere of academia, were rarely confronted with the harsh realities of life and death. Here, within these ancient, hallowed halls, death, especially murder, was an unwelcome and disorienting guest.

"Indeed," Rievaulx acknowledged, holding Sir Geoffrey's steely gaze. "This is a serious matter, and we'll want to conduct a thorough investigation."

"Of course you will," Sir Geoffrey replied with a huff, exasperation slipping through his facade. "You'll have the College's full cooperation but let me make one thing clear: Dr. Atherton was a complicated man. Let's put it this way—he didn't just rub people up the wrong way; he did it with a certain flair, as though antagonism were a personal calling, and he intended to see it through with distinction. Nevertheless, while he may have had his detractors, he was a valued member of our community. This is a great loss, Chief Inspector, not merely an inconvenience to be brushed aside like dust on a scholarly tome."

Rievaulx appreciated the Master's fervent response, though

he sensed a layer of desperation beneath the bravado. It was not uncommon for institutions to circle the wagons in the face of scandal, yet Sir Geoffrey's resolve to uncover the truth felt genuine. Still, Rievaulx was aware that cooperation in such cases often came with unspoken conditions, especially in a place like Cambridge, where reputation was held as sacred. Behind Sir Geoffrey's words, Rievaulx detected the underlying concern of what this tragedy could mean for the College's standing, a place where prestige and tradition were paramount, now shaken by the abrupt intrusion of violence.

"I appreciate your candor, sir," Rievaulx said, nodding. "Rest assured; we'll handle this with the utmost care."

"You have no idea what it means to be Master in these troubled times," Sir Geoffrey muttered, almost to himself. "The last thing we need is an inquiry that will make us the laughingstock of the academic elite. I suggest you move quickly, Chief Inspector. Find the perpetrator before the College becomes a footnote in a murder mystery more absurd than any thesis."

"As you say, Sir Geoffrey," Rievaulx replied with a measured calm, "in which case, we will want to speak with you further without delay, as well as the gardener who discovered the body. Any insight you can provide into Dr. Atherton's recent activities or any conflicts he may have had would be invaluable."

"Very well, if you must," Sir Geoffrey agreed, though his tone suggested he would rather be anywhere else. "I'll arrange for George Henson, the gardener, to meet with you right away. I'll do my best to answer any questions you have. This is a difficult time for the College, but we must face it head-on."

If only everyone thought that way, Rievaulx mused. "Facing it head-on" was easier said than done. He'd seen it before; people who claimed they wanted the truth, but when it came time to face it, they faltered. Would Sir Geoffrey stand firm, or would he crumble under the weight of the secrets they might uncover?

The ancient halls of St Michael's, usually humming with the quiet diligence of academic life, now felt heavy with an unsettling tension. The news of Dr. Atherton's death had spread like wildfire, leaving a trail of shock and anxiety in its wake. Students huddled in tight clusters, their voices barely above a whisper, as if the walls themselves were listening. Faculty members moved through the corridors with grim expressions, their conversations brief and laden with unspoken fears.

"Thank you," Rievaulx said, appreciating the Master's cooperation. "We'll also want access to Dr. Atherton's office and any personal records he kept. It's crucial that we gather as much information as possible."

"Of course," Sir Geoffrey agreed, though a shadow of discomfort crossed his face. "I'll have someone escort you to his office. It's just . . . well, you must understand, Chief Inspector, that Dr. Atherton was involved in some . . . sensitive research. His work was of great importance, and I would ask that you handle his papers with the utmost care."

Rievaulx nodded, recognizing the unspoken plea. "We'll be discreet, Sir Geoffrey. Our priority is to determine what happened to Dr. Atherton, and we'll approach his work with the respect it deserves."

"Thank you," Sir Geoffrey said, visibly relieved. "I'll leave you to it, then. If you need anything else, don't hesitate to ask."

With that, the Master turned and rejoined the group of fellows, his presence commanding their attention as he began to address them. Rievaulx watched him for a moment, then turned to Carter, who had been quietly taking notes throughout the conversation.

"Let's start with the gardener," Rievaulx said. "He's the one who found the body, so he may have noticed something unusual."

Carter nodded, scanning the quadrangle for George Henson. It didn't take long to spot him—a man standing apart from the others, his expression grim, hands clasped tightly in front of him. George was a man of few words, but his body language spoke volumes; he was deeply shaken by what he had discovered.

Rievaulx approached with a calm, reassuring manner. "Mr. Henson? I'm DCI Rievaulx, and this is DC Carter. We spoke briefly earlier," he reminded him when the elderly man stared blankly at him. Shock, Rievaulx surmised. "We'd like to ask you a few questions about what you found this morning."

George shuddered and appeared to pull himself together. He nodded, his gaze fixed on the ground. "I'll tell you what I can, Chief Inspector. I've never seen anything like this before . . . it's just terrible."

"We understand," Rievaulx said gently. "Can you start by telling us what you were doing when you found Dr. Atherton?"

George took a deep breath, as if bracing himself. "It was just after sunrise, like any other day. I always start my rounds in the quadrangle, making sure everything's in order. When I got to the garden, I noticed the gate was ajar. That's not usual. Only a few people have keys to that gate, and it's always kept locked."

He paused, his voice faltering slightly. "When I went in . . . that's when I saw him. Lying there on the bench, like he was just sleeping. But I knew right away something was wrong. He was so still, so pale . . . and that flower, the orchid, it was just lying there beside him. I've never seen anything like it."

Rievaulx listened carefully, noting every detail. "Did you notice anything else out of the ordinary? Anyone else in the garden, or anything that appeared unusual?"

George shook his head slowly. "No, sir. The garden was empty, quiet as the grave. I didn't touch anything, just blew my whistle and waited for help to arrive. I knew . . . I knew it wasn't something I should be messing with."

"You did the right thing," Rievaulx assured him. "You've been very helpful, Mr. Henson. We'll take it from here."

George nodded, though the haunted look in his eyes remained. "I just . . . I hope you find out what happened. Dr. Atherton . . . he wasn't always the easiest man to get along with, but no one deserves to end up like that."

"We'll do our best," Rievaulx promised.

As Rievaulx turned to leave, Carter remained, her gaze

scanning the faces of those nearby. The tension in the air was palpable, almost suffocating, like a thick fog that clung to every corner of the College. A prickling sensation at the back of her neck made her feel as if they were being watched, their every move monitored by unseen eyes.

Chapter 2

Rievaulx and Carter made their way to the office of Sir Geoffrey Howard, Master of St Michael's College, a room that exuded both authority and a certain mustiness. The space was an overwhelming testament to academic legacy, with polished oak furniture that bore the air of being in place for centuries, shelves crammed with leather-bound volumes, and an oversized window offering a carefully framed view of the College's pristine lawns. Sunlight filtered through the leaves outside, casting intricate patterns on the carpet, an illusion of tranquility that belied the gravity of their visit.

Here was Sir Geoffrey, a distinguished figure in his late sixties, as he sat behind a vast mahogany desk that appeared to dwarf even him. His mane of silver hair and impeccably tailored suit suggested a man for whom appearance was a matter of principle. He glanced up from the papers spread before him, his expression a mix of irritation and impatience, as though their presence was a necessary nuisance even though he knew they would be wanting to interview him.

"Detective Chief Inspector Rievaulx, Detective Constable Carter," he greeted, his voice smooth yet edged with a hint of frost. "Come in. Let's get this over with."

Rievaulx offered a polite nod as he took a seat opposite the Master, his manner calm but his gaze sharp. Carter followed suit, her notepad ready, poised for action.

"I last saw Dr. Atherton last night," Sir Geoffrey began, not waiting for any prompts, his tone carrying a trace of condescension. "He was heading toward the library, as usual. The man had an unquenchable thirst for books."

Rievaulx suppressed a wry smile. It was, after all, an academic institution—an obsession with books was hardly unusual, perhaps even a prerequisite. Yet, as he observed the Master, it became clear that this was less about Atherton's habits and more about the delicate balance of power and reputation within these ancient walls. The scholars here cared more about preserving their own status than truly engaging with the knowledge that surrounded them.

Carter seized the moment to dig deeper. "Did he seem . . . disturbed? More so than usual?"

Sir Geoffrey leaned back in his chair, a faint smirk playing on his lips as though the question amused him. "Disturbed? Dr. Atherton was always somewhat irascible, but last night? I'd say he was in his usual state of discomfort. Frankly, it's a wonder any of us tolerated him as long as we did."

Rievaulx sensed an opportunity and pressed on. "Were there any recent disputes that might have escalated?"

Sir Geoffrey's chuckle was tinged with bitterness. "Disputes? That's putting it mildly. Atherton and Dr. Sylvia Harper had a rivalry that bordered on the legendary. They could scarcely be in the same room without exchanging barbs. It was something of a spectacle."

Carter's pen moved swiftly across her notepad. "So, you believe Dr. Harper might have had a particular grievance?"

"Grievance?" Sir Geoffrey waved a dismissive hand. "Harper is known for her ruthlessness. Atherton's penchant for publicly belittling her work was something she would not easily forgive. If you're looking for someone with motive, she would be an excellent place to start."

"Noted," Rievaulx said, his mind already forming a strategy, dredging up what he had heard about the academic staff at St Michaels. "And what about Professor Lang? Didn't he have some involvement with Atherton?"

"Lang?" Sir Geoffrey scoffed. "He's charming, certainly, but don't let that fool you. Lang is as cunning as they come, playing every side to his advantage. If you're looking for hidden agendas, tread carefully around him."

Carter raised an eyebrow, intrigued. "And Dr. Forsyth? Was she close to Atherton?"

"Close?" Sir Geoffrey let out a mirthless laugh. "Forsyth is brilliant in her field but socially inept. I doubt she could form a meaningful connection with anyone, let alone Atherton, who, as I've said, thrived on antagonism."

Rievaulx tapped his fingers thoughtfully on the desk. "So, you suspect Harper and Lang may be central to this investigation?"

"Rivalry is merely the surface," Sir Geoffrey replied, leaning forward, his voice growing more animated. "Atherton enjoyed humiliating his colleagues, and Harper suffered for it. Her cold exterior hides a fiercely competitive nature. As for Lang, he revels in the chaos of academic politics. They both had reasons to see Atherton gone."

Carter leaned back, considering the implications. "If they were unhappy with Atherton, they might have had motives to . . . eliminate him."

Sir Geoffrey's gaze grew icy. "Motives are plentiful in academia, Constable. But I caution you, this is a delicate matter. An investigation could stir up trouble, and my colleagues are not ones to take such things lightly."

"Sir Geoffrey," Rievaulx began, his tone measured, "if there's anyone else who might have had significant contact with Dr. Atherton, it would greatly assist our investigation."

The Master hesitated, then spoke with a touch of reluctance. "Dr. Alistair Grayson. He and Atherton were rivals of a sort. Grayson is a cold fish, but he might have some insights worth hearing."

"And what . . ." Rievaulx paused, sifting through his memory. Arden? Yes, a recent addition, if he remembered rightly. The name had been tacked on at the bottom of the college's honors board, the brass letters still annoyingly shiny compared to the well-worn names above. "What about Arden?"

Sir Geoffrey's tone shifted, tinged with something almost like nostalgia. "Bright young man, but too idealistic for his own good. A bit out of his depth in this world, I'd say. Tread carefully there."

Rievaulx nodded, rising from his seat. "We appreciate your cooperation, Sir Geoffrey. If you think of anything further, please don't hesitate to contact us. We'll conduct our inquiries with the utmost discretion."

"Of course," Sir Geoffrey replied, his manner slipping back into aloofness. "But be aware, not all of my colleagues will be as accommodating as I. Lang, for one, could give you a fair run for your money, but he's harmless enough. I wouldn't pay him too much mind."

As they exited the office, Carter found herself taking one last look around, absorbing the weight of tradition and secrecy that permeated the space. Sir Geoffrey's office was a fortress, and she sensed that beneath its polished veneer lay a tangled web waiting to be uncovered.

IN THE CORRIDOR, RIEVAULX TURNED TO her. "Let's pay Dr. Harper a visit next. She might shed light on the intricate relationships Atherton had within the College. But," he paused, considering their options, "before we do that, let's inspect the library."

"Sir," Carter began carefully, "I respect your methods, but we're dealing with a murder here. Shouldn't we move a bit quicker? Start gathering evidence, questioning suspects?"

Rievaulx slowed his pace, turning to face her with a thoughtful expression. "I understand your concern, Carter. But rushing won't serve us well. Cambridge is a place of hidden depths, where secrets are buried deep. We must understand the dynamics at play here.

This isn't just about collecting evidence; it's about understanding the people, their motives, their fears."

Carter felt a flicker of guilt for her impatience. He was right, of course, but sitting still had never come naturally. *Time and tide wait for no man,* her father used to say, then, with a sidelong glance at her, *or woman.*

Growing up as the only girl among three brothers, she'd learned early that waiting her turn meant missing out. You acted fast, or you got left behind. Survival, in that household, meant being better at being a boy than the boys themselves. They'd joined the army. So she'd joined the police. Still competing, just less obviously.

"I get that, sir. I really do. It's just . . . it's hard to stand still when so much is at stake."

Rievaulx's expression softened, a rare occurrence. He placed a reassuring hand on her shoulder. "And you will make a difference, Carter. You've got a sharp mind. Sometimes the best way to make a difference is to slow down, take in the details others might miss. That's how we'll solve this."

They reached the entrance to the College library, where a small group of students had gathered, their faces a mix of apprehension and curiosity. The library, with its rare books and ancient manuscripts, was one of the last places Dr. Atherton had been seen alive.

"Excuse me," Rievaulx said, addressing the group with calm authority. "Were any of you here last night? Did you see Dr. Atherton?"

After a brief pause, a young man with disheveled hair and slightly askew glasses stepped forward hesitantly. "I . . . I was here," he began, his voice trembling. "I saw him around nine o'clock. He was heading towards the library, but that's the last I saw of him."

Rievaulx nodded, his gaze fixed on the young man's pale face. "Did he seem upset? Nervous?"

The student shook his head, looking down as he searched for the right words. "No, not really. He appeared . . . preoccupied, like he had something on his mind."

There was a murmur from the group, and another student, a slight figure with a nervous energy, spoke up. "You might want to talk to Hawk," he suggested in a whisper.

Rievaulx raised an eyebrow. "Hawk?"

The student shrugged, discomfort evident. "Yeah, he's. . . . an anarchist. Had a row with Dr. Atherton yesterday. Thought he was going to punch him. Hawk I mean, punch Dr. Atherton, not . . ." he faded, out casting his eyes around furtively.

"An anarchist, you say?" Rievaulx's tone was thoughtful. "And where might we find this Hawk?"

The student merely shrugged again, as though realizing he had already said too much.

As Carter jotted down notes, her mind raced to piece together the fragments of information. The student's account was intriguing but incomplete. Dr. Atherton had been seen heading toward the library, but what transpired afterward was still a mystery.

"Thank you," Rievaulx said, dismissing the students with a courteous nod. "If you remember anything else, no matter how small, please come forward."

As the students dispersed, the one who had mentioned Hawk hesitated, then turned back. "You might try the commune," he said with a note of urgency.

"The commune?" Carter asked, her curiosity piqued.

"Near Grantchester," he added before hurrying off, leaving them with a new lead. The commune, known for its unconventional lifestyle and eclectic residents, was a hub for those seeking an alternative to traditional society.

Carter turned to Rievaulx with a growing respect for his methodical approach. "So, what now? Should we check Atherton's rooms, see if we can find anything there?"

Rievaulx gave her a faint smile. "Patience, Carter. Yes, we'll check his rooms, and then we'll speak with the Fellows who moved in Atherton's circle."

Carter nodded, feeling a renewed sense of determination. She was here to do the work, to prove her worth. "And what about Atherton's connections in town? Maybe someone outside the College had a reason to harm him."

Rievaulx considered this, his mind turning over the possibilities. "A good point. We'll investigate that as well. But for now, our focus is here, within these walls. The answer lies somewhere in this College, and we're going to find it."

RIEVAULX AND CARTER PUSHED OPEN THE door to Dr. Atherton's rooms, the hinges emitting a low groan, almost as if the space itself resented their intrusion. What lay beyond was a curious blend of intellectual intensity and chaotic neglect; a room that encapsulated the mind of a man perpetually on the brink of either a great discovery or a complete breakdown.

The first thing was the lingering scent of burnt coal, hanging thick in the air despite the warmth of the season. It was late in the Easter term, a time when Cambridge was typically bathed in the gentle onset of summer, making the presence of a fire all the more incongruous. Yet the signs were unmistakable: a small hearth in the corner, filled with the ashy remnants of what had once been logs—and possibly, Rievaulx noted as he prodded the ashes with a poker, papers. What had Atherton been so keen to destroy?

The room itself was a testament to Atherton's life as a scholar; a chaotic, disordered testament. Bookshelves lined the walls, sagging under the weight of countless volumes on history interspersed with botany, their spines faded and brittle with age. The books were arranged with a kind of haphazard precision, some stacked neatly, others leaning precariously, as if defying gravity. Each shelf appeared to offer a glimpse into Atherton's mind, filled with the thoughts and theories of a man consumed by his work.

At the center of this intellectual storm was a desk, its surface barely visible beneath the mountain of paper that covered it. Handwritten notes, botanical sketches, and partially completed manuscripts were strewn about, creating a landscape of scholarly chaos. A brass lamp with a slightly tilted shade cast a dim light over the clutter, highlighting the frenetic scrawl of annotations that spoke of long nights spent wrestling with ideas. Beside the desk, an old leather chair, worn and creased from years of use, stood as silent witness to countless hours of research and contemplation.

Near the fireplace, an armchair draped with a thick woolen throw and a small side table cluttered with a cold, half-empty cup of tea and a pair of reading glasses added a touch of lived-in comfort to the otherwise oppressive atmosphere. The walls were adorned with framed botanical prints, their colors faded and the frames slightly askew, as if they too were succumbing to the weight of the room's intellectual disarray.

As they took in the scene, both Rievaulx and Carter felt a mix of curiosity and unease. The room, with its overwhelming evidence of a life dedicated to scholarship, suggested a man deeply immersed in his work, perhaps even seeking refuge in it. Yet there was something unsettling about the disarray, as if it hinted at a mind not entirely at peace.

"Quite the setup," Carter muttered, nudging aside a dog-eared copy of *The Orchid Thief*. "It's as if he was expecting an invasion of orchids at any moment."

"Or perhaps he thrived in the chaos," Rievaulx mused, surveying the clutter. "A true academic, or at least, what some would consider one."

As they began to sift through the mess, Rievaulx's hand brushed against a stack of manuscripts, each page filled with Atherton's meticulous handwriting. "Look at this," he said, holding up a page dense with notes. "His thoughts on orchid classification, or perhaps a manifesto on why he was always such a thorn in everyone's side."

Carter leaned in, her expression, skeptical. "If I had to guess, I'd say this reads more like the ramblings of a man convinced the world was out to get him. If this is anything to go by, Atherton certainly had a talent for making enemies."

"A talent, indeed," Rievaulx replied dryly. "He had a particular knack for rubbing people the wrong way—especially in these hallowed halls."

As they continued their search, a faded photograph caught Rievaulx's eye. He picked it up, revealing a group of students posed in front of the College, with a younger Atherton among them, his characteristic scowl already well-formed.

"Hard to imagine him ever being so . . . social," he remarked with a hint of irony.

"Maybe he was just terrified of giving a lecture," Carter suggested, half-joking but with a touch of genuine curiosity. "I can't picture him as anything other than a grumpy old man."

Rievaulx returned the photo to its place, his manner growing more serious as he resumed the search. "We need something more concrete. Correspondence, perhaps, or notes that could shed light on his relationships."

As they dug through the stacks of papers, a crisp envelope slipped out and fluttered to the floor. Rievaulx retrieved it, noting the elegant handwriting on the front. "A letter," he said, turning it over. "From Dr. Sylvia Harper, no less."

"Ah, the rival," Carter remarked, her interest piqued. "Shall we?"

"Absolutely," Rievaulx replied, carefully opening the envelope. As he unfolded the letter, the faint scent of aged paper mingled with the musty air of the room. The words within offered a glimpse into the tangled web of academia, where professional rivalry could easily slip into something more personal.

> *Dear Leonard,*
> *I trust this letter finds you well, though I cannot say it will elicit a warm response from you. As much as I find your recent forays into the classical interpretation of botanical nomenclature entertaining, if somewhat misguided, I must express my concern regarding your increasing encroachment into my field of expertise.*

You have frequently dismissed my work on Cattleya hybrids, yet I notice you now attempt to elevate your own standing by incorporating classical references into your botanical discussions. Let me remind you that the study of classics, like that of rare orchids, demands more than mere enthusiasm; it requires a deep, cultivated understanding that you seem to lack.

However, this letter is not merely an outlet for our ongoing feud. I have reason to believe that certain individuals within our College are actively undermining my work, and I suspect you are aware of these efforts. Your recent criticisms during the faculty meeting, though thinly veiled, did little to disguise the whispers circulating about the integrity of my research.

I urge you to reconsider your approach. Collaboration, not competition, should guide our efforts. We risk becoming the very caricatures we so despise, academics blinded by rivalry. I propose we set aside our differences and meet to discuss these matters. I would hate for either of us to fall prey to the petty politics that so often beset our field.

Yours in scholarly pursuit,
Sylvia

Rievaulx's brow furrowed as he finished reading. "Interesting," he murmured, looking up at Carter, who leaned over to read the letter herself.

"Harper's not just angry—she's threatened. Atherton's attempts to dabble in her domain must have riled her more than we thought."

"She's not just defending her territory," Carter observed, her mind racing. "She's practically accusing him of undermining her work—maybe even hinting at a conspiracy. If she felt cornered, who knows what she might have done?"

"Indeed," Rievaulx agreed, folding the letter carefully. "This rivalry was about more than just academic squabbles. There's something deeper here; something that might have pushed Harper or others to act."

With renewed determination, they resumed their search, every item a potential clue in the unfolding mystery. The letter had opened a door into Atherton's world, revealing a man enmeshed in rivalries and secrets. Before they left the room, as they sifted through the detritus of his life, it became increasingly clear that the answers they sought might not lie in straightforward evidence but in the intricate, often treacherous relationships that bound these scholars together.

RIEVAULX AND CARTER APPROACHED DR. SYLVIA Harper's rooms with a sense of anticipation, fully aware that the woman could be as frosty as a January wind. Their previous encounter with her had left a lasting impression. Neither of them could forget the brief exchange in the garden, where her reaction to the discovery of Dr. Atherton's body had been one of striking indifference. Rather than showing any concern for the deceased or curiosity about the identity of the perpetrator, Harper had been more preoccupied with the potential damage to the College's reputation. It was almost as if Atherton's death were nothing more than an inconvenience, an unwelcome disturbance in her meticulously ordered world.

Dr. Harper was known to be brilliant, but she was also famously difficult—a woman who did not suffer fools gladly and who expected the same level of precision from others that she demanded of herself. Rievaulx and Carter had braced themselves for another encounter with her imperious attitude, recognizing that beneath the polished veneer of her academic excellence lay a sharp tongue and a colder heart.

The hallway leading to Harper's office was dimly lit, the kind of corridor that looked as if it was designed to intimidate rather than welcome. The brass nameplate on her door gleamed with a meticulous polish, standing in stark contrast to the shadowy surroundings. The door itself, a heavy oak slab, radiated an unspoken message: entry was neither encouraged nor appreciated. Carter glanced at Rievaulx, looking for any sign that he shared her unease, but his face remained inscrutable, as always.

Harper's past interaction with them had been dismissive, almost contemptuous, making it clear that whatever they were to discuss now would be met with the same detached frostiness. Prepared for a less-than-warm reception, Rievaulx and Carter exchanged a brief nod before Carter reached out and knocked.

The door opened with a muted creak, revealing a room that was an exact reflection of its occupant: large, austere, and meticulously organized. The walls were lined with shelves filled to the brim with leather-bound volumes, their spines hinting at years of dedicated scholarship. The air was cool, almost unnervingly so, and the only sound was the steady ticking of an ornate clock on the mantel, as if even time dared not disrupt the orderliness of the space.

Dr. Harper sat behind a massive mahogany desk, her posture rigid, her hands clasped neatly in front of her. Her hair was pulled back into a severe bun, highlighting the sharpness of her features and the piercing intelligence in her eyes. As the officers entered, her gaze flickered over them with cool appraisal, and Carter felt a reflexive urge to straighten her spine.

"Chief Inspector," Harper greeted, her voice as crisp as the pressed papers on her desk. She barely acknowledged Carter; her attention focused solely on Rievaulx. The faint, musty scent of old books filled the room, intensifying the silence as she addressed the officers. "We meet again."

Rievaulx introduced himself and Carter. "Indeed, Dr. Harper. I am Detective Chief Inspector Jonathan Rievaulx, and this is Detective Constable Carter."

Harper's eyes momentarily flicked to Carter before returning to Rievaulx, her expression one of muted recognition mixed with a hint of respect.

"Ah, Chief Inspector Rievaulx," she remarked, a trace of reverence creeping into her tone. "Your name carries a certain weight here at Cambridge. I've encountered it in various academic circles over the years. It is . . . interesting to see it now associated with our current situation."

Rievaulx acknowledged the comment with a slight nod, masking any pride he might have felt. "Thank you, Dr. Harper. Our aim is to conduct a thorough investigation into Dr. Atherton's death, and we hope you can provide us with information that may assist in our inquiry."

Harper's manner shifted subtly, her lips pressing into a thin line. "I suppose I have little choice in the matter," she said, her tone edged with impatience. "I trust this won't take long. My time is precious, and I have pressing work to attend to."

The dismissive tone rankled Carter, but she kept her expression neutral. Rievaulx, however, was utterly unfazed.

"We'll be as brief as possible," Rievaulx assured her. "We're investigating the death of Dr. Charles Atherton. I believe you were acquainted?"

Harper's gaze didn't waver, though a slight tightening around her mouth betrayed her irritation. "Acquainted, yes. We were colleagues in the same College. Though "colleagues" might be overstating it."

"Your relationship was strained?" Rievaulx asked, his tone deliberately mild, but his eyes sharp.

Harper allowed herself a small, sardonic smile. "Strained? Atherton was brilliant, yes, but his arrogance was insufferable. He had little regard for anyone's opinions but his own and made no effort to hide his disdain for those he deemed inferior, which was nearly everyone."

Carter leaned forward, sensing an opportunity. "Did these disagreements ever become . . . personal?"

Harper's gaze shifted to Carter for a moment. "Personal? Hardly. Atherton wasn't the sort to hold personal vendettas. He was far too self-absorbed for that. Our disagreements were purely professional, though I won't deny they were often heated. Academia isn't for the faint-hearted, Constable Collins. We deal in ideas, and ideas are powerful things."

Carter felt a surge of irritation at the deliberate use of the wrong name. It felt like a calculated slight, a way to put her in her place. She bit back a retort.

"Where were you last night, Dr. Harper?" Rievaulx asked, shifting the focus back to the matter at hand.

"I was here, in my office," Harper replied without hesitation. "Working late, as usual. I have a considerable amount of research to conduct, and the evenings provide the peace I need. Several colleagues saw me if you need verification."

Rievaulx mentally noted this with the same care he might use when cataloguing a rare manuscript. "And their names?" he inquired. "Naturally, we'll need to speak with them."

Harper couldn't believe her word alone wasn't enough. "If you must know, Chief Inspector, Dr. Grayson checked in on me at around 10:15, and Irene Forsyth was here shortly thereafter."

Rievaulx raised an eyebrow at the specificity of "10:15," a detail that felt oddly precise. "And did you notice anything unusual? Anything that might suggest someone had a reason to harm Dr. Atherton?"

Harper's gaze sharpened and she said with a trace of impatience. "Chief Inspector, everyone in a place like this has secrets. But whatever they are, they have nothing to do with me. Now, if that's all, I have more pressing matters to attend to."

Rievaulx held her gaze steadily, then, to Carter's surprise, he switched to Latin. *"Non omnes qui errant pereunt, sed necesse est quaerere veritatem. Nonne ita, doctrix?"* (Not all who wander are lost, but it is necessary to seek the truth. Is it not so, Doctor?)

For a moment, Harper's face changed, and she blinked, clearly caught off guard. Then, slowly, a grudging smile appeared. "*Veritas semper elucet*, Chief Inspector," she replied, her tone softening just a fraction. (The truth always shines.)

Carter, who had endured the rigors of Latin at school, cast a sideways glance at Rievaulx, a newfound respect for her superior growing within her. Harper, on the other hand, was momentarily off-balance, though she regained her composure.

"Speaking of truths," Rievaulx switched back to English, "I'd like to discuss this letter from Dr. Atherton." He retrieved the neatly folded letter from his pocket and placed it on the desk. "It seems you had some rather pointed disagreements."

Harper's facial expression tightened. "I fail to see how my correspondence with Atherton is relevant to his death."

"And yet," Rievaulx pressed, "it contains some revealing sentiments, does it not? You express concern over his encroachment into your field. It sounds like you felt threatened."

Harper's eyes narrowed, and she sat up a little straighter. "Atherton was a fool, deluded into thinking he could excel in areas beyond his expertise. That is hardly a crime, Chief Inspector. It speaks more to his incompetence than anything else."

"Or perhaps," Rievaulx suggested, "he was a man determined to make his mark, even if it meant stepping on a few toes along the way."

Harper didn't break eye contact. "I am not responsible for the insecurities of others. Atherton's issues were his own."

"Thank you for your time, Dr. Harper," Rievaulx said, rising from his seat. "We'll be in touch if we require anything further."

Harper inclined her head, her cool manner returning. "Of course. I'm sure you know where to find me."

As they exited the office, Carter turned to Rievaulx, still processing what had just transpired. "Latin, sir?"

Rievaulx allowed himself a small smile. "My parents were classicists. It felt like an effective way to get her attention."

Carter shook her head, a mixture of admiration and amusement in her eyes. "It certainly worked."

Chapter 3

Their next interview took them to the rooms of Professor Robert Lang, and the contrast between his surroundings and those of Dr. Harper could not have been more pronounced. Where Harper's office had been imposing and austere, Lang's space was inviting, almost too much so. It was light and airy, with large windows that let in the afternoon sun, and the walls were adorned with modern art that was designed to put visitors at ease. Soft, comfortable furniture filled the room, and a gentle scent of lavender lingered in the air, as though everything had been carefully orchestrated to project an image of effortless charm. Beneath the surface, there was something about the space that felt ... calculated. It was as though every element had been meticulously chosen to convey a specific message: here was a man who was both approachable and sophisticated, modern yet deeply rooted in culture.

Lang himself matched his surroundings perfectly. Tall and silver-haired, with a polished smile, he greeted them with an easy warmth that felt more rehearsed than genuine. Carter, who had learnt to trust her instincts, sensed that this was a man who was well aware of his effect on others. The charm was like a weapon.

"Ah, the police," Lang said as they entered, his tone welcoming "Please, come in, sit down. Can I offer you something? Tea? Coffee?"

"No, thank you," Rievaulx replied, taking a seat in one of the overstuffed chairs. Carter remained standing, her eyes never leaving Lang's face, watching for the telltale signs of discomfort beneath the professor's practiced exterior.

"We're here to ask you about Dr. Atherton," Rievaulx began, his tone polite but firm. "I understand you were close?" He was taking a gamble, and he knew no such thing but Lang's response to whether it was true or not would be revealing.

Lang's smile faltered for a moment, but he regained his composure immediately. "Colleagues, yes. Atherton was . . . well, he was a unique character. Brilliant, but not exactly the easiest man to work with."

"Did you consider him a friend?" Carter asked.

Lang hesitated, his fingers tapping lightly on the arm of his chair—a nervous habit. "Friend? No, I wouldn't say that. We worked together, shared some common interests, but we were very different people."

"And last night?" Rievaulx asked, his voice in a casual manner. "Where were you?"

"Not on College grounds, Chief Inspector," Lang replied. "I was, as is my custom, at home with my wife. We had a quiet dinner, watched some television, and then retired for the night. A rather uneventful evening, I'm afraid."

Carter inquired. "Television?" she asked, lifting her head with an air of casual interest that she hoped masked the intensity of her question. "What were you watching?"

Lang's smile widened and with a flicker of amusement in his voice said. "Nothing particularly high-brow, Constable. My wife and I indulged in the Eurovision Song Contest. This year it was held in London, and my wife felt it was our patriotic duty to watch, albeit in vain, with hopes of a British victory. As it turned out,

Marie Myriam from France clinched the win. Should you require further confirmation, do feel free to ask my wife."

Rievaulx nodded, noting the subtle way Lang's manner shifted, a quick flicker of something almost like relief, as if he had been anticipating the question and was now satisfied with his answer. "We may do that. Thank you for your time, Professor Lang. If we have any further questions, we'll be in touch."

Lang said. "Of course, anything I can do to help. This whole situation is just terrible."

As they left Lang's office, the door closing quietly behind them, Carter frowned, her thoughts churning. "Charming and slippery. He's hiding something, but what?"

"Indeed," Rievaulx murmured, his mind turning over the possibilities. "Lang's type always hides something. The question is whether it's relevant to our case, or if it's simply part of the façade he's constructed for himself."

Carter nodded, her mind on the professor's smooth answers and the carefully curated environment he'd created. Everything about Lang screamed control; control over his surroundings, over his image, and, perhaps most importantly, over the narrative he wanted them to believe.

As they walked away from Lang's rooms, Carter felt that they had just scratched the surface of a much deeper mystery, one that Lang was determined to keep buried. She also couldn't dismiss the way Lang had readily provided his alibi, one that was conveniently unremarkable yet detailed enough to deflect suspicion or questions.

"Let's dig into his story," Rievaulx said, as though reading her thoughts. "If there's a crack in Lang's façade, we'll find it."

Carter nodded, her resolve hardening. They would find that crack, no matter how well-hidden it was. When they did, she was certain it would lead them closer to the truth about Dr. Atherton's death—and perhaps reveal more about Robert Lang than he ever intended them to know.

Their next interview took them to Dr. Irene Forsyth, a junior faculty member whose nerves were on full display from the moment they stepped into her office. The room was a small, cluttered sanctuary of academic chaos, where towering piles of books and precarious stacks of papers teetered on every available surface. The space itself reflected a mind teetering on the edge of either brilliant inspiration or utter overwhelm.

Dr. Forsyth's fragile manner was at odds with the imposing scholarly environment. Rievaulx found himself recalling the Master's earlier description of her: "She has the social skills of a particularly anxious cat." Now, more than ever, that comparison felt apt.

As they entered, Forsyth greeted them with a nervous smile, her hands fidgeting as she gestured for them to sit. There was an air about her of someone bravely trying to hold herself together in the face of adversity and the strain was beginning to show.

"Dr. Forsyth, thank you for agreeing to speak with us," Rievaulx began with his tone soothing, hoping to calm her.

"Of course, of course," Forsyth stammered, her hands twisting in her lap. "This is all just so . . . awful. I can't believe Dr. Atherton is . . . gone."

"Were you close to Dr. Atherton?" Carter asked, softening her tone.

Forsyth hesitated; her eyes flitted around the room as if searching for an escape route.

"I—I worked with him on a few projects," she finally managed, her voice trembled. "He was very . . . intense, but I admired him. He had such a passion for his work, even if it could be overwhelming at times."

"And last night?" Rievaulx inquired, his gaze steady and reassuring. "Where were you?"

"I was in my rooms, reading and working on some research notes," Forsyth whispered. "I didn't go out. I did pop along to see Dr. Harper sometime after 10:30, but I can't be more precise than that."

Carter exchanged a look with Rievaulx, her frown deepening. "Did Dr. Atherton ever mention anyone who might have held a grudge against him?" Carter asked.

Forsyth shook her head, her movements sharp and quick. "No, not to me. But... but he did have enemies. People who didn't like his ideas, who thought he was too... radical. But I don't know who they were."

"Thank you, Dr. Forsyth," Rievaulx said, rising from his seat with a measured nod. "If we need anything further, we'll certainly be in touch."

As they exited the cluttered office, Rievaulx noticed the visible wave of relief that washed over Forsyth. The tension in her shoulders dissipated, as though a great weight had been lifted.

"An excellent question, Carter," Rievaulx murmured, his gaze distant as he mulled over their encounter. There was something about Forsyth's manner that suggested she was not just nervous but genuinely fearful.

Trailing slightly behind, Carter furrowed her brow in thought. "She's frightened," she observed. "But what exactly is she afraid of? Or perhaps, whom?"

As they walked away, a thoughtful frown tugged at Rievaulx's features. The name Forsyth stirred something in the recesses of his mind, a vague recollection that danced just out of reach. Rievaulx had learnt over the years not to force such memories. Like bubbles in a still pond, he knew they would rise to the surface in their own time. For now, he resolved to keep a closer watch on Dr. Forsyth, convinced that the key to understanding her fear might also unlock more of the truth behind Dr. Atherton's death.

THEIR NEXT INTERVIEW BROUGHT THEM TO Dr. Alistair Grayson, a neuroscientist whose reputation extended well beyond his academic accomplishments into the realm of personal eccentricity. As Rievaulx and Carter stepped into his office, Grayson's office was a study in clinical detachment. The room was as sparse and unadorned as a freshly sterilized lab, with every surface meticulously arranged. Shelves held rows of neatly aligned journals, a minimalist desk stood devoid of any personal touches, and the environment was so sterile that it appeared to reject even the concept of comfort.

Grayson himself was a tall, thin figure whose every movement was precise and deliberate, almost as if choreographed. His face was a mask of impassivity, his gaze devoid of emotion, as though he viewed the world through a lens of professional detachment. His manner stood in sharp contrast to the usual academic chaos, embodying a cold, almost mechanical efficiency.

"Dr. Grayson," Rievaulx began as they entered, his voice calm but carrying the undertone of a question. "I'm Detective Chief Inspector Jonathan Rievaulx, and this is my colleague, Detective Constable Emily Carter." The formality of using their full names and titles felt almost obligatory in such a setting. "We'd like to have a word with you, if you don't mind."

Grayson acknowledged them with a brief, impersonal nod, his eyes as cool and unaffected as the room around him. "Detective Chief Inspector Rievaulx, Constable Carter. To what do I owe the pleasure?" His tone was polite enough, but there was an underlying sense that any deviation from his routine was an unwelcome inconvenience.

Carter was aware of Grayson's reputation for emotional detachment. She had briefly dated one of his students—an ill-advised experiment that confirmed her suspicion: scientific analysis was all well and good in a lab, but over dinner, it lost its charm rather quickly. She took the lead. "Dr. Grayson, we're investigating the death of Dr. Charles Atherton. We understand you might have some relevant information."

At the mention of Atherton's death, Grayson's expression flickered with what might have been surprise, a barely perceptible shift in his otherwise composed manner. "Dr. Atherton is dead?"

His tone conveyed mild astonishment, as if the news had interrupted a particularly engrossing thought.

Rievaulx and Carter exchanged an astonished quick glance. How could Grayson be unaware of Atherton's death when the entire College was buzzing with the news? The fact that Grayson was oblivious to it, in such an insular community, was almost as startling as the death itself.

"Yes," Rievaulx confirmed, masking his surprise as best he could. "I'd expected you might have heard by now. We're looking into the circumstances surrounding his death."

Grayson's gaze returned to its previous state of clinical neutrality. "I must admit, I had not been informed. It is indeed regrettable. Atherton was a man of considerable intellect, though our interactions were limited."

Rievaulx, observing the scientist's reaction with renewed interest, continued, "We'd like to know if you had any recent interactions with Dr. Atherton, or if you're aware of anyone who might have had a reason to bear him ill will."

Grayson's response was delivered with precision. "My interactions with Dr. Atherton were limited to the occasional exchange on professional matters. He was known for his radical theories, which, while not universally accepted, were part of academic discourse. As for personal grievances, I cannot speak to those."

Carter pressed further. "What about last night? Where were you?"

"I was engaged in my own research," Grayson replied. "In the laboratory until late. The specifics of my whereabouts can be corroborated by my work logs and security records."

"Is there anyone you can think of who might hold a grudge against Dr. Atherton?" Rievaulx asked. Grayson looked at him; he was silent for a moment.

"A grudge, Chief Inspector? I wouldn't know anything about grudges. What others think of someone is hardly my concern. But I can tell you that Dr. Harper and Professor Lang found him particularly irritating. I believe Lang borrowed some money from him at one point, and never bothered to repay it. That's rather his reputation, you know. But beyond that, I know nothing of grudges."

"Thank you, Dr. Grayson," Rievaulx said, knowing there might be further investigation. "We may need to follow up, but for now, that will be all."

As they exited the office, Carter was not entirely able to stop herself commenting on the extraordinariness of the encounter. "How could he not know about Atherton's death? The entire College has been buzzing with it. It's almost like he's living in a bubble." She couldn't hide her astonishment.

Rievaulx replied thoughtfully, "It's hard to say. Grayson certainly fits the profile of someone who might withhold information, but it could also be that he's so deeply absorbed in his work that the outside world barely registers. We'll need to investigate further."

Carter nodded, her mind racing with possibilities. Grayson's controlled manner could either be a protective facade or a reflection of his true nature. In either case, it made him a difficult subject to read.

As they walked away from Grayson's office, Rievaulx considered the next steps. "We have a few more pieces of the puzzle, but we're still missing the bigger picture. Let's see what the others have to say before we draw any conclusions."

Carter agreed. The investigation was just beginning. She knew the truth would not reveal itself easily. She was determined to uncover it, no matter how well it was concealed.

RIEVAULX AND CARTER APPROACHED THE ROOMS of Dr. Thomas Arden, noticing immediately that the door was slightly ajar, allowing a beam of sunlight to spill into the dim corridor. The soft rustle of papers and the distant ticking of a clock created an atmosphere that felt almost comforting. It was a stark contrast to the gravity of their investigation. The scene felt more like stepping into a comfortable retreat than into the office of an academic embroiled in a murder inquiry.

Rievaulx knocked lightly on the door frame. "Dr. Arden?"

"Come in," came the eager reply. Arden's voice was infused with the kind of energy that suggested he had been swept up in the whirlwind of academic chaos, perhaps oblivious to the world outside his books and papers.

As they stepped inside, they were greeted by a vibrant jumble of books, notes, and what appeared to be half-empty coffee cups precariously balanced on stacks of academic journals. The room was a kaleidoscope of intellectual clutter, with ideas spilling out onto every available surface. Dr. Arden himself was seated at a cluttered desk, his appearance a testament to the 70s youth culture that clung to the academic like a stubborn breeze. He wore a patterned shirt, unbuttoned at the collar, paired with slightly faded, flared trousers. His jacket, while clearly having seen better days, still carried an air of charm. His long, dark blonde hair, a tousled mane that hinted at a carefree spirit, was complemented by wide sideburns that framed his youthful face. His blue eyes sparkled with an earnestness that made him instantly approachable.

"Dr. Arden," Rievaulx began, introducing himself and Carter. "Would you mind if we ask you a few questions regarding Dr. Atherton?"

"Of course, Chief Inspector. Anything to help," Arden responded with genuine enthusiasm. He gestured towards the chairs across from him, "Please, have a seat."

"Thank you, Dr. Arden," Rievaulx said as he settled into the chair, careful not to disturb the precariously stacked papers. Carter followed suit, intrigued by the young man's palpable enthusiasm.

Arden leaned forward, his expression a mix of concern and curiosity. "Have you heard about Dr. Atherton?" he asked, his tone suggesting that the news had reached him with a mix of disbelief and concern.

"We're investigating his death," Rievaulx replied, his tone measured, gauging Arden's reaction. For a brief moment, he was confused. Why else would they be here? Or was there some other reason they might wish to interview the young academic about

Dr. Atherton? "We were hoping you could shed some light on his relationships within the department."

Arden's brow furrowed; the earnestness of his youth evident as he carefully considered his response. "Dr. Atherton? Yes, he was brilliant, but he didn't always play well with others." He paused, glancing around his office as though the answer might be hidden among the chaos. "He had a way of belittling those he felt were beneath him. I suppose it's not surprising that he had a few enemies."

Carter noted Arden's discomfort as he spoke. "Did you ever have any disagreements with him?" she probed, hoping to draw out more.

"Not directly, no," Arden said, shaking his head. "But I did see him clash with Dr. Harper. She always felt he was encroaching on her work. It's as if he thought he could stride into her territory without consequence."

"Interesting," Rievaulx remarked, making another mental note. "Do you think Dr. Harper had any reason to harm him?"

Arden leaned back in his chair, a look of indignation crossing his face. "No, of course not. She may have been prickly, but I can't imagine her resorting to violence. This is academia, not a battlefield."

Carter exchanged a glance with Rievaulx, noting Arden's idealism. "What about other colleagues? Any tensions with anyone else?" she asked. Maybe Arden might be more willing to speak openly than others they'd interviewed.

Arden hesitated as if weighing his words carefully. "Well, there is Professor Lang," he said finally. "He has a rather . . . ruthless reputation. Some of us have heard whispers about his methods, though I've never witnessed anything myself."

"Ruthless, how?" Rievaulx, intrigued by the young academic's candor.

Arden was clearly uncomfortable with the topic. "He's known for . . . pushing his agenda, shall we say? I've seen him undermine younger members in meetings, casting doubt on their work. It can be quite . . . disheartening."

"Like your fellow junior colleagues, I presume?" Carter suggested.

Arden chuckled, glancing down at his outfit as if aware of his youthful appearance. "Yes, I suppose so. I mean, I do dress like I'm still trying to impress my students," he said, gesturing to his eclectic ensemble. "I can't quite bring myself to adopt the tweed suits of my more seasoned colleagues. They seem so . . . intimidating."

"Did you witness any specific incidents involving Dr. Atherton?" Rievaulx asked, steering the conversation back to their investigation.

"Not involving him directly," Arden recalled, his voice growing more animated. "But I once overheard a heated exchange between them at a College meeting. Atherton had challenged Lang's conclusions about a study, and Lang . . . well, he didn't take it well. I remember thinking it was an unusually intense confrontation for our College."

Carter leaned forward, sensing the significance of the revelation. "And where were you last night, Dr. Arden?"

"I was here, in my rooms, working on my own research," Arden said, his voice firm with the confidence of a clear conscience. "I didn't see anything unusual, but I'm always willing to help if you need anything further."

Rievaulx sensed the young academic's eagerness to assist. "Thank you, Dr. Arden. Your insights are invaluable. If you recall anything else or hear of any developments, please do let us know."

"Of course. I'll keep my ears open," Arden assured them, his sincerity evident in his tone.

Just as they were about to take their leave, Rievaulx, guided by a hunch, turned back. "Tell me, Dr. Arden, do you happen to know a student by the name of Hawk?"

"Hawk? Oh, everyone knows Hawk," Arden replied, his expression a mixture of recognition and mild disdain.

"What's your opinion of him?" Rievaulx inquired, curious to see if the young academic had any additional insights.

Arden wrinkled his brow, contemplating the question. "Youthful arrogance and a lot of hot air, mostly. He rails against what he calls the Cambridge elite, yet here he is, attending his tutorials as if nothing's amiss. He fancies himself an anarchist, but his work is consistently of an excellent standard."

"Indeed," Rievaulx filed away this new information. "I take it you wouldn't happen to know his real name?"

To Rievaulx's surprise, Dr. Arden chuckled. "His real name? Ah, that's part of the charm, I suppose. His name is Hawk Ravenwood. I'd venture to say his parents had a rather gothic sense of humor."

As they stepped back into the corridor, Rievaulx glanced at Carter. "He's got potential as an informant, someone on the inside, hasn't he?"

"Provided he can navigate the treacherous waters of academia," Carter replied, her tone thoughtful. "But I suspect he'll do just fine." The investigation was gradually piecing together the puzzle, and Dr. Arden, with his youthful enthusiasm and unguarded honesty, had offered more than he likely realized.

Chapter 4

THE STREETS WERE ALIVE WITH THE usual assortment of students, tourists, and locals. There was an undercurrent of tension in the air, a subtle but unmistakable shift from the familiar hustle and bustle. As she stood by the entrance gates to St Michael's, watching the steady stream of traffic pass by, she decided it was wiser to leave her car parked for the moment. She felt that there was something off. Beside her, Rievaulx ambled along, pushing his faithful old bicycle with the nonchalance of a man who'd seen it all before as they made their way towards Parkside police station.

"Do you ever think about it, sir?" Carter asked, her voice thoughtful as she watched a group of students in their academic robes pass by, their laughter ringing out over the cobblestones. "The way this city is split in two?"

Rievaulx glanced at her, his expression as unreadable as ever. "You mean the divide between the town and the gown?"

Carter nodded, her gaze drifting over the ancient stone buildings of Cambridge, standing in silent testament to centuries of academic pursuit. "It's like two different worlds, coexisting in the same place but never really meeting. The university has all this power, all this wealth, and the town . . . well, the town just gets by."

Rievaulx took a moment before responding, his eyes looking over the familiar streets of Cambridge, their cobblestones worn smooth by generations of feet. He had spent years in this city, but it was easy to overlook the hidden tensions that simmered beneath its venerable surface.

"It's always been like this," he said at last, his voice carrying a note of quiet reflection. "The university, with its imposing towers and hallowed halls, stands as a bastion of knowledge and privilege. The town, on the other hand, exists in a different world altogether. The friction between the two has been simmering for centuries, each side entrenched in its own sense of entitlement." He paused, then added, almost as an afterthought, "Take the Spinning House, for example."

Carter tilted her head, curiosity sparking in her eyes. "The Spinning House, sir?"

Rievaulx nodded, a faint, almost imperceptible smile playing at the corners of his mouth. "Ah yes, the Spinning House—Cambridge University's little-known chapter of darkness. Established in the 17th century, it lingered well into the 19th, casting a long shadow over the city. It was a place where the University exerted its control, a detention facility for women deemed "disorderly" or accused of "immoral behavior." Often, the charges were little more than vague accusations, trumped-up by the University's proctors, those ever-vigilant guardians of student conduct. These women could be arrested on a whim and confined there for up to three weeks, without trial, without recourse."

He let the weight of those words settle in the air between them. "It was a grim reminder of the power dynamics at play here, Carter. The University has always wielded its authority with a certain ruthlessness, and the Spinning House was just one manifestation of that. The town . . . well, the town has never quite forgiven, nor forgotten."

As they turned a corner, they were met with the sight of a small group of townspeople gathered outside a pub. The men, rough-looking and weathered, eyed with suspicion the two police officers. One of them, a burly man with a scowl etched into his face, spat on the ground as they passed.

"Bloody university types," the man muttered, loud enough for them to hear. "Think they own the bloody place."

Carter felt a flash of anger but kept her expression neutral. "You see what I mean, sir? There's real resentment here."

Rievaulx nodded. "Yes, and it's something we can't ignore. Atherton was a part of the University, but his life didn't stop at the College gates. If there's a connection between his work and the town, we need to find it."

They continued in silence for a while, the noise of the city swirling around them. Carter had a growing sense of urgency, a feeling that they were racing against time to find answers before the simmering tensions in the city boiled over into something more dangerous.

When they finally skirted Parker's Piece and reached the police station, Carter turned to Rievaulx and asked, "Do you think the town could have had something to do with it? Someone who resented the university, who saw Atherton as a symbol of everything they hated?"

"It's possible," Rievaulx said, as he considered the question. "But we can't jump to conclusions. We must follow the evidence, wherever it leads. The town, the College, the university—these are all pieces of the puzzle. We just must find out how they fit together."

Carter nodded, yet the unease hadn't left her. The case was growing more complex with every new discovery, and the line between the town and the gown blurred in ways she had anticipated.

As they entered the police station, Carter couldn't shake the feeling that they were on the brink of something that would reveal the true nature of the city she thought she knew. Whatever that something was, it was drawing them deeper into the shadows of Cambridge, into a world where knowledge had a price, and the past was never truly buried.

THE AFTERNOON SUN FILTERED FEEBLY THROUGH the tall windows of Rievaulx's office, casting long, meandering shadows across the cluttered room. The familiar, somewhat acrid scent of instant coffee mingled with the musty odor of old case files and the lingering tang of cigarette smoke, a stubborn relic of countless late-night interrogations. The room, crammed with the flotsam of a detective's life, presented an incongruous mix of scholarly rigor and chaotic disorder, a space where thought and action collided, often with unexpected results.

Rievaulx, seated behind his desk, was absorbed in a small slip of paper that carried the weight of a far larger burden. His usual air of methodical calm was tinged with an intensity that was palpable, drawing Carter's attention as she stood by the window. The summer light that had made its way inside highlighted the dust motes in the air, added to the sense of stillness that hung between them.

There was something about the way Rievaulx stared at that note—something in the slight furrow of his brow, the tightness in his jaw that suggested he was seeing far more than just the words on the page.

"What is it, sir?" Carter ventured, stepping closer. The soft creak of the floorboards underfoot was the only sound that disturbed the moment.

Before Rievaulx could respond, the door swung open with a well-worn squeak, revealing Desk Sergeant Harold Pritchard. A stout figure with a ruddy complexion and a disposition that exuded no-nonsense pragmatism, Pritchard entered the room bearing a steaming cup of tea in one hand and a plate overflowing with biscuits in the other, rich tea, digestives, and the Garibaldis, all jostling for space like children at a fair.

"Thought you might be needing this," Pritchard announced, stepping into the room with the confidence of a man who knew that a good cup of tea was often the best remedy for the world's ills. He placed the cup and plate on Rievaulx's desk with a flourish, clearly pleased with his offering.

Rievaulx looked up, the intensity in his expression softening slightly at the sight of the tea. "Thank you, Sergeant. Just the thing to keep the mind sharp." He reached for a biscuit, his hand hovering above the plate as if considering which one to take. He hesitated, catching the weight of Pritchard's watchful gaze.

"Miss Carter," Pritchard nodded in her direction, his face a mix of emotions. There was a fatherly concern there, a protective instinct for the young woman who had found herself entangled in the murky world of murder investigations. It was a sentiment he struggled to articulate, his years on the force having shaped him into a man more comfortable with action than words. At the same time, there was a flicker of unease about the whole notion of "women's lib," that he found unsettling. The idea of women in the police force was, to his mind, a sign of the changing times—a sign he wasn't entirely sure he was comfortable with. To him, women had their place, and it wasn't in the grim business of solving murders, though he'd be hard-pressed to define exactly what that place was.

Shaking off these unwelcome thoughts, Pritchard added, "Just make sure you two don't get too carried away with all this. Murder investigations are serious business."

Rievaulx caught the glance of understanding that passed between Pritchard and Carter silent acknowledgment of the shifting tides that neither could completely ignore.

With a final nod, Pritchard turned on his heel and strode out, leaving Rievaulx and Carter once again enveloped in the quiet hum of the office.

Rievaulx resumed his scrutiny of the slip of paper, a flicker of amusement now dancing in his eyes. "Don't mind him, Emily. Old-school values die hard, especially in a place like this. But he means well."

Carter watched him for a moment, a small smile tugging at the corners of her mouth. "Well, then, let's not keep him waiting. What's on that note that has you so engrossed?"

Rievaulx didn't respond immediately. His eyes remained fixed on the note, his thoughts clearly elsewhere. When he finally looked up, his expression was thoughtful, almost distant. "It's a cryptic note," he said, his voice carrying the weight of something just beyond reach. "Found in Dr. Atherton's pocket. At first glance, it might seem like nonsense. But there's something more here if you look closely."

Carter leaned over, scanning the elegant, almost calligraphic handwriting. The note was brief, just a few lines, but it resonated with an unsettling ambiguity.

> *The ancient manuscript lies hidden, only for those who seek with true intent. The dealer knows the price, but beware; knowledge has its cost.*

Carter frowned slightly, the words swirling in her mind. "A manuscript? Do we have any idea what it's referring to?"

Rievaulx shook his head slowly, leaning back in his chair as if trying to gain some perspective. "Not yet. But the phrasing suggests something concealed, something Dr. Atherton was deeply involved with—something he didn't want to fall into the wrong hands. And this dealer, whoever they are, is central to understanding what that was."

Carter's mind was already racing ahead, piecing together fragments of information. "A rare manuscript, perhaps? Atherton was a botanist by academic inclination, but did he have a fascination with historical texts? Could he have been tangled up in some sort of illicit trade?"

Rievaulx's gaze sharpened as he considered the idea. "It's a possibility," he mused, fingers tapping thoughtfully on the desk. "Cambridge is a place with deep, hidden currents. There's a long history of people trying to exploit the secrets locked away in its libraries and archives. But this note . . . it reads more like a warning than a mere transaction."

Carter read the note again as a prickle of unease crept up her spine. There was something almost ominous about the language, a more sinister meaning beneath its surface. "What should be our next step, sir?"

Rievaulx's voice firm with purpose. "We need to track down this dealer," he said. "Whoever they are, they might hold the key to unravelling what Atherton was involved in. And we'll dig deeper into Atherton's life; his interests, his acquaintances, any connection that might lead us to this manuscript or whatever it is he was hiding."

Carter agreed the note was only one piece of a much larger puzzle. As she turned to look back to the window, she thought that the secrets of Cambridge were far from fully revealed. Whatever Dr. Atherton had been caught up in, they would want all their wits about them to uncover the truth.

Just then, the telephone on Rievaulx's desk erupted into its jarring characteristic, clamor. Rievaulx picked up the receiver.

"Certainly, put them through," he instructed, covering the mouthpiece and murmuring to Carter, "It's the pathologist," before returning his attention to the call. A brief acknowledgement followed, and Rievaulx listened intently. After a moment, he responded, "A knitting needle? Thinner? That's interesting," then thanked the caller and requested the report be sent over as soon as possible.

Carter, her impatience barely contained, leaned forward. "Well?"

Rievaulx was unhurried. He took his time, mulling over the information before speaking. "Time of death appears to be between ten and midnight. The manner of death: stabbed through the heart with something long and thin, thinner than a knitting needle."

They lapsed into silence, both wondering what could be thinner than a knitting needle.

Chapter 5

Detective Constable Emily Carter had never been one to wax lyrical about grand architecture or the intricacies of classical design, but even she couldn't deny the imposing presence of the Fitzwilliam Museum. The neoclassical façade, adorned with stately Corinthian columns that soared proudly against the Cambridge skyline, stood as a monument to the city's deep roots in history and culture. As she approached the entrance on Trumpington Street, the shadow of King's College Chapel loomed nearby, its majestic form a silent reminder that in this corner of the world, history was not merely preserved; it was a living, breathing entity that shaped the present.

Students whizzed by on their bicycles, their black academic gowns billowing behind them like capes caught in the wind. The lively energy of the city was palpable, but today it was tinged with an underlying tension. She was here on official business, investigating a series of art thefts that had occurred over the last few months, the latest only a week ago, that had left the Fitzwilliam reeling. The university community was in a state of shock, while the townspeople appeared to regard the situation with a mix of indifference and quiet satisfaction, as if to say, "Let the university types deal with their own mess".

Carter's involvement in the case had been something of a reluctant favor to Sergeant Pritchard, who had hinted that art thefts were more "suitable" for a female officer than the grim business of murder investigations; even though she was, in fact, a detective. The patronizing attitude wasn't unusual; many of her male colleagues still viewed her as more of an errand-runner than a serious investigator.

As she stepped into the museum's grand vestibule, Carter felt a slight shiver, and it wasn't just the coolness of the stone floor beneath her feet or the echo of her footsteps in the cavernous space; the weight of history pressed in on her. Somewhere within these walls, secrets lay hidden, and one of them could be worth killing for.

A stern-looking woman greeted her at the entrance, her manner as formidable as the museum itself. With her grey hair pulled back into a severe bun and her eyes sharp and unyielding, she looked every bit as unyielding as the stone pillars that surrounded them.

"Good afternoon. How can I help you?" the woman asked, her voice was clipped and precise.

"Detective Constable Emily Carter," she replied, flashing her warrant card with a crisp efficiency that she hoped would set the right tone. "I'm here to speak with Mr. Shaw regarding the recent thefts."

The woman, whose name badge identified her as Mrs. Forbes, gave a curt nod. "Please have a seat, Constable Carter. I'll inform Mr. Shaw of your arrival."

Carter took a seat on a wooden bench near the entrance. The Fitzwilliam Museum was no ordinary museum; it was a fortress of art and antiquities, protected by layers of security that had somehow been breached by someone with knowledge, skill, and, most disturbingly, a plan had been executed with a level of precision that suggested the work of a professional. The recent thefts hadn't limited themselves to old masters. A number of ancient manuscripts had also quietly disappeared; less flashy, perhaps, but no less valuable to those who knew what they were looking for.

The first theft had occurred over six months ago, but it took a few more before the Fitzwilliam admitted there was a problem. Security had its gaps, understandable, perhaps, for a museum of its stature. Important, yes, but hardly the Louvre.

As she waited, Carter's thoughts drifted to the Backs, that picturesque stretch of the River Cam where students often punted in lazy circles, seemingly unburdened by the weight of the world. She remembered her own rare excursions onto the river, feeling like an outsider in a world of privilege and tradition. The students, with their carefree laughter and confident poise, belonged to a realm she had only ever glimpsed from the outside. University life, with its ancient libraries and cloistered courtyards, had never been her path. Instead, she had chosen a life of service, of justice. While she didn't regret the choice, hardly much of one, really, for a working-class girl from the industrial sprawl of the Midlands, there were moments, like now, when she found herself wondering how things might've turned out differently.

"Constable Carter?" The voice of Mr. Shaw pulled her back to the present. He was a tall man with a scholarly air and greying hair. His tweed jacket, slightly worn at the cuffs, added to the image of a man whose mind was often preoccupied with matters far removed from the mundane concerns of everyday life and a life spent poring over dusty manuscripts.

"Thank you for meeting with me," Carter said as she stood, extending her hand.

"Of course, of course," Shaw replied, shaking her hand with a distracted air. "Please, follow me to my office."

As they walked through the museum's labyrinthine corridors, Carter was struck by the silent majesty of the place. Each gallery they passed was a world unto itself, filled with treasures from every corner of the globe. The air was thick with history, the kind that pressed down on you, demanding reverence. Carter was awed; she was also here to find answers.

Shaw's office was, in stark contrast to the rest of the museum, a chaotic mess. Papers were piled high on every available surface, and books were stacked haphazardly on shelves that groaned under their weight. It was a room that spoke of a mind too absorbed in its own intellectual pursuits that did not pay attention to organization or tidiness.

"Please, have a seat," Shaw said, gesturing to a chair opposite his desk. "I understand you're investigating the thefts?"

Carter nodded, extracting her notebook with a practiced flick, but then paused as a thought struck her. The phrase from the note found in Atherton's pocket echoed in her mind: *The ancient manuscript lies hidden, only for those who seek with true intent. The dealer knows the price, but beware; knowledge has its cost.* An ancient manuscript? It felt like a lead worth pursuing.

"Yes, Mr. Shaw," she began, her tone both deliberate and pointed. "We're particularly interested in exploring any potential connection between the thefts and the recent murder of Dr. Atherton. I understand he had some involvement with the museum?"

Shaw's brow furrowed deeply, his expression one of intense concentration as he sifted through his memories. "Atherton? Ah, yes. He was a botanist, wasn't he? Or a historian of botany? I'm not sure. One or the other but not someone we typically interact with. Our focus tends to be more . . . well, on the artistic and antiquarian side of things."

"Exactly," Carter said, "but we found a note in his belongings that suggests he was involved with a manuscript—something ancient, rare, valuable. Do you know if the museum has had any dealings with him recently?"

Shaw hesitated, his fingers drumming a jittery rhythm on the edge of his desk. "Well," he began, "there was indeed something. A few weeks ago, Atherton came to us with a manuscript. He insisted it was an ancient botanical text, one that purportedly held significant insights into the history of botany in this region. He was quite adamant about its importance. I recall there was an antiquarian involved in some capacity, though I can't quite remember all the specifics."

Carter inquired. "And? What happened?"

Shaw rubbed his temples as if trying to ward off a headache. "It was complicated. Our experts couldn't agree on its authenticity. Some believed it was genuine, others thought it might be a forgery, or at least heavily altered. Atherton was furious when we refused to authenticate it without further study. He withdrew the manuscript and stormed out."

"Do you have any idea where he might have taken it?" Carter asked. She sensed the importance of this manuscript in the tangled web she was trying to unravel.

Shaw shook his head. "No idea. He was very secretive about the whole thing. If it was genuine, it would have been incredibly valuable, both academically and financially. But if it was a forgery . . ." He trailed off, the implications hanging in the air between them.

Carter jotted down the latest information, her mind abuzz with potential connections. "And these thefts," she questioned, her voice measured, "could they be linked? Is it possible that someone might have stolen the manuscript, or that Dr. Atherton was somehow involved in these thefts?"

"It's possible," Shaw conceded, there was a lack of certainty to his voice. "The thefts have been remarkably selective. Whoever committed them clearly knew what they were after. If Atherton had a hand in it, it suggests a much more elaborate scheme, something beyond a mere academic's quick profit."

The thought was unsettling to the both of them. The notion that Atherton might have been entangled in such a scheme—or worse, that his death could be part of it—added a disturbing layer to the case.

The stakes were evidently much higher than she had initially anticipated. They were the intricacies of deceit, avarice, and perhaps even murder.

"Thank you for your time, Mr. Shaw," Carter said as she rose from her seat.

"I'll be in touch if we need any further information."

Shaw nodded; a look of concern etched on his face. "I hope you find the answers you seek, Constable. It's disquieting to think that someone might kill over such matters. Although," he hesitated, a thoughtful frown crossing his features, "now that I think about it, the very next day after Atherton left in a fury, one of the thefts occurred."

"Did it?" Carter answered. "Did it indeed."

With a newfound sense of purpose, Carter made her way out of the museum, her thoughts a whirlwind of connections between the art world and Atherton's murder. She knew she had to share this information with Rievaulx, convinced that the intertwining threads of academia, ambition, and theft could lead them closer to uncovering the truth.

As she stepped back into the sunlit streets of Cambridge, the vibrant atmosphere enveloped her, and the ringing of bicycle bells chimed like a clarion call. She would pursue this lead, determined to find the resolution of a murder that had rocked the heart of the College.

THE RIVER CAM WOUND ITS WAY through the heart of Cambridge, a quiet ribbon of stillness that mirrored the golden afternoon light with a serene grace. Punts glided softly along the water, their passengers immersed in hushed conversations or simply savoring the beauty of the day. Jonathan Rievaulx stood at the stern of his punt, the long pole in his hand slicing through the water with the ease of someone who had long since mastered the art. His movements were unhurried, almost meditative, as he guided them forward with each deliberate push.

Opposite him sat Lydia, his companion and emotional anchor, her poise as natural as the gentle breeze that played with her auburn hair, catching the sunlight in warm, coppery hues. Her hair, cut in a stylish yet practical manner, framed a face that was both beautiful and sharp, much like her mind. Lydia's green eyes, perceptive and kind, took in the world with a quiet confidence that drew people to her. There was an elegance about her that was never ostentatious, a subtle sophistication that reflected her life as a journalist in London.

Today, Lydia wore a tailored jacket over a blouse, paired with well-cut trousers that spoke of someone who valued both style and substance. She had a way of dressing that was always impeccable, yet never showy, a reflection of her personality. As they drifted down the river, Lydia's gaze was thoughtful, as if she were mentally sifting through the day's events, weighing them with the same care she brought to her work. Independent and intelligent, Lydia had a passion for uncovering the truth, a quality that made her an excellent journalist. She was also empathetic, a good listener who offered well-considered advice and support.

Lydia wasn't one to be easily swayed. She had a strong will and wasn't afraid to challenge Rievaulx, particularly when she felt he was neglecting their relationship in favor of his work. Honesty and communication were cornerstones for her, and though this sometimes put her at odds with Rievaulx's more reserved nature, it was what made their relationship work. Lydia balanced him out, grounding him when his thoughts threatened to carry him away into the complexities of his cases. Still, he brought something to the table. Not just the brooding intellect or the ability to make sense of tangled messes that left others floundering, though that helped. It was more the way he could take a problem—hers or anyone's—and look at it from an angle no one else had thought of. It was oddly reassuring, like having a private hotline to a sharper sort of logic.

Lydia kept him grounded when his cases threatened to pull him too far into abstraction. He, in turn, reminded her that not every problem had to be solved on instinct and adrenaline. Between them, they found a kind of balance—admittedly a precarious one, but it worked well enough most of the time.

For Jonathan, Lydia was the link that kept him connected to the world beyond his own mind. He enjoyed the quiet solitude of

Cambridge, but he knew that it was Lydia who reminded him to live in the present, to engage with life beyond the cases that consumed him. She was the more extroverted half of their partnership, always unafraid to engage with him and with the world, even when he retreated into his introspections.

Today, though, there was a comfortable silence between them, the kind that only comes from a deep understanding of one another. The river flowed on, the poles dipping in and out of the water, and for a while, it felt as if nothing else existed but the two of them, drifting together in the golden afternoon light.

"Cambridge really is special, isn't it?" Lydia's tone was neutral, more of an observation than an expression of admiration.

Jonathan nodded, pushing the pole against the riverbed with a bit more force than necessary. "It's a place where history and the present coexist, sometimes uneasily. The past is always there, in the buildings, the traditions, even in the air you breathe."

Lydia looked at him with a bemused smile. "You sound almost wistful, Jonathan. I wouldn't have pegged you as the nostalgic type."

"Not nostalgic," Jonathan replied, guiding the punt under the low-hanging branches of a willow. "But it's hard not to feel the weight of it all. The poets, the philosophers, the centuries of thought and debate; it's all here, layered like sediment."

"And what's your point?" Lydia asked, her gaze drifting to the passing scenery. "That Cambridge is some kind of timeless haven, untouched by the outside world?"

Jonathan paused, considering his words carefully. "Not untouched, but insulated, perhaps. It's a place that can make you forget there's a world beyond these banks. But that's not necessarily a good thing."

Lydia's smile turned wry. "No, I suppose not. It's easy to get lost in a place like this—to start thinking that all that matters is what happens within these walls, when in reality, the world moves on without you."

Jonathan leaned on the pole for a moment, letting the punt drift as he recited softly, "*Stands the Church clock at ten to three? And is there honey still for tea?*"

Lydia arched an eyebrow. "Rupert Brooke? Now there's a surprise. I didn't know you had a poetic streak."

He chuckled softly. "I wouldn't call it that. But Brooke had a way of capturing the essence of this place, its beauty, yes, but also its sense of loss. He wrote that poem from Berlin, you know, yearning for a place he could never fully return to."

"Ah, so it's a cautionary tale then," Lydia said, her tone more reflective now. "Longing for a past that's gone, while the present slips away unnoticed."

"Something like that," Jonathan agreed, resuming his steady rhythm with the pole. "Cambridge can do that to you, make you look back, even as you try to move forward."

They drifted in silence for a while, the only sounds the gentle lapping of the water against the punt and the distant hum of the city beyond the riverbanks. For Rievaulx, this moment of quiet was both a comfort and a weight. The case, with all its complexities and uncertainties, lingered in the back of his mind, and Lydia's words had struck closer to home than he cared to admit.

As they approached Grantchester, the village's ancient spires and rooftops came into view, softened by the late afternoon light. The famous Orchard Tea Garden awaited them, a place of calm and simplicity where the weight of the world could be set aside, if only for a short while.

"Jonathan," Lydia said, breaking the silence as they neared the bank, "you've been quiet lately. Is it the case, or something else?"

Rievaulx didn't answer immediately, the question pulling him in several directions at once. "The case," he said finally, though he knew it wasn't the whole truth. "It's more complicated than I expected. There are connections I can't quite see yet, pieces that don't fit."

Lydia nodded, her expression thoughtful. "And you're worried it's all you have, aren't you? That solving these puzzles is the only thing that gives your life meaning."

Rievaulx flinched inwardly, though he kept his face impassive. Lydia had always had a knack for cutting through his defenses, seeing the truths he preferred to keep hidden. "It's what I'm good at," he said simply, though the words felt hollow to him.

Lydia didn't press further, sensing when to leave a subject alone. They moored the punt and made their way up the path to the Tea Garden, the scent of flowers and freshly cut grass filling the warm summer air. Grantchester was as idyllic as ever, a place where it felt as if time stood still, where the world's complexities felt far away.

But as they settled at a small table under an apple tree, Jonathan couldn't shake the feeling that the case was drawing him deeper into a labyrinth of secrets and lies, one where the past and present were so tightly woven together that it was impossible to see where one ended and the other began.

Their tea arrived, along with a plate of scones, strawberry jam, and clotted cream, and for a moment, it was like everything might be all right. The peace was fleeting, the calm before a storm that Rievaulx knew was gathering on the horizon.

Lydia, ever pragmatic, steered the conversation towards lighter topics, sharing stories of her work in London and the latest gossip from the art world. Rievaulx listened, grateful for the distraction, but always, at the back of his mind, the case continued to churn, unresolved and relentless.

As they finished their tea and prepared to leave, Lydia to catch her train back to London, the shadows had lengthened, casting a golden light over the garden. Jonathan knew he would have to return to the demands of the investigation, but for now, he allowed himself this brief moment of calm.

As they walked back to the punt, Lydia by his side, Rievaulx wondered in spite of himself if the truths he sought would ever fully come to light or if they would remain forever hidden in the shadows of Cambridge's ancient walls.

Rievaulx's flat on Bateman Street was a place of quiet refuge, unassuming from the outside, yet within its walls, it held the rich scent of old books and the quiet hum of a mind constantly at work. It was his sanctuary, a retreat from the world where he could immerse himself in the intricate puzzles that his profession presented. Tonight, though, as he closed the door behind him, the familiar comfort of the space eluded him, the weight of the day pressing down with an unrelenting force.

After leaving Lydia at the train station, he had walked back through the twilight streets of Cambridge, his thoughts were on the day's events and the words Lydia had spoken. Her insight, as ever, had cut through to the heart of the matter, uncomfortably so. He was consumed by his work, driven to disentangle the web of mysteries laid before him. Was that all there was?

Rievaulx poured himself a glass of Scotch and settled into his favorite armchair, the one perfectly positioned to gaze out of the window overlooking the narrow street below. The last rays of daylight were fading, soon to be replaced by the warm, golden glow of the lampposts that dotted the pavement. This view had been his solace on many a solitary night, but tonight, it felt different; the shadows outside creeping closer, threatening to overtake the light.

As he sipped his drink, Rievaulx's thoughts drifted inevitably back to the case, particularly the conversation he'd had with Carter earlier that day. Her recounting of the interview with Mr. Shaw at the Fitzwilliam had been thorough, her enthusiasm almost infectious as she spoke of the elusive manuscript. The idea of Atherton, a man so desperate to prove the document's authenticity, had stayed with Rievaulx. It was a desperation that had spilled over into something darker—possibly even theft.

The connection between Atherton's murder and the recent art thefts felt tenuous, the puzzle pieces refusing to fit neatly together. Yet Carter's persistence suggested there might be more to discover. Rievaulx knew better than to dismiss unlikely connections; often, the truth was buried in the most unexpected places, hidden in the shadows of seemingly unrelated events. The manuscript, its dubious authenticity, and the involvement of an antiquarian; all these elements hinted at something more sinister lurking beneath the surface of Cambridge's genteel academic exterior.

He set his glass down and leaned back in the chair, his gaze wandering to the shelves of books that lined the room. Most of the volumes were related to his work: criminal psychology, forensic science, the history of detective methods, but there were others too, books on philosophy, botany, and art, each representing a different facet of his curiosity. Rievaulx had always been drawn to the intersection of knowledge and mystery, to the notion that the past held the keys to understanding the present.

His eyes fell on a collection of rare plants on the windowsill, their delicate leaves and blossoms thriving under his care. The plants were a personal passion, a reminder that life, in all its fragility, required patience and nurturing. In a world where death and decay were often his focus, tending to something living provided a much-needed balance. It was a small act of defiance against the darkness that so frequently occupied his thoughts.

As he watered the plants, allowing his mind to wander, the image of Atherton's manuscript resurfaced. The scientist's fervent insistence on its authenticity had undoubtedly been driven by more than academic interest. If the manuscript was genuine, it could have been immensely valuable, enough to tempt someone into drastic action. If it was a forgery, then Atherton's desperation could have led him into dangerous territory, one where the stakes were higher than he had anticipated.

Rievaulx's thoughts meandered through the gallery of individuals he had encountered during the investigation: Harper, whose cold anger barely concealed her resentment; Lang, with his polished charm masking deeper secrets; Forsyth, trembling with nervousness and fear; Grayson, detached and clinical as always; and Arden, whose friendly openness was almost too easy. Rievaulx had long learnt to be wary of those who presented themselves as the most agreeable; more often than not, they were the ones harboring the darkest intentions. Each of these characters had their own connections to Atherton, their own motives, but which one had the capacity for murder? Also, how did the manuscript fit with what he already knew?

He set the watering can aside and returned to his armchair, picking up his glass once more. The warmth of the Scotch spread through him, but it did little to alleviate the tension coiled in his chest. Outside, the city was settling into the quiet of the evening, the gentle glow of the streetlights casting long shadows across the cobblestones.

Rievaulx thought of Lydia; her patience, her insight, and the subtle but persistent doubts that had crept into their relationship. He knew she was right; his work had consumed him, leaving little room for anything else. He also knew he couldn't turn away, not when the truth felt so close, just out of reach, waiting to be uncovered.

He took another sip of Scotch, his mind already going over the next steps in the investigation. There was still so much to unravel, so many unanswered questions, but for now, in the quiet of his flat, he allowed himself a moment to acknowledge the toll that the case, and his relentless pursuit of answers, had taken on him.

As the evening deepened, the city outside began to hush, the stillness settling in. Rievaulx knew sleep would be elusive tonight, with the weight of the case and Lydia's words pressing on his thoughts. He also knew he would push forward, driven by the need to find the truth, no matter what the cost.

And as he finished his drink and set the glass aside, Rievaulx knew he was committed to bringing the answers into the light, to keep searching until the mysteries that haunted him were finally laid to rest. It was because in the end, that was who he was, a detective, bound to the pursuit of truth, even when the shadows closed in around him.

Chapter 6

Cambridge, with its ivy-clad Colleges and cobblestone streets, also concealed a world beneath its scholarly veneer, a vibrant subculture thriving in the bohemian cafés and pubs tucked away in the city's backstreets, particularly in the Kite area. This district, marked for demolition by relentless developers, stood as a defiant bastion of old working-class charm, increasingly worn but stubbornly resistant to change.

Among these eclectic establishments was Waffles Café, a world apart from the hallowed halls of academia where tradition and decorum held sway. The café buzzed with an air of vibrant rebellion, its walls plastered with faded posters from bygone protests and revolutionary movements, remnants of a restless spirit that appeared to linger in every corner. The mingling scents of strong coffee, cheap ale, and the acrid tang of cigarette smoke created a heady atmosphere that spoke of resistance and defiance.

Waffles Café, perched on the corner of Gold and Fitzroy Streets, famous for its unusual and decidedly bohemian Sunday breakfast of bacon, eggs bolognaise with maple syrup, was more than just a place to grab a bite. It had become the epicenter of the "resistance" against the demolition of the Kite area. Its iconic charm was unmistakable; from the flared trousers of the owners to the whimsical lollipop-style pillars outside and the Victorian sweet-shop interior. It was a haven for those who cherished its unique blend of aesthetic flair and political fervor.

It was in these enclaves of counterculture that several of the University's students gathered, drawn together by a shared disdain for the establishment and a hunger for radical change. The conversations that hummed through the dimly lit rooms were filled with fervor, ranging from heated debates about politics and philosophy to impassioned discussions of art and literature. It was a world that thrived on challenging the status quo, where ideas flowed as freely as the drinks, and where the lines between thought and action often blurred.

Rievaulx and Carter pushed open the door of the Café, a place that had clearly seen better days. The tinkle of a small bell above the door announced their arrival, immediately drawing the attention of those within. The interior was a chaotic blend of mismatched furniture, as if the tables and chairs had been collected from various house clearances and hastily assembled into a café. The tables were strewn with half-empty mugs of coffee and glasses of ale, remnants of earlier, more carefree conversations.

The patrons, an eclectic mix of students, academics, and local eccentrics, turned to scrutinize the newcomers, their chatter faltering as they registered the unwelcome sight of authority figures in their midst. Suspicion flickered in their eyes, and the atmosphere, once filled with the hum of animated discussion, became tense. It was as if Rievaulx and Carter had intruded upon a private club, where the mere presence of the law was enough to disturb the fragile equilibrium.

Rievaulx, ever the master of subtle observation, took in the scene with a calm detachment. He could sense the unease his appearance had caused, the way conversations had petered out and glances were exchanged across the room. Carter, standing just behind him, felt the shift in the air too, the cold draft of hostility that greeted them as surely as if someone had opened a window to let in the chill.

They had little choice; it was in this very sanctuary of youthful rebellion that they had finally cornered the elusive Hawk. His name had surfaced in hushed whispers, accompanied by vague shrugs and uneasy frowns whenever they inquired about him. No one was particularly eager to discuss Hawk's whereabouts, as though even acknowledging his existence might invite trouble. Known for his radical views and open disdain for the academic establishment, Hawk had a reputation that preceded him. His recent argument with Atherton made him a person of interest that no diligent investigator could afford to ignore.

Rievaulx was undeterred as he scanned the room. He had been in far less welcoming places and knew better than to let a few hostile stares put him off his stride. He nodded to Carter, who returned the gesture with a determined look of her own. They had work to do, and no amount of resentment from this motley crowd would deter them from their task.

Carter too scanned the room, her gaze finally settling on a figure slouched in the far corner, half-obscured by a cloud of smoke. The young man was dressed in a battered leather jacket, his hair long and unkempt, and his expression one of practiced indifference. This, she knew, was "Hawk"—the notorious figure within the University's counter-culture scene.

"Hawk," Carter said, approaching the table with a calm but with authority. "We would like to have a word."

Hawk looked up, his eyes narrowed as he took in the sight of the two police officers. "What do you want, pig?" he sneered, the insult delivered with the kind of casual arrogance that only the very young or the very foolish could muster.

Rievaulx remained unfazed, pulling out a chair and seating himself opposite Hawk, gesturing for Carter to do the same. "We're investigating the death of Dr. Atherton," he said evenly, his voice carrying the weight of authority that Hawk's bravado could not diminish. "We've been told you had a disagreement with him shortly before he was killed. We'd like to hear your side of the story."

Hawk snorted, taking a long drag on his cigarette before exhaling a plume of smoke in their direction. "Atherton was a pompous old git," he said with a shrug. "Always lording it over us, acting like he knew everything. We didn't exactly see eye to eye, but that's hardly a crime, is it?"

Carter locked eyes with Hawk. "Witnesses saw you arguing with him," she said, her tone brooking no nonsense. "They said you were shouting, that you looked ready to punch him. What was it about?"

Hawk flicked ash from his cigarette, his gaze drifting lazily over the room before settling back on Carter. "The old man caught me trying to sell a manuscript," he said finally, the words delivered with a nonchalance that belied the seriousness of the situation. "Said it was a fake. Told me he was going to report me to the authorities, get me expelled. I told him to shove it. He didn't scare me."

Rievaulx studied Hawk, noting the bravado in his tone but also the underlying tension. His mind was making the connection. "Where did you get the manuscript?" he asked, his voice insistent but calm.

Hawk hesitated, his eyes flicking away as he stubbed out his cigarette in a chipped ashtray. "Picked it up from a bloke down by the river," he said finally. "Said it was genuine, worth a fortune. I figured I could make a quick quid off it, maybe even fund a few projects. Atherton saw right through it, called me out."

"Did you know it was a forgery?" Carter asked, cutting through the haze of smoke and deception that surrounded Hawk.

Hawk gave a half-hearted shrug, a gesture that spoke of indifference but didn't quite manage to hide the flicker of uncertainty in his eyes. "Maybe. But it wasn't my problem. I was just trying to make some cash."

Rievaulx exchanged a glance with Carter as he raced through the implications in his mind of Hawk's story. The connection between the student and Atherton was becoming clearer. His argument with Atherton had been about the authenticity of the manuscript, not something more sinister.

"Where's the manuscript now?" Rievaulx asked as he probed for more information.

Hawk's eyes flashed with annoyance, and he shifted uncomfortably in his seat. "Atherton took it, didn't he? Said he was going to turn it over to the authorities, get me kicked out of varsity. I never saw it again."

Carter leaned back in her chair, frustrated. Hawk was clearly no killer. He was a brash, arrogant student, more concerned with making a quick profit than with taking a life. His connection to the forged manuscript raised more questions than it answered. There was a thread here.

"What do you know about the art thefts that have been happening around Cambridge?" Rievaulx asked, pushing past the surface of Hawk's bravado.

Hawk raised an eyebrow, a smirk playing on his lips. "You think I'm mixed up in that, too? Sorry to disappoint, but I'm no thief. I've got enough on my plate without adding larceny to the list."

Rievaulx regarded him, his gaze steady as he measured Hawk's words against the backdrop of the case they were trying to piece together. "Someone's been moving stolen art and antiquities through the black-market in Cambridge. You must have heard something."

Carter froze as this was the first time she'd heard any mention of a black-market in Cambridge. Was Rievaulx privy to information he hadn't yet shared with her, or was he merely fishing, casting a line to see what he might reel in? His tone, always so measured, gave nothing away. Was he playing a hunch or working from something more solid?

Hawk hesitated, his eyes flickering with something that looked like unease, a chink in his otherwise impenetrable armor of indifference. "Maybe I've heard a few things," he said slowly, his voice dropping to a more cautious tone. "But I'm not involved. There's a bloke who deals in that sort of thing. Some antiquated git." He stopped and gave a chuckle. "Antiquated antiquarian. Calls himself *The Curator*. Word is he's been moving some serious merchandise, but I don't know what, where or how."

Carter exchanged a glance with Rievaulx, her pulse quickening at the mention of a mysterious figure known as *The Curator*. It was an intriguing lead and if this Curator was involved in the art thefts, it could be a significant and one they would have to unravel.

"Where can we find this Curator?" Rievaulx asked, his tone firm.

Hawk shook his head, and he leaned back in his chair, regaining some of his earlier bravado. "You don't find him, mate. He finds you. And trust me, you don't want him finding you."

Carter felt that Hawk was clearly holding back, but she knew that pushing him too hard might cause him to clam up entirely. They wanted more information, but they would have to be careful about how they went about getting it. The last thing was for Hawk to go underground, taking any useful leads with him.

Rievaulx stood, studying Hawk with a level gaze that didn't so much challenge his composure as quietly dismantle it. "If you think of anything else, you know where to find us," he said, his tone both a warning and a statement.

Hawk watched them leave, a flicker of uncertainty crossing his face.

As they stepped out into the cool Cambridge air, the noise and energy of the café fading behind them, Carter turned to Rievaulx. Her exasperation was apparent in the tightness of her voice. "What do you think, sir? Is Hawk telling the truth?"

Rievaulx ever thoughtful and his eyes were distant as he considered the possibilities. "I think he's telling us what he wants us to believe. There's more going on here than we realize. The manuscript, *The Curator*; these are pieces of a larger puzzle, one that we've only just begun to understand."

Carter nodded.

"We must keep an eye on that erstwhile young man," Rievaulx said, pulling Carter into the doorway of a derelict building where they could observe the doorway of Waffles without being observed themselves. They didn't have to wait long for Hawk to appear.

THE NARROW STREETS OF CAMBRIDGE WERE a veritable labyrinth of cobblestones, winding alleys, and ancient buildings that loomed like stern sentinels over the city's historic heart. Through these serpentine passages, Hawk led them on a chase that cut through time itself. Skirting past Christ's Pieces, dodging the crowds near the bus station, and threading his way through Bradwell's Court, Hawk moved with the agility of someone who had long mastered the city's hidden corners. Despite his disheveled appearance, he navigated the throngs of students and tourists with a nimbleness that spoke of the deep familiarity with Cambridge's backstreets.

Rievaulx and Carter pursued him as their footsteps rang off the weathered stones, struggling to keep up. Hawk had glanced over his shoulder realizing he was being followed, bolted into Market Square. His long legs carried him away with an unexpected swiftness that only heightened their urgency.

"Damn it," Carter muttered as she was forced to sidestep a group of tourists clustered around a street performer. A mime, his face painted white and frozen in an exaggerated expression, held his pose as the crowd, oblivious to the chase unfolding nearby, erupted into applause. Carter pushed through them, her eyes never leaving Hawk's retreating form. "We can't let him get away."

Rievaulx, hot on her heels, was forced to dodge a group of students cycling carelessly down Sidney Street, their gowns billowing behind them as they chatted animatedly, unaware of the drama playing out around them. The students, startled by the sudden appearance of two officers in pursuit, veered off course, causing a brief but chaotic entanglement. Rievaulx managed to maneuver around them, trying to predict Hawk's next move. Though Hawk had the advantage of knowing the city's twists and turns, Rievaulx's own intimate knowledge of Cambridge's quirks and shortcuts promised to even the odds.

"Hawk!" Rievaulx's voice cut through the bustling market, firm and commanding. "Stop running! We just want to talk."

Hawk had no intention of stopping. He threw a frantic glance over his shoulder before veering sharply into St Edward's Passage, nearly colliding with Snowy, a familiar fixture on the Cambridge streets in his usual mix of antique military garb and eccentric headwear, with a mouse on one shoulder and a goat trailing behind.

Hawk didn't slow down, and neither did Carter, who narrowly avoided Snowy's goat herself as she followed him into the narrow passage.

Carter rounded the corner, her boots slipping on the uneven cobblestones still slick from an earlier downpour. Ahead, Hawk was a blur of movement, his figure disappearing and reappearing between the shadows cast by the tall, ancient buildings. Each step was a struggle as she fought to maintain her footing while keeping up the relentless pace.

Rievaulx, maintaining his calm, followed closely behind, his breathing measured despite the chase. He sidestepped a couple walking arm in arm, their startled expressions betraying their surprise at the sudden disruption of their peaceful stroll. Experience had taught him that this pursuit would require both speed and strategy. He hoped Hawk's youth and impulsiveness could be turned to their advantage.

Bursting out of the narrow passage onto King's Parade, Hawk picked up speed, darting onto Trumpington Street before making a sharp turn onto Silver Street. The street was busy with pedestrians, and Hawk weaved through them with a deftness born of desperation.

"Where's he headed?" Carter shouted over her shoulder; her voice taut with determination as they pursued him toward the

Silver Street bridge. Rievaulx, striving to keep pace, was gradually losing ground as the chase continued.

At the bridge, Hawk hesitated, casting a wary glance over the side as though considering a daring leap into the Cam below. The river, with its gentle flow and peaceful punts, contrasted sharply with the frantic chase that had led them here.

"He's going to jump!" Carter's pulse quickened. "We have to stop him!"

Instead of plunging into the Cam, Hawk swerved down the steps leading to the riverbank, heading straight for Scudamore's Punting Company, where the punts bobbed gently on the water, the late afternoon sun casting a sheen over the scene. His eyes locked on the river as if it offered the key to his escape, Hawk made for one of the punts with single-minded determination.

Carter and Rievaulx skidded to a halt at the river's edge, dodging a family of tourists who were photographing the iconic view. The parents, clutching maps and cameras, looked up in surprise as the two police officers rushed past, their expressions shifting from confusion to curiosity. There was no time to explain; their focus was entirely on Hawk, whose figure was now unsteady on a punt as he tried to push off from the bank.

Hawk leapt onto the punt, nearly capsizing it in the process. The vessel wobbled precariously, water sloshing over the sides, but Hawk managed to steady himself, grabbing the long pole used for punting.

For a brief moment, it appeared Hawk might actually escape, gliding across the river. Then, with a fateful slip, the pole slid from his grasp and disappeared into the water, leaving him stranded in the middle of the Cam, helplessly adrift.

Carter let out a dry chuckle, the tension of the chase dissolving into the absurdity of the situation. "He's stuck," she said, shaking her head in disbelief. "What now, sir?"

Rievaulx, catching his breath, reached for his radio with a calm, measured hand. "Now," he replied, his voice steady, "we reel him in." For once, he had remembered his radio and called for reinforcements, his tone betraying no doubt. "He's not going anywhere."

As they waited for a boat to retrieve Hawk, Carter kept her eyes on the young man, who now sat miserably in the punt, his earlier bravado replaced by the reality of his predicament. The chase had ended in the most anticlimactic way possible, but it had also confirmed something important. Hawk was more scared than dangerous. His connection to Atherton's death appeared tenuous at best, and it was clear he had more to fear from the authorities.

When the boat finally arrived to bring Hawk back to shore, Carter was relieved. They had caught him, but the chase had only highlighted the gaps in their understanding of the case. Hawk wasn't their killer of that, she was certain. His involvement in the underground dealings of Cambridge's student subculture and the potential black market was a thread they couldn't afford to ignore.

As they led Hawk back to the station, the sun was beginning to dip below the horizon, casting long shadows across the city, Carter felt a renewed sense of determination. The case was far from over, and there were too many unanswered questions. With this new piece of information, they were getting closer to knowing what happened.

She decided that she wasn't going to stop until they had it.

THE POLICE STATION BUZZED WITH A quiet energy when Rievaulx and Carter returned, Hawk in tow. The stark contrast between the intense, labyrinthine chase through Cambridge's cobblestone streets and the bustling, organized chaos of the station hit Carter like a cold splash of water. Officers moved with purpose between desks, telephones rang with an insistent urgency, the rhythmic clatter of typewriters, some staccato, some leisurely, mingled with the low hum of conversation. For a moment, Carter felt disoriented; the sudden shift in atmosphere threw her off balance.

Hawk, now handcuffed, was promptly escorted to an interview room by two uniformed officers. The cocky bravado that had fueled his flight had evaporated, leaving behind a nervous young man who was painfully aware of how deeply he was in over his head. Rievaulx and Carter watched him go, both acutely aware that while Hawk was unlikely to be the mastermind behind Dr. Atherton's murder. Every lead, no matter how small, had to be pursued.

"Let's debrief," Rievaulx suggested, nodding toward the small office that had become their ad hoc headquarters for the case. The room was a microcosm of their investigation, cluttered with files, maps, and hastily scribbled notes, all arranged in a precise yet chaotic order mirroring the complexity of the case itself. Rievaulx's methodical nature had turned the space into a tactical nerve center, every item strategically placed to extract the most information.

Carter followed him inside, closing the door behind them as Rievaulx settled into the chair behind the desk. His expression was thoughtful, almost distant, as he steepled his fingers; a gesture Carter had come to recognize as a sign that he was mentally piecing together the puzzle.

"What do you make of Hawk?" Rievaulx's tone was contemplative, less about seeking answers and more about inviting reflection.

Carter leaned against the edge of the desk. "He's small-time, sir. He got caught up in the thrill of rebellion and easy money, but I don't think he is our killer. The manuscript he tried to sell was probably a forgery, and his involvement with Atherton is driven more by youthful arrogance than anything of real substance."

Rievaulx nodded, his fingers drumming lightly on the desk. "Agreed. But the mention of *The Curator*, that's something we can't ignore. If there's a figure operating in the shadows, moving stolen art and antiquities, that's a lead worth digging into."

Carter crossed her arms. "Do you think this Curator could be linked to the art thefts we've been investigating? Or even to Atherton's death?"

"It's possible," Rievaulx replied. "We know Atherton was involved in something concerning a manuscript, whether it was genuine or not, it held value. If *The Curator* is involved in black-market dealings, it's not far-fetched to think Atherton might have crossed paths with him."

Carter agreed. "We will have to investigate this Curator's operations," she said. "If he's moving stolen goods, someone in the art world or academic circles must have heard of him. We can start by talking to the people closest to Atherton, his colleagues, his students. Someone must know something."

Rievaulx leaned back in his chair, "Agreed. But we also need to tread carefully. If this Curator is as elusive as Hawk suggests, we're dealing with someone who's adept at covering their tracks. We can't afford to spook him."

They spent the next hour meticulously reviewing the details of the case, piecing together what they knew and identifying the gaps that still needed to be filled. It was methodical work, the kind that required patience and precision, qualities Rievaulx possessed in abundance. For Carter, though, the process was as maddening as it was necessary. She longed to act, to drive the investigation forward, but she also understood that they couldn't afford mistakes. The stakes were too high, the case too complex.

As they wrapped up their debrief, Rievaulx said to her. "We're making progress, Carter," he said, his voice steady and reassuring. "It may not feel like it, but we are. This case isn't going to be solved overnight, but we're getting closer."

Afterwards, they made their way to the interview room, where Hawk sat trying to maintain his earlier bravado, though his confidence was noticeably frayed. As Rievaulx and Carter entered, Hawk's eyes flicked up, and for a fleeting moment, there was a glimmer of wariness before it was quickly masked by a sneer that didn't quite reach his eyes.

Rievaulx took the lead, his voice calm yet carrying the weight of authority. "Hawk, let's talk about that manuscript you tried to sell. We know it's probably a forgery, but what's more intriguing to us is your connection to it. Who's *The Curator*?"

Hawk leaned back in his chair, his shoulders rolling in

an exaggerated shrug as if the question was beneath him. *The Curator*? He let out a short, dismissive laugh. "I don't know. Never met the guy. He's just a name, a shadow. I don't deal with shadows; I deal with opportunities." His eyes darted to Carter, then back to Rievaulx, searching for any sign of how much they might already know.

Rievaulx allowed the silence to stretch. It was a tactic to make the suspect fill the void with more than they intended. Hawk shifted in his seat, a crack appearing in his façade. "Look," he said defensively, "I got the manuscript through some people I know. I wasn't asking for a pedigree. It was just another deal, that's all."

"And these people you know," Carter interjected. "They wouldn't, by any chance, be connected to that commune outside Cambridge, would they? The one where "dropping out" is taken rather more seriously than just a lifestyle choice?"

Hawk's sneer faltered, yet he recovered, leaning forward with feigned casualness. "You might hear things at the commune, sure," he admitted, "but it's all just talk. Smoke and mirrors. You'd be wasting your time sniffing around there. Nothing solid, nothing real."

Rievaulx exchanged a glance with Carter. The commune could be something that might lead them closer to *The Curator* and, by extension, to the truth behind Atherton's death.

Rievaulx observed Hawk weighing the truth in his words. "Perhaps," he said slowly, "but we'll be the judge of that. If there's even a whisper that leads us to this Curator, we'll find it."

Hawk's bravado flickered, the reality of his situation pressing down on him, yet he wasn't ready to give in completely. "Suit yourself," he muttered, though the confidence in his voice had a hollow ring. "But don't say I didn't warn you when you come up empty-handed."

Rievaulx stood, signaling the end of the interview. "We'll see," he said with quiet finality. "In the meantime, I'd suggest you think carefully about your position, Hawk. Cooperation might be the only card you have left to play."

As they left the room, Carter noticed the subtle shift in Hawk's manner, still trying to play the part of the confident rebel, but the cracks were starting to show. The mention of the commune had struck a nerve.

Back in the corridor, Rievaulx turned to Carter. "The commune might be our next step. Something tells me Hawk knows more than he's letting on, but we'll get there in time."

Carter was already mentally preparing for the next stage of their investigation. The commune outside Cambridge might hold answers to questions they hadn't even thought to ask yet.

"What do we do with him in the meantime? We've no real grounds to hold him," Carter said. "Technically, he hasn't done anything wrong."

She was already losing interest in him. He'd likely said all he was going to.

"Quite," Rievaulx nodded. "Tell Pritchard to let him go. For now. But make it clear we may need to speak to him again. And if we do, he'd be wise not to take us on another scenic tour of central Cambridge."

Carter tilted her head. "Why do you think he ran? Could be he knows more about this 'Curator' than he's letting on?"

Rievaulx paused, the sort of pause that meant his mind was already running ahead. "Possibly," he said at last. "But until we know who *The Curator* actually is, there's little point playing guessing games with someone who clearly enjoys the spotlight." He frowned. "That said, the mention of the commune unsettled him. No question about that."

Chapter 7

THE LATE AFTERNOON SUN CAST A somber glow over the weathered stone walls of St Michael's College, its warm light slowly giving way to the encroaching shadows of evening. The once-inviting golden hues now emphasized the College's imposing, almost forbidding façade, a stark reminder of its ancient traditions and the weight of its history.

Rievaulx and Carter made their way to Dr. Sylvia Harper's office. The recent emergence of the so-called Curator, an antiquarian, by all accounts, and his connection to Dr Atherton's mysterious manuscript had brought them back to Dr Harper. If anyone's expertise in classical studies could shed light on the matter, it was hers.

As they approached her door, which stood slightly ajar as it had on their previous visit, the change in Dr. Harper's manner was immediately apparent. Gone was the thin veneer of cordiality she had displayed before; in its place was palpable impatience, as though their presence was nothing more than an unwelcome interruption to her work.

When they entered, Dr. Harper remained seated at her desk, her eyes narrowing in irritation as she looked up from a pile of papers. She made no effort to rise or offer them a seat, the chill in the room a stark contrast to the warmth of the setting sun outside.

"Back again, Chief Inspector?" she said, her tone dripping with annoyance. "I would have thought our last conversation covered all you needed to know."

The ever-unflappable Rievaulx responded with a polite nod, refusing to be unsettled by her brusqueness. "Indeed, Dr. Harper. However, new information has come to light, and we were hoping you could shed some more light on it."

Harper leaned back in her chair with an air of resignation. "Very well but do be quick about it. Unlike some, I have actual work to do."

This comment irritated Carter, but she kept her expression neutral as Rievaulx took the lead. She suspected that Dr. Harper's sharp tongue was a defense mechanism, yet it did little to make the interaction any easier with her.

"Dr. Harper," Rievaulx began, his tone as measured as ever, "we've come across evidence suggesting that the manuscript Dr. Atherton was working on is more complex than it initially appeared. We wanted to revisit your concerns about its authenticity."

Harper's eyes flicked to the side. Carter recognized the subtle gesture as a tell. There was something she wasn't saying. "My reservations were purely academic, Chief Inspector. I have little patience for flights of fancy, and that's precisely what Atherton's so-called manuscript was a fantasy, a fabrication. I made that clear to him on more than one occasion."

"And yet," Rievaulx continued, "you didn't lodge any formal complaint with the College about his research, did you? Why was that Dr. Harper?"

Harper hesitated. It was only for a fraction of a second, but it was enough for Carter to catch a glimpse of something beneath the surface, uncertainty, perhaps, or even fear. The moment passed quickly, and Harper's sharp gaze returned to Rievaulx.

"I didn't see the need," she said with a dismissive wave of her hand. "Atherton was stubborn, yes, but he wasn't a fool. I assumed he would eventually come to his senses. Besides, the College has more pressing matters to attend to than indulging in every academic spat."

Rievaulx considered her words carefully. "And yet, the nature of your disagreements with Dr. Atherton might suggest otherwise. Some might even interpret them as a motive, Dr. Harper."

Her eyes flashed with anger, and for a moment, the mask of detached professionalism slipped. "A motive? For what, exactly? Atherton's death?" She let out a short, mirthless laugh. "Don't be absurd, Chief Inspector. I may have disagreed with him, but I certainly didn't wish him dead. If anything, I found him rather pitiable; so desperate for recognition that he clung to that ridiculous manuscript as if it were the key to his legacy."

Harper's manner clearly indicated she was rattled yet she was doing her best to maintain control. Carter carefully watched the exchange as there was clearly more to the story.

"Dr. Harper," Carter spoke, "we're simply trying to understand the dynamics at play here. It's clear that Dr. Atherton's work was important to him, perhaps too important. If there's anything more you can tell us, anything that might help us understand what drove him, now is the time."

Harper's irritation was now tempered by a hint of calculation and appeared to be weighing her options. Finally, Harper leaned forward, her voice dropping to a more conspiratorial tone.

"Atherton wasn't the only one with something at stake," she admitted. "There are others in this College, others who have far more to lose if certain truths come to light. You'd do well to remember that, Chief Inspector."

Rievaulx shifted his posture, subtly tightening his focus. "And who might these others be, Dr. Harper?" he asked, his tone deceptively casual.

Harper was done talking. She straightened in her chair, the moment of vulnerability gone as quickly as it had appeared. "That's for you to find out, Chief Inspector. I've already told you more than I should have. Now, if you'll excuse me, I have work to do."

Rievaulx knew better than to press further, as it was a clear dismissal. He rose from his chair, and Carter followed suit. As they were about to leave, Rievaulx paused and turned back. "Tell me, Dr. Harper, what do you know about a student called Hawk?"

"Hawk?" she repeated, her surprise evident. "I know absolutely nothing about him." She quickly looked down at her desk. "Now, if you don't mind..."

Rievaulx's expression was as inscrutable as ever, but Carter knew him well enough by now to sense the gears turning in his mind. There were more players in this game than they had initially realized, and Harper's cryptic warning only confirmed that they were on the right track. As they walked back through the dimly lit corridors, Carter had the feeling that there was more to their investigation than they first thought, and it was far from over. One thing was certain: the deeper they explored the world of St Michael's College, the more intriguing it became.

THE SCENT OF STALE BEER AND cigarette smoke clung to the air as Rievaulx and Carter stepped into the dimly lit confines of *The Eagle* on Bene't Street. The pub, with its low wooden beams and darkened corners, was a haven for locals, a place where shadows obscured faces, and the presence of outsiders was met with suspicion. The wooden floorboards creaked under their feet as they moved toward a secluded corner booth where Professor Lang sat hunched over a glass of Scotch.

Rievaulx and Carter had noted his furtive exit from St Michael's earlier and had decided to follow him. Now, as they approached, Lang looked up, his eyes narrowing in recognition.

"Detective Chief Inspector. Detective Constable. What brings you here?"

Rievaulx slid into the seat opposite Lang, his expression polite. "We're following up on some leads, Professor. May we ask what brings you here this evening?"

Lang hesitated, his hand tightening around his glass. For a moment, Carter thought he might refuse to answer, but then he set the glass down with a soft clink.

"If you must know, I'm here to settle a debt," he admitted, his voice heavy with resignation. "Gambling, I'm afraid. Not exactly the most respectable pastime, but one must have one's vices."

Carter felt a pang of disappointment. She had been so sure that Lang was involved in something more sinister, but now, her suspicions had been nothing more than a red herring.

"And this debt," Rievaulx asked gently, "has nothing to do with the recent thefts or Dr. Atherton's death?"

Lang shook his head vehemently. "Absolutely not. My ... habits are unfortunate, yes, but I've no involvement in anything criminal, I assure you. The man I was meeting is just an old acquaintance, someone who's been helping me out of a tight spot. That's all."

Rievaulx studied Lang for a moment, trying to see through the layers of the professor's weary exterior. Finally, he accepted the explanation for what it was.

"Thank you for your honesty, Professor," Rievaulx said. "If you think of anything else that might be relevant to our investigation, please don't hesitate to contact us."

Lang offered a smile that did not reach his eyes. "Of course, Chief Inspector. I only wish I could be of more help."

With that, Rievaulx and Carter rose from the booth, leaving Lang to his thoughts. As they exited the pub, Carter couldn't hide her dissatisfaction with the outcome of what they did not learn.

"I was so sure we were onto something," she muttered, her hands clenched into fists at her sides.

Rievaulx's calm manner was in stark contrast to her simmering anger. "Sometimes the obvious lead turns out to be a red herring, Carter. But don't worry, there's still plenty of ground to cover. And speaking of which, I think it's time we consider investigating that commune outside Cambridge could turn out to be more relevant than we know."

Carter's determination renewed. "Tomorrow?" she suggested but Rievaulx shook his head.

"Soon," he replied, "but if they've caught wind of Hawk's arrest, they'll have already taken steps to clear up any loose ends. Best to wait a couple of days; they'll let their guard down by then."

Carter suppressed her impatience again.

As they stepped out of the pub, the crisp evening air was a welcome antidote to the smoky, dim atmosphere they had just left behind. Carter inhaled deeply, letting the coolness refresh her weary lungs, and tried to dispel the frustration that had taken hold.

"Tell me more about this commune," Carter said as they made their way back to her car. The streets were now serene, the soft glow of the streetlamps casting elongated shadows on the cobblestones.

Rievaulx's expression was reflective. "The commune's a few miles outside Cambridge, near Grantchester. It's been around for years, but it's recently drawn some unwelcome attention. The local rag has been making a fuss about it—drug use, petty theft, and even whispers of black-market dealings. Most of it's probably sensationalism, but it's worth investigating."

Carter mentally taking note of the details, especially his reference to "black-market dealings". "And you think there's a link to Atherton?"

Rievaulx shrugged. "It's a possibility. Atherton was entangled in something, that's clear enough. Whether it directly involves the commune is yet to be seen, but I wouldn't be shocked if some of the locals have more to say than they're letting on."

They reached Carter's car, and as she slid into the driver's seat, she couldn't shake the sense that they were on the cusp of a significant breakthrough regarding the overall picture yet some it remained elusive.

"Can I give you a lift anywhere, sir?" she offered, starting the engine.

"No, thank you," Rievaulx said. "I'll manage with my bicycle. I have to be somewhere," he glanced at his watch, "sooner rather than later. As for the commune, I suggest you head out there tomorrow," he advised. "For now, Let's call it a day. We'll need to be sharp for whatever comes next."

THE POLICE STATION TOOK ON AN eerie stillness in the late hours of the night, the fluorescent lights casting a cold, pallid glow over the empty desks and silent corridors. The usual hustle and bustle of the day shift had long faded, leaving behind only a skeleton crew of officers working the late shift, their voices hushed as they handled the mundane tasks of the night. The quiet was so profound that every creak of a chair, every rustle of paper was amplified, turning the station into a mausoleum of unfinished business.

Carter sat at her desk, surrounded by a chaotic array of files. The faces of the suspects blurred in her mind, merging into an indistinct mass as the hours wore on.

She picked up the file marked *Art Theft Investigation*, its neatly typed pages charting a troubling pattern. What began at the Fitzwilliam had spread to London, and now the latest theft had hit the Ashmolean in Oxford. It was no longer local. It was organized.

According to the report, the Monet taken from the Ashmolean—*Twilight over the Waterlilies* (1892)—was thought to have been stolen to order. Acquired by the museum in 1960, it was valued at £250,000. Not exactly the sort of thing that wandered off without help.

Carter let out a low, silent whistle. This wasn't just another opportunistic smash-and-grab. It had the feel of something more organized, more deliberate—and inevitably, more complicated. She toyed with the idea of contacting the Art and Antiques Squad at Scotland Yard, who were knee-deep in the London thefts. Or perhaps Thames Valley, given the Oxford connection.

She checked her watch. Too late now. Any calls at this hour would raise eyebrows, and probably questions she wasn't in the mood to answer. Best to run it past Rievaulx first. Charging off in all directions looked good in theory but rarely got you anywhere worth going.

As for the commune tucked away near Cambridge—well, it wasn't the most obvious choice for hiding stolen Monets and rare manuscripts, but then, criminals rarely rented billboard space. She shook her head. Eccentric cover or convenient red herring, it was worth keeping on the radar.

Still, the real priority was tying it all back to Atherton's murder. It was the closest thing they had to a motive, and for now, the only thing holding the mess together. Carter spent the better part of the evening combing through notes, reports, and anything else that might offer a thread to tug. So far, it was mostly educated guesswork. Heavy on the guess.

"What am I missing?" she murmured to herself, tapping her pen against the desk in a rapid, anxious rhythm that mirrored the disarray of her thoughts.

The missing manuscript, it might indeed be a forgery, but could that alone make it worth killing for? What if the manuscript wasn't just a fake but a piece of something far more insidious?

Rievaulx had suggested the possibility of a black-market for dubious manuscripts, a shadowy world where the value of a text wasn't in its authenticity but in the reputation it could bolster. If such a market existed, how had this particular manuscript become the center of such a perilous situation? The question created a relentless specter that refused to be dismissed.

The deeper she investigated, the more elusive the answers became. Every angle she explored turned into a web of increasingly convoluted possibilities. Was the manuscript part of a larger scheme, more complex than they had anticipated?

The idea that a mere document could be tied to something so nefarious appeared far-fetched, yet the facts stubbornly suggested otherwise. Were there other manuscripts, perhaps more valuable or dangerous, circulating in the shadows? Had this forgery been a mere pawn in a more elaborate game?

Each line of inquiry she pursued led to new, perplexing questions rather than straightforward answers. The manuscript's significance was deliberately obscured by layers of deception and intrigue, and every revelation only added to the mystery. The more she thought about it, the more she felt as though she were chasing shadows.

Her office, usually a sanctuary of order, closed in on her. The piles of paperwork, the scattered notes, and the hastily scribbled thoughts on yellow legal pads were beginning to resemble a battlefield. The telephone's ring interrupted her reverie. As she answered it, her thoughts remained tethered to the mystery of the manuscript. There was no one there, the dial tone a strange hum in her ear. The weight of unanswered questions pressed down on her, and the sense of an impending breakthrough felt tantalizingly close yet maddeningly out of reach.

She glanced at the clock on the wall; it was well past midnight. The rational part of her brain told her it was time to go home, get some sleep, and return with fresh eyes in the morning. In spite of this, the thought of leaving, of walking away from the case even for a few hours, felt like abandoning her post, letting the mystery slip further out of her grasp.

She rubbed her temples, trying to stave off the headache that was threatening to form. Rievaulx was preoccupied earlier; he was distracted in a way that wasn't typical for him

Rievaulx had a knack for seeing things clearly, for cutting through the noise and focusing on what really mattered. Carter admired that about him, even if it made her feel like she was flailing in his wake. She wanted to prove herself, to show that she could hold her own, but the pressure was beginning to weigh on her too.

"All right," she said aloud, as if giving herself a pep talk. "One more hour, then I'll go home."

She picked up the file again, determined to find something—anything—that might tie the pieces together. She flipped through the pages, scrutinizing every detail, every inconsistency. The night stretched on, the station growing quieter with each passing minute, but Carter kept at it, fueled by a mix of stubbornness and caffeine. She wasn't going to let this case beat her. She couldn't afford to. The minutes ticked by; the clarity she sought remained elusive. The more she tried to force the pieces together, the more they resisted.

She rubbed her eyes, her thoughts drifting back to Rievaulx. She wondered if he was still awake, still turning over the same questions in his mind. He had a way of seeing patterns where others saw only chaos, of finding the thread that would unravel the entire mystery. She envied that ability, but more than that, she respected it.

"Come on, Emily," she muttered to herself. "You can do this."

Even as she said the words, doubt crept in. What if she couldn't do it? What if she was missing something crucial, something that Rievaulx would have spotted in an instant? The thought was a constant reminder of the pressure she was under, the expectations she had to meet for herself.

She glanced at the clock again. Almost one in the morning. She began to gather her things, finally admitting defeat for the night. The case would still be there in a few hours, waiting for her, but for now, she must rest to clear her head.

As she left the station and stepped out into the cool night air, Carter couldn't shake a sense that events were moving forward. The city was quiet, the streets deserted, but her mind was anything but. The questions, the doubts, the frustration; they followed her home like shadows, lingering even as she tried to push them away.

JONATHAN RIEVAULX MIGHT HAVE FELT OUT of place at the Garden House Restaurant, Lydia's choice, but years of college dining had left him well-versed in the quiet choreography of cutlery and conversation. It wasn't the formality that unsettled him; it was the pretension. The abstract art on the walls appeared to mock interpretation, and the surrounding diners discussed quantum theory and postmodern collapse as if the fate of civilisation hinged on it.

Jonathan knew how to hold a fork. What he struggled with was the point of the performance.

The polished, self-consciously modern Cambridge this place represented made him feel slightly out of step, as though the city had evolved into something slicker and less recognisable. However, he'd always been a little out of sync, an unexpected arrival to elderly parents, born one winter's evening when his mother, well into her fifties, mistook labour pains for indigestion. They'd never quite recovered from the shock. In truth, neither had he.

They were seated by the window, where the flickering candlelight did little to soften the sharp angles of their faces. The historic streets of Cambridge were visible just beyond the glass, but he found it hard to appreciate them. His mind was elsewhere in the complexities of his latest case. Lydia, as poised and immaculate as ever, was midway through recounting a story about her latest project at the gallery in London. He nodded at what he hoped were the right moments, his responses automatic, his thoughts far from the conversation.

"Jonathan, are you even listening to me?" Lydia's voice cut through his reverie, sharp with irritation. Her expression was one of exasperation, tinged with disappointment, as she set her fork down with a deliberate clink.

"Sorry," he said, offering a sheepish smile that didn't reach his eyes. "It's this case ... it's complicated."

"Complicated," Lydia repeated, her tone heavy with skepticism. She rolled the word around as if it were something bitter. "It always is, isn't it? Every time we have a moment together, you're here in body, but your mind is a thousand miles away."

She wasn't wrong, and Rievaulx knew it. Lydia had a knack for piercing through his defenses, exposing truths he preferred to avoid. "I'm trying," he said, and he meant it. "But this case ... it's like one of those Russian dolls. Every time I think I'm getting somewhere, there's another layer underneath."

Lydia's look softened just a fraction. "And what about us,

Jonathan? Have you given any thought to our future? I've been thinking . . . maybe it's time you considered moving to London. We could be together more often, build a life there."

Rievaulx felt a familiar tightening in his chest, the walls of the restaurant closed in on him. He had known this conversation was coming. Lydia had been dropping hints for weeks, and now it was laid out on the table like an unsavory dish he hadn't ordered. "Lydia, you know how much I love Cambridge. My work, my life—it's all here."

Lydia's lips pressed into a thin line of frustration. "And where does that leave us, Jonathan? Are we supposed to carry on like this forever? Me coming up every other weekend, and you buried in your work the rest of the time?"

The problem with Lydia, Rievaulx thought, was that she was too sensible. She had a way of cutting through the fog of his life with brutal clarity, leaving him scrambling for an answer that wouldn't make him seem like a complete cad. He took a breath, searching for the right words, but everything that came to mind felt inadequate.

"Lydia, it's not that simple," he said at last, knowing how weak the argument sounded even as he voiced it. "I want to be with you, but Cambridge . . . it's who I am. I can't just walk away from it."

She folded her hands in her lap, her gaze cool and detached. "I'm not asking you to abandon everything, Jonathan. Just to consider it. But to me you're more married to your work than you could ever be to me."

He wanted to protest, to tell her she was wrong, but the words stuck in his throat. Lydia was right, in a way that made him deeply uncomfortable. He did love his work, and Cambridge, the place had a hold on him that was hard to explain. The ancient streets, the cloistered Colleges, the sense of history at every corner; it was all a part of him, as much as he was a part of it. He'd left once—for Oxford, of all places. His one act of rebellion, fully aware of just how much it would annoy his parents. It hadn't gone well. The truth was, he was a Cambridge man through and through.

In Cambridge, he knew who he was. He belonged. A man who could move easily between town and gown, never quite one or the other, but perfectly at ease in both. In London? Well, that was another matter entirely. In London, he wasn't sure who he'd be, if anyone noticed at all.

But it wasn't just about him, not this time. Was he being selfish? Quite possibly. Self-awareness was never much comfort when it arrived five minutes too late.

"I need time," he said finally, his voice subdued. "Just . . . give me some time to work things out."

Lydia's smile was tight, resigned. "Time, Jonathan, is something we're running out of. I'm 35, you're 42."

The words hung in the air between them, unspoken subtext doing most of the heavy lifting.

And there it was, the unvarnished truth laid bare. The rest of the meal passed in near silence, the atmosphere between them as cool as the evening air outside. He picked at his food, the flavors lost on him, while Lydia made a few half-hearted attempts at conversation, each one falling flat. By the time dessert arrived, they were both simply going through the motions, their minds elsewhere.

As they left the restaurant and walked through the quiet streets of Cambridge, Jonathan felt the weight of their conversation pressing down on him, heavier even than the case that had occupied his thoughts all evening. The city, usually a source of comfort and inspiration, loomed over him with a sense of foreboding.

At the corner where Lydia would catch her taxi, she turned to him, her voice softer now, tinged with a sadness that made his chest ache. "Goodnight, Jonathan."

"Goodnight," he replied, leaning in to kiss her cheek. The gesture felt hollow, a formality rather than a true expression of affection.

She turned away, took a step, then paused. A moment later, she turned back to him—never a good sign in Rievaulx's experience. People rarely turned back to deliver good news without some sort of catch.

"There's something I should mention," Lydia said, with the kind of calm she used when testing the water. "I've been offered an assignment covering the Concorde landing in Sydney. It's a proper piece. Byline, international angle, the lot."

She looked at him, not quite asking, not quite explaining. Just waiting. Rievaulx didn't reply straight away. He rarely did. But in the silence, a conversation had already begun.

"I'll telephone when I get there," she said, a little too quickly, brushing a kiss against his cheek.

She stepped back, looked up at him, and added, "It'll be good for us."

He didn't trust himself to speak, so he settled for a nod. It was safer that way.

He watched her climb into the taxi and drive off into the night, the taillights disappearing into the fog-shrouded distance. For a moment, he stood there, feeling as though something vital had slipped through his fingers, something he might never recover.

As he walked back to his flat, he looked at the buildings of Cambridge with their shadows long and dark under the flickering streetlights. Normally, Rievaulx found comfort in the city's embrace, but tonight it felt oppressive, a reminder of the choices he couldn't make, and the life that was slowly changing for him.

Chapter 8

The tearoom near the station offered a much-needed respite from the sterile walls of the police station. Inside, the air was thick with the comforting aroma of freshly brewed coffee and the mouthwatering scent of fried bacon, a warm haven for their tired minds. Rievaulx and Carter settled into a small table by the window, their breakfast plates largely untouched as they sifted through the clutter of case notes spread before them.

Carter's eyes, shadowed with fatigue, hinted at the long hours she'd spent poring over the case. She gripped her coffee cup like a lifeline, the weariness in her posture undeniable, yet her voice remained steady. "I stayed late last night, went through everything again. But it's like we're chasing shadows. Every lead fizzles out just when it feels like we're onto something."

Rievaulx stirred his tea absently, his gaze focused on the disarray of papers between them. "Sometimes," he began, a trace of weariness in his tone, "the most obvious clues are the ones we're too close to see. We've been so buried in the details that we might be overlooking the bigger picture."

Carter frowned, considering his words. "You think we're overcomplicating things?"

"Possibly," Rievaulx replied, a faint smile tugging at the corners of his mouth. "Or maybe the culprit is counting on us getting lost in the complexity. We must step back and try to look at this with fresh eyes."

Carter's exasperation clung to her like a heavy fog. The case offered pieces of truth but never quite revealing the whole picture. "So, what's the plan?"

"We must re-evaluate," Rievaulx said, his voice taking on a more decisive edge. "We've been focusing on academic motives, but what if the motive is more personal? We should look into their personal lives, their relationships. There might be something we've missed because it didn't fit our assumptions."

Carter's mind raced, trying to connect the dots in this new direction. "So, we start over, but with a different perspective?"

"Exactly," Rievaulx agreed, his smile growing just a bit wider. "And this time, let's make sure our assumptions don't cloud our judgement."

The conversation shifted to logistics, the tension easing as they mapped out their next steps. They would re-interview the suspects, scrutinize any inconsistencies, and revisit the crime scene with a fresh perspective. It was the kind of methodical detective work in which Rievaulx excelled, and Carter felt a renewed sense of determination.

As they finished their breakfast and prepared to leave, Rievaulx's expression became more serious. "Before we dive into re-interviewing, there's one more thing we need to consider," he said. "The commune near Grantchester."

Carter looked up. "Yes, what about it?"

"I think now it's time we took a closer look," Rievaulx replied with conviction. "It's been under suspicion for various unsavory activities, including receiving and selling stolen goods. With the manuscript's disappearance and Hawk's involvement, it might be more connected to our case than we initially thought."

Carter's shifted gears. Do you think there's a link between the commune and our case?"

"It's worth exploring," Rievaulx said. "Given the circumstances and the people involved, it could offer us some crucial insights. I suggest you head out there tomorrow and see what you can uncover. For now, let's focus on re-examining our current information and preparing ourselves for this new approach."

Stepping out into the crisp morning air, Carter felt a spark of optimism. With a new strategy and Rievaulx's steady guidance, she had a renewed sense of purpose.

THE COMMUNE ON THE OUTSKIRTS OF Cambridge was like stepping into another world, a patchwork of eccentricity and artistic abandon tucked away in the countryside. As Detective Constable Emily Carter guided her Mini down the narrow, winding dirt road, she felt a mixture of curiosity and unease. She had studied its reputation, a reputation that preceded it. It was a haven for those who rejected the rigid conventions of the academic city nearby and a refuge for artists, dreamers, and perhaps even those with less-than-legal pursuits. The sprawling compound, with its crumbling farm buildings, caravans, and makeshift shelters, lived in a realm of its own. Depending on whom you asked, the commune was either a sanctuary for free spirits or a hotbed of suspicious activities.

The gravel crunched under her tires as she pulled up in front of what appeared to be the main building, a weathered farmhouse with peeling blue paint, its age and wear evident in every creaky board. The yard was a chaotic mix of rusted bicycles, discarded furniture, and half-finished sculptures, strewn about as if dropped by some careless giant. People moved through the yard in a state of leisurely disarray; some engaged in intense conversations, others absorbed in their creative endeavors, each person oblivious to the outside world. Carter felt like she was entering into a universe carefully curated to exist apart from society's rules.

Stepping out of her car, she adjusted her blazer and inhaled the damp, earthy air, tinged with wood smoke and a faint, unmistakable hint of cannabis. Her heart sank slightly. The last thing she wanted was to stumble into a drug raid. She was here to follow a lead, not get sidetracked by the commune's extracurricular activities.

As she made her way to the farmhouse, her boots crunching on the gravel, she caught snippets of conversation, words like "authenticity," "expression," and "breaking free from society's chains" floated through the air, accompanied by the gentle strumming of an acoustic guitar. She felt like she was stepping into a different era and a place where the concerns of the outside world held little sway.

"Here goes nothing," Carter muttered under her breath, her hand hovering over the weathered door. The knock echoed in the quiet yard, drawing curious glances and a few guarded looks from the commune's residents.

The door creaked open, revealing a tall, lanky man with a wild mane of curly hair and a shirt so splattered with paint that its original color was a mystery. He eyed Carter with a mix of amusement and suspicion, his eyes flicked to the warrant card she held up.

"Detective Constable Carter, Cambridge CID," she said, her tone was professional yet cordial. "I'd like to ask a few questions about some stolen artworks."

The man raised an eyebrow, a wry smile playing on his lips as he leaned against the door frame. "Stolen artworks? That's not really our scene. We're more into creation, not theft."

Carter replied, "I'm not accusing anyone of theft. But we've received information that some stolen items might have passed through here. I'd appreciate your help in tracking them down."

The man shrugged, a gesture that was equal parts indifference and quiet defiance. After a moment, he stepped aside, gesturing for her to enter with a lazy wave. "Sure, come on in. I'm Rowan, by the way."

As Carter stepped inside, she was immediately hit by a sensory overload. The commune's interior was a riot of color, scent, and sound. The walls, far from being mere structures, were canvases bursting with vibrant murals, swirling abstracts that appeared to pulse with life. The floor was a patchwork of worn rugs and splintered wooden planks, adding to the space's bohemian charm.

The air was thick with the mingling aromas of incense, paint, and the pervasive scent of herbal smoke, a smell so potent that Carter had no doubt about its source. The entire place felt like a living tapestry of artistic expression, a celebration of creativity that swirled around her, both captivating and disorienting.

In her plain clothes and sensible boots, Carter felt slightly out of step. Her practical get-up, wide-legged jeans, a soft cream muslin shirt, a rust-coloured waistcoat, and a navy blazer, might have passed for modern and efficient elsewhere. Here, among the commune's residents draped in layers of tie-dye, patchwork, and purpose, she looked more like someone dropping off a report than joining the revolution. Their outfits, a mix of bold colors and flowing fabrics, came from far-off markets, each piece a testament to the commune's free-spirited ethos.

Rowan led her through a maze of cluttered rooms, each more chaotic than the last. Artists were everywhere, some painting with feverish intensity, others hunched over sculptures or pottery wheels, while a few sat in circles, lost in what sounded like deep philosophical debates. The atmosphere buzzed with unbridled creativity, making Carter wonder how anyone could find order in such chaos.

"So, what exactly are you looking for?" Rowan asked as they entered a large communal studio. Canvases leaned against every available surface, their bold colors clashing in a riot of hues. The smell of turpentine was sharp enough to sting her eyes.

"We're investigating a series of art and antiquities thefts in Cambridge," Carter explained, glancing around at the disarray. "We have reason to believe that some stolen items might have ended up here, either for sale or as part of a larger operation."

Rowan frowned, scratching his chin thoughtfully. "Can't say I've seen anything like that around here. We do a lot of trading, sure, but it's usually just our stuff. We sell a few pieces now and then, but mostly to keep the place running. You're welcome to look around, though. Maybe talk to some of the others."

Carter's optimism was fading. The commune felt like a place where people were more interested in their art than in dealing with stolen goods. She couldn't afford not to follow up any lead though.

For the next hour, Carter wandered through the commune, speaking with its residents and examining the various artworks scattered about. It quickly became clear that most of what was being produced here was of minimal value—abstract paintings thrown together in bursts of emotion, sculptures made from found objects that defied conventional aesthetics, and pottery that looked more like misshapen experiments than art. There wasn't a scrap of anything that could reasonably pass for genuine art, and as for valuable manuscripts—well, Carter had a creeping suspicion they'd already been destroyed.

Carter returned to the front of the building, where she found Rowan sitting on the porch, casually rolling a cigarette. He looked up as she approached, a small, knowing smile on his lips.

"Find what you were looking for?" he asked, though his tone suggested he already knew the answer.

"Not exactly," Carter admitted, keeping her voice neutral. "But I appreciate your cooperation."

Rowan nodded, lighting his cigarette with a nonchalant flick of his wrist. As he took a long drag, Carter couldn't help but notice the thick, pungent smoke curling into the air—unmistakably cannabis. Rowan exhaled a dense cloud, the herbal aroma filling the space between them.

"We're not bad people, you know," Rowan said, his voice earnest despite the haze of smoke. "We just don't fit into your world, the world of rules and regulations. We're trying to create something different here, something pure."

Emily met his gaze steadily, her expression unreadable. There was a glint in Rowan's eyes, a subtle challenge, as if he was testing her, hoping to provoke the stereotypical response he might expect from a police officer. Emily wasn't going to rise to the bait.

"I understand your desire to live outside conventional society," she said. "But my job is to investigate potential links to a series of art thefts. Whether or not your community follows society's rules doesn't change that."

Rowan's grin deepened slightly, as if waiting for her to get flustered. Carter remained composed, focused on her task.

"See anything you'd like to buy?" he asked, with the kind of casual tone that made it clear he was hoping to put her on the back foot. "We survive by selling our artwork."

Carter shook her head. "No," she said, without embellishment. Art had never really been her thing. The walls of her childhood home had been filled with photos—mostly of her three brothers in various muddy states and latterly in their army uniforms—and a couple of sun-faded watercolours her parents had been given as a wedding present. In a house where noise and practicality reigned, art was something other people had time for.

"Thank you for your time," she said, turning to walk back to her car. The scent of marijuana clung to her, but she brushed it off, her mind moving onto the next steps. The commune had been an interesting detour, but it had yielded no concrete leads, yet, as she drove away, Carter was not entirely about to stop herself feeling a pang of disappointment. The case was becoming more intricate with each twist, and another dead-end weighed heavily on her. She knew she couldn't dwell on it. There were still answers to find, and she was determined to uncover them, no matter how many false leads she had to chase.

THE POLICE STATION FELT LIKE A world away from the chaotic vibrancy of the commune. Here, the walls were a drab shade of grey, illuminated by the unforgiving glare of fluorescent lights that cast a sterile, almost oppressive glow over the rows of desks and filing cabinets. Carter sat at her desk and leaned back in her chair, pressing her fingers to her temples as she tried to make sense of the information she'd gathered. The commune had been a disappointment: no stolen artworks, no forged manuscripts, no leads on Dr. Atherton's murder. But was she missing a crucial piece, a detail that hadn't yet slotted into place?

Her eyes drifted to the board on the wall in front of her, where the evidence she'd meticulously assembled sat like pieces of a jigsaw puzzle. Photographs of the stolen items, notes on the suspects, timelines, and connections, all carefully arranged, yet none of it coalescing into a clear picture. It was as if she were trying to read a book with entire chapters ripped out.

The door creaked open, Carter looked up to see Rievaulx enter the room, his expression as composed as ever. A flicker of tension in his eyes suggested he'd been grappling with the case as much as she had.

"Any luck at the commune?" he asked, though his tone indicated he already knew the answer.

Carter shook her head. "It was a bust, sir. The place is full of artists and free spirits, but nothing of any real value. They're more interested in their own creative pursuits than in profiting from stolen art."

Rievaulx took a seat across from her desk. "It's important to follow every lead, Carter, even the ones that don't pan out. At the very least, we can rule them out as suspects."

"I know," Carter replied, "but it feels like we're running in circles. Every time we think we're onto something, we hit another dead end."

Rievaulx's eyes shifted to the board, his eyes focusing as he took in the array of evidence. "We might be missing the bigger picture," he said. "We've been so focused on the forgeries and the stolen art, but what if those are just symptoms of a deeper issue? What if the real motive behind Atherton's murder isn't about the manuscript or the art thefts after all?"

Carter mulled over his words. "You think we've been looking in the wrong direction?"

"Not entirely," Rievaulx responded. "But I think it's time to broaden our scope. Atherton's connections and relationships might be just as significant as the objects he was dealing with. We must consider the people who were closest to him, those who stood to gain or lose the most from his death."

Carter concurred. "We've been so focused on the art thefts that we haven't looking into his personal life. His colleagues, his students, anyone who had a reason to want him gone."

"Exactly," Rievaulx said, a note of approval. "It's time to start Investigating his relationships, the people in his orbit. The key to solving this case might not be in the objects he dealt with, but in the lives he touched."

"I'll start by compiling a list of his closest contacts," Carter said, reaching for a notepad. "His colleagues at the university, his students, anyone who might have had a motive."

Rievaulx looked at the board. "And I'll inquire about any connections he might have had outside the university. There's more to Atherton than we've uncovered so far, and I am beginning to suspect the answer might well lie in his personal life."

As they began to map out their next steps, Carter had a renewed sense of purpose. The commune had been a dead end, but she had ruled out one lead.

THE SUN DIPPED LOW OVER CAMBRIDGE. The warm evening air carried the scent of summer: a blend of leaves and distant blossoms, as the city gradually settled into the quiet rhythms of twilight. Rievaulx and Carter walked side by side down the tranquil lane of Melbourne Place with its delightful Victorian townhouses on one side and the less delightful architecture of Parkside Community College on the other as they made their way to the *Free Press*, a traditional backstreet pub on Prospect Row.

"This," Rievaulx said, pausing in front of the place and casting an appreciative glance at the quaint little pub, "stands as a tribute to the town's spirit against anyone attempting to dictate its ways. It first got its license in 1834, when Sarah Horne opened her cottage to serve her own ale. Just as she began, the temperance movement launched its publication, *The Free Press*, urging the town to reject drinking entirely. Hence the name."

Carter smiled, feeling a moment's solidarity with Sarah Horne. "Thumbing her nose at the establishment. Much like the commune crowd," she said.

They slipped inside, finding a couple of seats nestled in a corner as the pub began to fill with workers on their way home and students drifting in from the Kite. It was a small place, one of the smallest in Cambridge, and quickly packed to the brim. Squeezed together with their drinks, the rising chatter all but swallowing conversation, they sat in companionable silence, each left to their own thoughts.

Carter stole a glance at Rievaulx. The entire day had been spent chasing leads that ultimately led nowhere, leaving her with a sense of inadequacy. She had, she realized, placed her hopes on the commune, expecting it to yield some breakthrough, but instead, it had only deepened her doubts about the path they were on.

They finished their drinks, and with a silent nod to each other, stood and squeezed their way through the crowd and the smoke-filled air until they were outside on the pavement, the crowd closing over their passage as if they'd never been there.

"Sir," she started, as they made their way down Warkworth Street and then right onto Warkworth Terrace toward the station; Carter heading for her car, Rievaulx for his old Raleigh bicycle, "do you ever get the feeling we're just going round in circles? That no matter how much effort we put in, we're just chasing our own tails?"

As they walked, the soft sound of their footsteps filled the silence between them. When he finally spoke, his tone was weary and hinted at the challenges of their work. "Every case has its challenges, Carter. This one is particularly intricate. But we can't let frustration cloud our judgement. We have to trust the process, even when it feels like we're treading water."

Carter nodded though the tight knot of anxiety in her chest refused to loosen. "I know that sir. But it's hard not to feel like we're overlooking something and we're just not seeing it."

Rievaulx came to a halt, turning to face her. His expression was serious, but there was a gentle understanding in his eyes that eased some of her tension. "This case is like a puzzle, Carter. Sometimes the clues don't immediately fit. Sometimes, you have to step back and take in the whole picture before the connections become clear."

Carter's thoughts clouded with self-doubt. "I just . . . I want to prove myself, sir. I want to show that I'm capable of handling this kind of case. But every time we hit another dead end, I start to wonder if I'm really cut out for this."

Rievaulx placed a reassuring hand on her shoulder. "Carter, you're one of the most dedicated detectives I've had the privilege of working with. You have the instincts, the intelligence, and the determination to solve this case. You also must learn to be patient—with yourself, and with the process. Doubt is natural, but it can't be allowed to undermine your confidence."

She looked up at him and asked. "Do you ever doubt yourself, sir?"

A smile tugged at Rievaulx's lips, one that spoke of years of experience and the burden of leadership. "Every day, Carter. I've learnt that doubt is just another important part of the process. It keeps you sharp, keeps you questioning. And in the end, it's what drives you to find the answers."

Carter had a flicker of hope stir within her, a sense that maybe, just maybe, she was on the right path after all. The case was challenging, yes, but she wasn't alone in facing those challenges. With Rievaulx's steady guidance, she knew they would navigate this labyrinth together one step at a time.

They resumed their walk, continuing down the quiet street. The city was bathed in the soft, warm glow of the setting sun, and for a brief moment, it felt as though the weight of the investigation had lifted, if only slightly.

As they reached the end of the street, Rievaulx turned to her once more, his voice steady and resolute. "We'll find the answers, Carter. It may take time, and we may face more setbacks, but we'll get there. Trust in the process, and trust in yourself."

Carter felt a renewed sense of determination. The road ahead was still long, and many challenges lay in wait, but she felt ready to face them. She knew they would find the truth.

The sun dipped below the horizon, leaving Cambridge bathed in the soft embrace of twilight.

Chapter 9

THE UNIVERSITY LIBRARY LOOMED IN THE early morning mist, an austere sentinel against the fading twilight, its towering façade a testament to the ambition of minds long past. The building's formidable presence, reminiscent of Giles Gilbert Scott's industrial masterpieces, dominated the landscape, its 157-foot height cloaked in fog, rendering it both imposing and elusive.

As Detective Chief Inspector Rievaulx and Detective Constable Emily Carter approached, the library gave the impression of receding into itself, the grandeur of its tall windows and industrial design shrouded by the veil of mist. For the past week, it had felt as though summer had lost interest in Cambridge altogether. The heat of the earlier weeks had vanished without so much as a goodbye, leaving behind the sort of damp greyness that made you wonder if you'd only imagined the sunshine in the first place.

The structure, completed in the 1930s on the grounds of a former military hospital, stood between Robinson College and the Memorial Court of Clare College, a bridge between the past and present. The ornate detailing of the roof, usually a symbol of academic prestige, now whispered secrets from a bygone era.

Rievaulx's voice cut through the heavy air, steady and purposeful as he gestured towards the imposing edifice. "It started in the

Old Schools near the Senate House," he remarked, "but it outgrew that space quickly."

The library's grandeur was lost on Carter, who viewed it more as a relic of industrial ambition than a beacon of intellectual prowess. The building had always left her unimpressed, its significance more underwhelming with each passing visit. Today, however, the atmosphere was different. The library, typically a sanctuary for scholars, was imbued with an unsettling stillness; its usual occupants conspicuously absent, leaving only the rustle of leaves and the distant toll of a bell to break the silence.

As they stood at the foot of the broad stone steps leading to the entrance, the library was foreboding. Rievaulx adjusted the scarf around his neck, the unseasonal chill of the morning biting through his layers. He glanced at Carter, noting the determination etched on her face. She was ready.

"Ready?" he asked, his voice low, steady in the quiet of the morning.

Carter said. "Ready as I'll ever be, sir."

Together, they ascended the steps, the heavy wooden doors groaning as they swung open. Inside, the library's usual hush had transformed into an oppressive silence, broken only by the occasional echo of footsteps on the polished stone floor. The air, thick with the scent of old paper and dust, carried a sharper, acrid undertone; a scent that spoke of something final.

A uniformed officer awaited them just inside, his face pale, his hands fidgeting. He was young, likely new to the force, and clearly rattled by what he had witnessed.

"The body's in the *Rare Books Room*, sir," he said, his voice quivering slightly. "It's . . . it's not a pretty sight."

Rievaulx offered a curt nod, his expression betraying nothing. "Lead the way."

As they followed the officer through the labyrinth of corridors, Rievaulx surveyed the surroundings with a sharp eye. The towering bookshelves and vaulted ceilings, once symbols of scholarly pursuit, now felt oppressive, as if the weight of history itself bore down upon them. The library, a sanctuary of knowledge, now felt more like a crypt.

The *Rare Books Room* lay deep within the library, accessible only to a privileged few. Here, the university's most treasured volumes were kept: rare manuscripts, first editions, artefacts of immense value. It was also here that the lifeless body of Peter Matthews, the librarian, now lay.

Entering the room, Carter was struck by the contrast between its elegance and the grim scene before them. The tall windows, usually casting warm light over the room, were dim and shadowed, lending the space a cold, somber air. The familiar scent of old leather bindings and polished wood was tainted with the unmistakable stench of decay.

Matthews sat slumped over a grand mahogany desk, his head resting on an open book as though he had drifted off mid-sentence. But the unnatural angle of his neck betrayed a more sinister reality. His skin, waxy and pale, bore the early signs of rigor mortis. An empty bottle of pills and a half-full glass of water nearby suggested the possibility of suicide.

Rievaulx was not one to accept such things at face value.

He approached the body with the deliberate caution of a man who trusted his instincts. Peter Matthews, in his early sixties, had dedicated his life to the preservation of knowledge. His thinning grey hair was neatly combed, and his clothes, though slightly rumpled, suggested a man of meticulous habits. Rievaulx's gaze fell upon the book beneath Matthews's head; an exquisite edition of Chaucer's *Canterbury Tales*, its gilded pages gleaming faintly in the dim light.

"Carter, what do you make of it?" Rievaulx's voice broke the silence yet underscored with urgency.

Carter stepped closer; her brow furrowed in concentration. "At first glance, it looks like a suicide," she began cautiously. "But . . . something feels off. The pills, the glass of water; it's all too neat, too convenient. And the book? Why Canterbury Tales? It's valuable, yes, but why would he choose to die with it?"

Rievaulx nodded, his sharp eyes absorbing every detail. "Exactly. Matthews was clearly a man of order and precision. This," he gestured to the scene, "doesn't fit. It feels staged, like someone wanted us to believe it was a suicide."

Carter's eyes widened as the implications sank in. "If it's staged, then the killer wanted to send a message or cover something up. But what? And why Matthews?"

Rievaulx's focus returned to the book, his mind trying to find connections that were too elusive to grasp. "What if this wasn't about Matthews at all? What if it's about what he knew, or what he discovered?"

Carter leaned in, careful not to disturb the scene, and glanced at the open pages of the book. "The *Canterbury Tales*. It's a classic, but why would it be relevant here? Unless . . ."

"Unless it's a distraction," Rievaulx finished, his tone grim. "Someone wanted us to focus on the book, on the obvious. The real clue might lie elsewhere: in Matthews's work, in what he was cataloguing or studying. If he uncovered something threatening, it could explain why he was silenced."

Carter nodded, her mind racing through the possibilities. "We will investigate his recent work, see if anything stands out, anything that perhaps connects him to Atherton or the manuscript we've been investigating."

"Precisely," Rievaulx agreed. "And we must be meticulous. Whoever orchestrated this went to great lengths to cover their tracks."

Carter straightened up. "I'll start by interviewing his colleagues, see if anyone noticed anything unusual. I'll also check the library's records. If Matthews was working on something sensitive, there might be a trace of it there."

Rievaulx gave her a brief look of approval. "Good. I'll stay here and examine this room. There might be something subtle, something easy to overlook but significant."

As Carter left the *Rare Books Room*, Rievaulx turned his full attention back to Peter Matthews' body. This death was no mere tragedy; it was a deliberate act, a message written in the language of fear, power, and secrecy. Someone had been threatened enough by Matthews to end his life, and Rievaulx was determined to uncover the reason.

The library, with its silent shelves and ancient tomes, had become a battleground, a place where the past and present clashed with lethal consequences. Rievaulx methodically searched the room for any overlooked clues. He sensed one thing for certain: the stakes had just been raised, and time was running out, but he was not sure by whom or why.

Then he noticed it, perched on the windowsill and partly obscured by an oversized bookcase: an orchid. Not the same as the one found by Dr. Atherton's body, the common Ophrys apifera or Bee orchid, its presence alone, a fresh, spotless, well-cared-for bloom, was out of place in the dusty corner, hinted, no, suggested strongly, at a connection. A quiet certainty settled over Rievaulx. Matthews' death and Atherton's murder were connected. The clock was ticking, and with each passing moment, a danger loomed larger. Now he was resolute. He would find the answer, no matter what it took.

THE LIBRARIAN'S OFFICE WAS A SNUG, cluttered space, steeped in the aura of countless years spent in the pursuit of knowledge. The walls were lined with bookshelves, each packed to the brim with volumes of varying sizes, their spines cracked and faded from years of handling. Every surface was buried under stacks of papers, catalogues, and handwritten notes, leaving only a small, clear area on the desk where Peter Matthews had likely spent countless hours at work.

Rievaulx and Carter paused in the doorway, absorbing the scene. Rievaulx's face was set in a hard line, while Carter, still processing the news of his discovery of the orchid, was pale. They were caught in a relentless race to reach its center.

The room was a perfect reflection of its late occupant; meticulous in its organization yet hinting at an undercurrent of obsession. The scent of old paper and ink filled the air, a testament to the countless hours Matthews must have spent surrounded by the treasures of the written word.

"There's a lot to sift through," Carter remarked, her voice carrying a note of determination. "But if Matthews was tangled up in something, the evidence must be here."

Rievaulx stepped further into the room. He focused on the cluttered desk. "We're searching for anything that connects him to Atherton or the manuscript we've been investigating. If Matthews was indeed part of the same conspiracy, he may have left behind a crucial clue."

The two detectives began their methodical search, sorting through the mountains of papers and books with precision and care. It was slow, tedious work, but they both knew that even the smallest detail could prove invaluable.

Carter started with the desk drawers, carefully opening each one to examine its contents. Most of it was mundane: stationery supplies, old receipts, a few personal items, but in the bottom drawer, something caught her eye.

"Sir, have a look at this," Carter said, holding up a journal.

Rievaulx crossed the room and took the journal from her, flipping through its pages. The handwriting was meticulous, almost obsessively neat, and the entries detailed Matthews's daily activities, his thoughts on the books he was cataloguing, and his interactions with the university's staff and students.

"This is intriguing," Rievaulx murmured, skimming through the entries. "It appears Matthews was keeping a thorough record of everything he was working on—every manuscript, every book. He mentions Atherton several times."

Carter leaned in; her curiosity piqued. "Does he mention the manuscript we've been investigating?"

Rievaulx continued reading, his brow furrowed in concentration. "Yes, here it is. He notes that Atherton brought him a manuscript a few weeks ago, one Atherton claimed was of significant historical value. Matthews was skeptical but agreed to examine it. There's a reference here to a meeting with Atherton the day before his death."

Carter felt a chill crawl down her spine. "So, Matthews was one of the last people to see Atherton alive. And now he's dead too."

"It's more than that," Rievaulx replied, his voice sharpening with urgency. "Matthews's notes suggest he uncovered something—something that made him uneasy. He doesn't provide details, but there's an underlying tension in his writing, as if he knew he was onto something dangerous."

Carter's mind raced as she considered the implications. "If Matthews discovered the manuscript was a forgery or uncovered the true nature of Atherton's involvement, it could have made him a target. Whoever is behind this must have realized Matthews was getting too close."

Rievaulx nodded, his expression grave. "We will find out exactly what that was. We can track down the manuscript, whatever it may be. And we can see what Matthews was working on recently—there could be a connection."

As they dug deeper into Matthews's records, a sense of urgency thickened the air. The library's shadows pressed in on them, whispering secrets just out of reach.

"We should also look for any recent correspondence," Carter suggested. "If Matthews was worried, he might have reached out to someone for help."

"Good thinking," Rievaulx agreed, gesturing toward the stack of papers on the desk. "Let's see if there are any letters."

They resumed their search, their focus unwavering. Each document, each scrap of paper held the potential to unravel the mystery that surrounded Matthews's death. It felt as though they were unearthing buried treasure, and with every revelation, the puzzle grew more intricate.

Rievaulx's attention was suddenly drawn to a small, unmarked envelope tucked beneath a pile of manuscripts. He carefully pulled it free, inspecting it closely. The envelope was yellowed with age, its contents seemingly unassuming, yet Rievaulx sensed it held something of importance.

"Carter, have a look at this," he said, sliding the envelope across the desk.

Carter opened it with nimble fingers, revealing a stack of letters, each dated within the last few months. The letters were from various institutions and individuals, all expressing interest in rare manuscripts and acquisitions, but one letter, in particular, caught her eye: a formal request from a collector in London, inquiring about the very manuscript Matthews had catalogued.

"Sir, this letter references the manuscript Atherton brought to Matthews," Carter noted, her eyes widening. "It looks like someone was trying to acquire it."

Rievaulx leaned closer, reading over her shoulder. "And they were willing to pay a significant sum for it too. This could be the motive we've been searching for. If the manuscript was a forgery, this collector might have been trying to acquire it without realizing its true nature."

Carter's expression turned serious. "If that's the case, then Matthews's death wasn't just about protecting a secret. It was about money, power . . . something that threatened to expose the truth."

They exchanged a knowing glance, the weight of their discoveries settling heavily between them. The tapestry was far from complete.

"We will follow up with this collector and see what they know. And we investigate Matthews's final days, who he spoke to, what he was working on. We're getting closer to the heart of this mystery, but we must tread carefully. Whoever is behind this clearly won't hesitate to eliminate anyone who stands in their way."

As they gathered the documents and prepared to leave the librarian's office, Rievaulx felt a lingering sense of unease. The shadows in the room pulsed with hidden dangers, a reminder that they were venturing into perilous territory.

He paused, his instincts prickling. Something felt off, something elusive, yet essential.

"There's more here," he said. "Something hidden. We need to keep searching."

They resumed their search, and as they reached the back of the room, Rievaulx noticed a slight irregularity in the wall behind one of the shelves, a recessed section, as if it had been deliberately concealed.

"Carter, help me move this," Rievaulx instructed, gesturing to the heavy wooden shelf.

Together, they pushed it aside, revealing a hidden compartment in the wall. Inside was a small, locked box, its exterior battered, yet the lock was intact.

"Looks like Matthews was keeping something hidden," Carter observed, eyeing the box with a mix of curiosity and caution. "Do we have a way to open it?"

Rievaulx pulled a set of tools from his pocket: a burglar's lockpick, given to him by a once-prominent thief who, realizing that advances in forensics would soon make his capture inevitable and prison was bad for his arthritis, had resigned himself to retirement and taken up gambling instead, an occupation at which he was suspiciously good. Ignoring Carter's raised eyebrows, he deftly worked the lock until it clicked open. Lifting the lid, he revealed a neatly arranged collection of documents and photographs, each one carefully preserved in a plastic sleeve.

Carter reached in and pulled out the first document, her eyes widening as she realized its significance. The pages were yellowed and slightly crumpled, as though they had been hastily stashed away.

"Sir, this must be it. The manuscript Atherton brought to Matthews," she exclaimed, holding it aloft as if it were a sacred relic unearthed from history. "It's the one that caused all the controversy. Look, Matthews clipped a note to it: *Atherton's folly*.

With careful hands, she lifted the note, her brow furrowing as she read the manuscript's title: *The Garden of Shadows*. The words reverberated ominously in the room, carrying the weight of the tensions that had surrounded it.

Rievaulx frowned, peering over her shoulder at the manuscript, his expression darkening. "A rather spiteful note," he remarked, his voice contemplative. "This must be the key, Carter. Whatever Matthews discovered about this manuscript, it's what got him killed."

The atmosphere thickened with unspoken implications. The manuscript, once merely a subject of academic debate, now loomed large in their investigation, a beacon of the dark secrets hidden beneath the surface.

As they continued to examine the box's contents, more evidence of Matthews's investigation came to light; there were letters, notes, even photographs of Atherton and other university staff members. It was clear that Matthews had uncovered something significant, something that had placed him in grave danger.

"This goes deeper than we ever imagined," Carter said, her voice tinged with awe and fear. "The manuscript, the forgeries, the murders—it's all connected."

Rievaulx nodded, his mind already planning their next moves. "We will get this back to the station, analyze every piece of it. If Matthews was, as we suspect, onto something, we might finally have the evidence to expose the truth."

As they gathered the documents and prepared to leave the office, the weight of their discoveries pressed down on them. The shadows in the library felt oppressive, a reminder of the perils and danger that lay ahead. As they walked out, Rievaulx had the feeling that they were on the brink of a breakthrough.

AS THE FOLLOWING DAYS BLURRED INTO a relentless cycle of research, interviews, and late nights, Rievaulx and Carter found themselves plunging deeper into the murky depths of the case. The university library had become their second home, its musty scent a constant reminder of the secrets it held within its ancient walls.

The routine of sifting through dusty, weighty books and old documents became both their refuge and their battlefield, a place where the line between discovery and dead ends was razor thin.

Carter spent the next few hours speaking with Matthews's colleagues, piecing together fragments of information that might bring them closer to the truth. Each conversation with students and library staff revealed a different facet of the enigmatic librarian. There was admiration, suspicion, and a healthy dose of intrigue surrounding Matthews, but one sentiment was universal: no one believed he was the type to end his own life.

Meanwhile, Rievaulx immersed himself in the labyrinth of the manuscript's history. He reached out to academic institutions far and wide, chasing leads that led him into a tangled web of forgeries and hidden histories. Each answer only spawned more questions, each revelation slipping through his fingers like sand.

The next afternoon, as Rievaulx pored over yet another stack of documents, the tension in his shoulders became almost unbearable. The library, usually a sanctuary of quiet study, felt more like a pressure cooker, its walls closing in as the weight of the investigation bore down on him. He glanced at the clock, realizing it was time for their daily debrief.

"Time for a tea break," he suggested, sensing that a change of scenery might offer them both some much-needed clarity.

Carter agreed without hesitation, and they made their way to a nearby tearoom, a bustling spot frequented by students and academics alike. As they settled into a corner table with a pot of strong, steaming tea, Rievaulx couldn't help but notice the fatigue etched into Carter's face.

"I spoke with a few of Matthews's colleagues," Carter began, her tone serious. "They all mentioned how paranoid he'd become in the weeks before his death. He was convinced someone was watching him, that there was a threat lurking just out of sight."

Rievaulx frowned, the new information turning over in his mind. "Did anyone have an idea of who it might have been?"

"Not specifically," Carter said, shaking her head. "But there were rumors about an antiquarian who'd been visiting the library frequently, asking a lot of questions about certain manuscripts. No one seems to know much about him, but Matthews was definitely wary."

"Interesting," Rievaulx mused, his thoughts racing. *The Curator*, perhaps? That might be our lead. If Matthews was onto something, it's possible this collector knew more than he was letting on."

Carter's eyes brightened with the thrill of the chase. "I'll reach out to some of Matthews's contacts, see if anyone remembers a name or description."

With their course set, they finished their tea and headed back to the library, where they plunged once more into the archives. The hours passed in a haze of papers, books, and hushed discussions with staff, but Rievaulx felt a renewed sense of purpose driving him forward.

As the sun began to dip below the horizon, casting a warm light across the stone walls of the library, Carter returned from her latest round of interviews, her expression animated. "You won't believe what I found," she said, her voice trembling with excitement.

Rievaulx looked up from a stack of manuscripts, intrigued. "Go on."

"The rare book collector is Victor Drake," Carter revealed, her eyes gleaming. "Several people mentioned he was especially interested in botanical manuscripts, and Matthews appeared to be particularly wary of him."

"Drake," Rievaulx repeated, the name clicking into place like a puzzle piece. "I've heard of him; he's well-known in the rare books community, always on the lookout for valuable acquisitions, and he was known for not being particularly scrupulous as to how he acquired them. If he was hanging around Matthews, that raises a lot of red flags."

"Exactly," Carter said, nodding. "It seems like Drake was trying to get his hands on that manuscript, and Matthews might have been in his way. He even went as far as to ask around about Matthews's work, trying to gauge how much he knew."

A surge of adrenaline coursed through Rievaulx. "If Drake was involved, we will track him down. He could be the key to unlocking this entire case."

Just then, the phone beside Rievaulx gave a muffled ring, its sound dulled by the thick stacks of books and manuscripts, yet echoing faintly in the cavernous room. He picked up the receiver.

"DCI Rievaulx," he answered, listening for a few moments before nodding. "Ah," he murmured, glancing at Carter. He covered the mouthpiece and mouthed, *pathologist*.

"Strangled?" Carter echoed with a frown once Rievaulx relayed the findings after the call. "Well, it confirms our suspicions—definitely murder. But . . . strangled?"

"Quite," Rievaulx replied thoughtfully, letting out a sigh. "Are we looking at the same killer, changing his methods, or could there be two of them?"

RIEVAULX'S FLAT WAS A SANCTUARY OF order. The first floor of a Victorian townhouse, with the bay window overlooking Bateman Street, gave him a front-row seat to the daily procession of students drifting to and fro. In his more introspective moods, of which there were plenty, he'd find himself staring out, not so much watching as vaguely observing. It was one of Cambridge's little quirks: first-years safely tucked inside the college walls, and then, as if gently nudged from the nest, sent off to college-owned houses for the rest of their student lives.

The walls of his flat were lined with carefully organized bookshelves, each volume meticulously placed, the titles forming a pattern of knowledge accumulated over years. Soft light from a few strategically placed lamps bathed the room in a warm glow, creating an atmosphere of calm that contrasted sharply with the turbulence of the case that consumed his thoughts. Here, in this quiet refuge, surrounded by the wisdom of ages, Rievaulx did his best thinking.

He sat at his desk, the documents and photographs from the librarian's hidden box spread out before him. The discovery had been a step forward, but it also raised more questions than it answered. The connections between Atherton, Matthews, their murder, the manuscript, and the orchid were all there, intertwined, but tangled, elusive.

As he sipped his tea, Rievaulx allowed his mind to drift over the details. One killer or two? It was a question that nagged at him. Whether one or two, the manuscript was the linch-pin, that tied everything together. What was its true significance? Was it a genuine historical artefact, or as they'd come to believe, a cleverly crafted forgery? What mattered was why had it driven both Atherton and Matthews to their deaths?

His thoughts lingered on the orchid, that rare and beautiful flower left at the scene of Atherton's murder. It was a symbol, a message, but of what? And who was the sender? The connection between the manuscript and the orchid was tenuous at best, but Rievaulx couldn't shake the feeling that they were linked in some way. The orchid on Matthews's windowsill only deepened the implication of a connection. Unlike the one left openly beside Atherton's body, a blatant signal of foul play, Matthews's death had been veiled as a suicide, with the orchid subtly positioned on the sill, almost out of sight, yet undeniably there. Had it belonged to Matthews himself? None of the staff, when questioned, could recall ever seeing it, but that meant little; it was tucked away. It might have been placed there by Matthews, or by the killer.

His contemplation was interrupted by a knock at the door. Startled, Rievaulx glanced at the clock and realized it was late evening.

He opened the door to find Carter standing there. She clutched a folder in her hand, the strain of the investigation evident in the lines etched on her face.

"Sir, I've been going over the records from the library," she said, stepping inside as he motioned her to enter. "There's something you should see."

Rievaulx chuckled quietly. "Don't you have a home to go to, Carter?"

He knew she rented a room in a shared house on Mill Road with two other girls, standard setup for someone at her stage.

Carter gave a smile that leaned more towards grimace. "Home's a bit crowded at the moment," she said. "My housemates, nice enough, generally, have recently become involved with a pair of lads who aren't exactly thrilled about me keeping company with the local constabulary. I'd rather not witness anything I might feel professionally obliged to report."

She paused, then added, with a hint of defensiveness, "Besides, I like my desk. And when you're not around, Sergeant Pritchard makes the tea and lets me in on his biscuit stash, which is more than I can say for my housemates."

Rievaulx smiled and led her to the desk where they both sat down. Carter opened the folder and spread out a series of documents, pointing to an entry that instantaneously caught Rievaulx's attention.

"It's a record of the library's acquisitions," she explained. "About six months ago, Atherton made a significant donation—a collection of rare botanical texts, including the manuscript we've been investigating. Look at the timing. It coincides almost exactly with the arrival of the orchid in Cambridge. I think Atherton brought it back with him after his last research trip."

Rievaulx's eyes narrowed as he scrutinized the documents. "The orchid wasn't just a random plant. It was connected to the manuscript. And Atherton knew its significance."

Carter said "But there's more. I cross-referenced the dates with Matthews's journal entries. He started cataloguing the collection almost immediately after it arrived, and that's when he began to grow suspicious. I think he realized that the manuscript was a forgery and was trying to figure out who was behind it."

Rievaulx leaned back in his chair, his mind racing. "And when he was too close to the truth; they silenced him."

"It makes sense, sir," Carter said, her voice tinged with both excitement and apprehension. Something is still missing. Why would someone go to such lengths to forge a manuscript? And why kill to protect it?"

Rievaulx considered the question, his thoughts turning to the broader implications. "It's not just about money," he said. "It's about reputation, power. In the world of academia, a discovery like this could make or break a career. If Atherton had exposed the forgery, it could have destroyed someone's life's work."

Carter began to understand. "And the orchid, it's a symbol of that power, that influence. Whoever is behind this wanted to send a message, to show that they control the narrative."

A chill ran down Rievaulx's spine. The stakes were higher than he had realized, and the adversary they were facing was more formidable than he had anticipated. The truth was out there, buried beneath deception and ambition.

As they continued to piece together the puzzle, Rievaulx knew they were getting closer to the heart of the conspiracy. With the new discovery, the danger grew more acute for them. Whoever was behind these murders would stop at nothing to protect their secrets. The path ahead was fraught with peril. Rievaulx and Carter exchanged a determined glance; they both knew there was no turning back. The truth was within their grasp, but it would come at a cost. They were ready to pay whatever it took.

THE FOLLOWING DAY FOUND RIEVAULX AND Carter en-route to London, the city's early morning bustle slowly waking beneath the pale sunlight. Their destination was a stately Georgian town house, nestled on a street lined with grand trees and even grander residences. The air here carried the faint scent of old money, the kind that whispered its presence rather than announced it as they approached Victor Drake's residence.

"Ready for this?" Carter asked, her voice low, the gravity of their mission evident in her eyes.

Rievaulx said. "As ready as we'll ever be."

They rang the bell, and after a moment, the door swung open to reveal a tall man with a meticulously groomed beard and a manner that exuded both charm and calculation.

"Officers! What a delightful surprise," Drake greeted them after Carter introduced them and they flashed their warrant cards. His smile was disarming and his eyes sharp. "What brings you to my humble abode?"

"Mr. Drake," Rievaulx began, "we'd like to ask you a few questions regarding your recent visits to the Cambridge University Library and your interest in a particular manuscript."

For just a split second, Drake's smile faltered, a flicker of something unreadable crossing his face, "Ah, the manuscript. Yes, I've heard quite a bit about it," he replied, gesturing for them to enter. "Please, do come in. I'm more than happy to assist."

The elegant parlour they stepped into was a quiet declaration of Drake's refined tastes; calculated, deliberate, and just a little too perfect. The air was cool, faintly scented with something expensive and herbal. Rare books lined the shelves in neat, almost obsessive order, their spines uncracked, as though chosen more for their titles than their contents. Botanical prints, all framed identically, hung with precision along the walls. Exquisite specimens, yes, but sterile somehow, as if any sign of life had been carefully pressed out of them.

Carter took a step further in, her boots muffled by the thick Persian rug underfoot. There was no dust. Not a single smudge on the polished surfaces. It was the sort of room where people sat with their backs straight and voices low, a place designed more for impression than comfort.

She glanced at Rievaulx. He was already scanning the space, not for aesthetic appreciation but for signs that something didn't fit. The tension in the room wasn't obvious, but it was there, lingering just beneath the civility. A little too much order. A little too much care taken to present exactly the right image.

It was a beautiful room, but beautiful rooms, as Carter had learned, could hide very ugly things.

"Tell us about your interest in the manuscript," Rievaulx said, getting straight to the point.

Drake chuckled lightly, a dismissive wave of his hand accompanying the sound. "It's merely scholarly curiosity, Chief Inspector. I've always had a penchant for rare texts, particularly those that delve into botany. The manuscript in question . . . what was its title again?" He feigned a casual forgetfulness.

"*The Garden of Shadows*," Carter supplied, her regard steady as she watched for any sign of disingenuousness.

"Ah, yes. Quite the evocative title," Drake responded. "But I assure you, my interest is purely academic."

Rievaulx exchanged a quick glance with Carter, both sensed the undercurrents of deception. "We have reason to believe that Mr. Matthews, the librarian at Cambridge, had reservations about the manuscript. We also know you were in contact with him."

Drake's charm became more calculated, his posture defensive. "Mr. Matthews was a respected librarian, but, as you know, the academic world is often fraught with a certain . . . drama. People grow rather attached to their work and the narratives they've built around it."

"Did you have any disagreements with him?" Carter asked while watching his reaction.

"Disagreements?" Drake repeated, his tone indignant. "Not at all. I merely sought to understand the manuscript's provenance. Scholarly pursuits can sometimes be misunderstood."

Rievaulx leaned forward with intent. "We understand that you visited Matthews frequently. Did he mention anything that could suggest he was in danger?"

For the briefest moment, Drake betrayed a crack in his composure. Just as hastily, he masked it with a smooth smile. "Officers, I had nothing to do with Mr. Matthews's unfortunate demise. I am, as I said, merely a collector. If something more sinister was afoot, I'm afraid I wouldn't be privy to it."

Carter stepped closer, her voice insistent. "You were trying to acquire that manuscript, weren't you? And when Matthews started uncovering its true nature, he became a liability."

Drake replied. "I assure you, Detective Constable, I'm not quite sure what you're insinuating. The academic world is a volatile place, people can be resistant to change, especially when it threatens their life's work."

"Is that what happened with Matthews?" Rievaulx inquired. "Did his discoveries make him a threat?"

Drake's expression hardened; the charm slipped to reveal something colder beneath. "You're barking up the wrong tree Chief Inspector. Feel free to investigate to your heart's content, but I assure you, my dealings are entirely legitimate."

Rievaulx exchanged a knowing glance with Carter. They were hitting a wall, and Drake's carefully constructed facade was proving difficult to penetrate. "We'll be in touch, Mr. Drake ," Rievaulx said, rising from his chair. "If you remember anything else, don't hesitate to contact us."

As they stepped back out into the crisp London air, the tension of the exchange still hung between them.

"Well, that was enlightening," Carter said, her voice edged with sarcasm. "He's a slippery one, isn't he?"

"Indeed," Rievaulx replied, his thoughts moving to the next steps. "Drake is hiding something, and it's more than just a passing interest in rare manuscripts."

"Where to next?" Carter asked.

"We can investigate Drake's past," Rievaulx said. "If he's been involved in forgeries or any other shady dealings, it might shed light on his true intentions. And we will look through Matthews's records again. He might have left something behind that we missed."

As they made their way back to Cambridge, the momentum of the investigation began to build once more. Rievaulx sensed they were edging closer to a confrontation that would unravel everything they thought they knew.

Chapter 10

St Michael's College, once a beacon of scholarly pursuit, now felt more like a fortress under siege to Rievaulx and Carter. The ornate wrought iron gates, typically symbols of academic tradition, now served as a barrier against the relentless throng of journalists and curious onlookers gathering outside. It appeared the news had finally made it beyond the boundaries of Cambridge. Summer, usually a sluggish season for headlines, had left the broadsheets and tabloids scrabbling for something—anything—to fill their pages. With nothing juicier to hand, they'd latched onto the death of an academic, almost a fortnight old now, and under normal circumstances, barely worth a paragraph halfway down page three.

The air was thick with tension, as if the ancient stone buildings themselves were holding their breath, bracing for what was to come.

Detective Chief Inspector Jonathan Rievaulx stood just outside those imposing gates, his tweed jacket rumpled from a long and taxing day. He adjusted his collar and cast a wary eye over the crowd of reporters, armed with notepads and cameras. The flashbulbs went off like a staccato of lightning, illuminating the scene in harsh bursts that felt more like the frantic heartbeat of prey than the steady pulse of reason.

Beside him, the College porter, a grizzled veteran who bore the stoicism of a man who had seen too much, stood unmoved by the chaotic scene. His eyes, shadowed by memories of war and the horrors he had witnessed near the River Kwai, regarded the reporters with a disdain born from experience. These modern-day vultures, with their incessant questions and flashy equipment, were mere amateurs compared to the real dangers he had faced. The sight of them, particularly the female reporters, stirred echoes of the past; they were the gaunt, skeletal faces of British and Australian women he had seen in a grim internment camp in Sumatra. The jarring voices of these journalists paled in comparison to the harrowing silence of those days, a silence that spoke more profoundly than any headline ever could.

The press was relentless, determined to uncover the latest scandal that now wrapped itself around the College. Their voices merged into a cacophony that bounced off the ancient stone walls, blending with the history embedded within them. Among the chaos, one intrepid reporter dashed toward a nearby telephone box, eager to file his story, while another wielded his notebook like a weapon, firing off questions in every direction.

Rievaulx couldn't suppress a wry smile at the sight. It was as if two worlds were colliding before his eyes: the dignified, age-old traditions of academia meeting the chaotic, ravenous world of modern journalism. Neither side appeared fully prepared for the encounter.

"Look at them," Rievaulx remarked, his voice a low rumble. "Like wolves circling their prey."

Carter stood beside him, surveying the scene with a cool detachment. "The media is bored, it smells blood, and the College's reputation is at stake. They won't stop until they've wrung every last drop out of this story."

Rievaulx offered a nod that carried more thought than enthusiasm. His mind was elsewhere. Lydia hovered at the edges of his thoughts . . . Lydia in Sydney, reporting with crisp professionalism on that sleek marvel of engineering, the Concorde.

Would she come back? That was the question. Not just to England, but to him.

Australia had its charms, of course, sunshine, space, a certain laid-back appeal, but Lydia was no beach-dweller. She was London through and through. She was sharp, fast-moving, intolerant of waffle. The easy charm of the Antipodes would wear thin soon enough of that he felt confident. Still, geography was one thing. People were another; whether she'd return to *him*—well, that was a different matter entirely.

"Sir?" Carter's voice brought him back to the present.

She didn't press him about the vague reply; Rievaulx disappearing into his thoughts was hardly a new development. In her experience, it happened often and without warning. It was also, infuriatingly, part of what made him so annoyingly effective at what he did.

Rievaulx released a breath as if trying to shed a thought, his brow furrowing. "And the administration won't take kindly to this level of scrutiny. They'll do whatever it takes to protect their ivory tower. It could hinder our investigation further." He said crisply focusing on the matter at hand.

They were there at the urgent request of Sir Geoffrey, who had telephoned the station earlier, his voice cracking with barely concealed panic. "You must do something about this blasted press!" he had demanded, the words sharp and insistent.

"I understand, Sir Geoffrey. We'll manage the situation as best we can," Rievaulx had replied, his tone calm. The thought of dealing with the press filled him with about as much enthusiasm as a cold breakfast.

"Sir Geoffrey wants to see us immediately," he had informed Carter afterward, pinching the bridge of his nose as if to stave off the impending headache. "He's worried about the press and is desperate to control the narrative before it spirals out of control."

Carter rolled her eyes, a gesture that was more suited to the stage than a police station. "Surprise, surprise. They're more concerned with public image than solving a murder."

They had arrived separately, as they had on that fateful morning when Dr. Atherton's body had been found. Rievaulx, ever the pragmatist, had arrived on his old Raleigh bicycle, while Carter had navigated the narrow streets in her red Mini, the strains of Rod Stewart's *Tonight's the Night* replacing her usual ABBA.

As the gates creaked open, Rievaulx strode through with purpose, Carter following close behind. She had parked her car with the finesse of a novice driver on her first roundabout. They made their way up the cobblestone path toward the Master's office, the air heavy with the scent of impending scandal.

A reporter called out, "Chief Inspector! What can you tell us about Dr. Atherton's murder? Are there any suspects?"

"No comment at the moment," Rievaulx replied curtly, unwilling to offer more. This was not the time for public pronouncements, and he had no intention of giving the press anything they could twist into sensationalism.

As they approached the Master's office, the noise from the crowd began to fade, replaced by the solemn echo of their footsteps on the ancient stones, each one a reminder of the seriousness of their task.

"Enter," came the voice from within, sharp and impatient.

Rievaulx opened the door to find Sir Geoffrey standing by the window, his arms crossed, his face lined with worry. The late afternoon sun cast long shadows across the room, deepening the creases of concern etched into his features.

"Chief Inspector," Sir Geoffrey began, his voice clipped and tense. "Thank you for coming so quickly. We find ourselves in a delicate situation, and I trust you understand the gravity of what's at stake." His gaze flickered to Carter, as if her presence added an unwelcome draft to an already chilly room, before he continued, "The press . . . they're becoming a real problem."

"Of course, Sir Geoffrey," Rievaulx replied and met the Master's regard with the steady resolve of someone who had faced many such storms before. "But our priority is the investigation. The College's reputation will have to take a backseat to the truth."

The Master bristled, a flush rising to his cheeks. "I understand your priorities, Chief Inspector, but you must also understand ours. If any scandal is linked to the College, it could jeopardize our funding, our standing in the academic world. We cannot afford any further complications."

Rievaulx leaned casually against the desk, his posture deceptively relaxed. "We'll do our best, Sir Geoffrey. We would like full access to all relevant information. Any attempt to obstruct our investigation will have serious consequences."

Sir Geoffrey's face tightened, his fingers drumming nervously on a fountain pen that lay on the desk. "I understand," he finally conceded, though his tone suggested otherwise. "But I implore you to be cautious. The press can be . . . relentless."

"And so can we, Sir Geoffrey," Rievaulx replied, his voice firm. "Rest assured; we'll tread carefully. The truth will come out, with or without your approval."

The tension in the room was palpable, the Master's unease hanging in the air like a cloud of smoke. It was clear that the path ahead would be fraught with challenges, a careful balancing act between duty and reputation.

Sir Geoffrey's shoulders sagged under the weight of the situation. "Very well, Chief Inspector. You will have access to whatever you need. But please, keep me informed of your findings, especially if they might reflect poorly on the College."

"Understood," Rievaulx replied, sensing a slight easing of the tension. For now, they had reached a tenuous agreement.

As they stepped out of the Master's office, Rievaulx turned to Carter, his brow furrowed in thought. "I wonder what scandal has him so on edge," he mused, the hint of intrigue in his voice unmistakable.

"Unless, of course, the murder of an academic on College grounds qualifies as a scandal in its own right," Carter replied dryly. "If that's the case, we're in for quite the performance."

Rievaulx chuckled, though the situation was far from humorous.

"If this is just the beginning, I dread to think what's still hidden beneath the surface."

They were about to descend the grand staircase, their footsteps echoing through the hall, when a door swung open unexpectedly. Dr. Thomas Arden emerged, his face pale, his manner anxious.

"Chief Inspector, I need to speak with you," Arden called out, his voice a frantic whisper. His eyes darted nervously around the corridor, as if the very walls were listening.

"Now?" Rievaulx asked, surprised by the interruption. "We're rather busy, Dr. Arden."

"Please, it's important," Arden insisted, his tone desperate. "I've uncovered something that could be vital to your investigation."

Rievaulx hesitated. "All right but make it quick."

Arden led them into his office, closing the door behind them with a hurried hand. "There are secrets in this College, secrets about a group operating in the shadows. If you give me a moment, I can show you something that might change everything."

As Arden spoke, Rievaulx noted the fear in his eyes that hinted at something deeper, something more dangerous.

"What is it?" Rievaulx asked.

"Not here," Arden replied, his voice low. "Follow me."

With a glance at Carter, who raised an eyebrow in silent agreement, Rievaulx nodded. There was no mistake, this was something far more significant than they had ever anticipated.

THE ATMOSPHERE THICKENED WITH TENSION AS Arden led Rievaulx and Carter through the dim, echoing corridors of the College. Their footsteps, muffled yet distinct on the cold stone floor, added a rhythmic pulse to the eerie silence. The portraits of long-deceased scholars adorned the walls, their painted eyes seeming to follow the trio with a mix of curiosity and silent reproach, as if they were aware of the turmoil brewing within the College's ancient halls.

"Where exactly are we going?" Carter whispered, her curiosity piqued as they ascended a series of winding staircases.

"To a place few know about," Arden replied in a hushed tone. "A hidden room used by a secret society. It's where the true power of the College resides."

Rievaulx raised an eyebrow. "A secret society? You're not pulling our leg, are you?"

Arden shook his head, his hands trembling slightly. "It's very real. They call themselves *The Fellowship*. They've been manipulating events from the shadows for years, and I fear . . ." he hesitated and took a breath, "I fear they're involved in Dr. Atherton's murder."

At the end of a narrow corridor, they paused before a nondescript door, half concealed by a faded, age-worn tapestry. So unremarkable was the tapestry that it nearly rendered the door invisible. Arden hesitated, casting a nervous glance over his shoulder before unlocking it. As the door creaked open, it revealed a small, cluttered room that appeared untouched by time.

The air inside was thick with the musty scent of old books and dust, mingled with a faint trace of Scotch that lingered like a ghostly presence. Shelves lined the walls, crammed with papers, folios, battered books, and ancient manuscripts, forming a barricade of forgotten lore that felt as if it were pressing in on the room. At the center stood a long, heavy table, its dark wood scarred and aged, strewn with scattered papers marked with cryptic symbols and strange, arcane patterns. Above the table loomed an imposing portrait of a stooped figure cloaked in academic robes, his face cast in shadow, concealing his identity yet leaving his gaze unnervingly sharp. A dark cape rested over his shoulders; a cape devoid of any connection to Cambridge tradition, giving him an unsettling air of mystery and quiet authority. The shadows closed in quiet and dense, as if the room itself held its breath, weighed down by secrets best left undisturbed.

"This is it," Arden said, stepping inside with a grim finality. "The heart of *The Fellowship*."

Rievaulx surveyed the room, every sense heightened. This was the last thing he'd expected though, on reflection, perhaps he should have. St Michael's was old, steeped in shadows of its own history. Rumors of secret societies drifted around Cambridge like mist, their truth uncertain, yet the city harbored a dark past, one that slipped through its cobbled streets and lingered in shadowed doorways. Discovering one here should not have come as a shock. "And just what is it they do here?"

"They control everything," Arden said, his voice edged with both fear and resolve. "Academic appointments, research funding, even student admissions. They've been orchestrating things from the shadows for decades. I believe it goes beyond that. Around Cambridge, there are whispers, suggestive glances, a hint that this influence extends far beyond the College, that *The Fellowship's* reach is long indeed."

"Reaching where?" Carter asked, eyes widening in disbelief. "Are you saying Atherton was just a pawn in something far bigger?"

"Exactly," Arden said, pacing nervously. "Atherton was a member, but he started questioning their methods and wanted out. I believe they saw him as a threat."

Rievaulx's mind raced. "And you're certain of this? Do you have any proof?"

Arden reached into a drawer and pulled out a worn, leather-bound journal. "This belonged to Atherton. I found it hidden in his office. It contains everything; the members, their activities, their plans."

He handed the journal to Rievaulx, his hands trembling with unease. "If you read this, you'll understand everything. Be very cautious; they'll go to any lengths to protect their secrets."

Rievaulx accepted the journal, sensing its importance. "This might be the breakthrough we've been waiting for," he said, casting a glance at Carter, who offered a firm nod of agreement.

Turning back to Arden, Rievaulx asked, "Dr. Arden, what prompted you to search Atherton's office? And just how did you come to know about all this?" he asked, gesturing broadly around the room. "What are you keeping from us?"

Arden let out a long breath. "I'd heard rumors. I've noticed people slipping in and out of this room, always locking it carefully behind them, glancing around to make sure no one was watching."

"If that's true, how were you able to observe them without being noticed yourself?" Rievaulx asked.

Arden straightened his shoulders. "I went to public school," he remarked. "Learning to linger unseen in corridors is a survival skill you pick up quickly."

Rievaulx knew this from his own experience. "And," he added thoughtfully, "how did you get a key? Were you aware of this journal? And if you found it in his office, why bring it here?"

Arden steadied himself. "I found the key taped inside the journal, which was lying on his desk beneath some irrelevant papers. I suppose he liked the idea of hiding it in plain sight, and anyone not in the know would likely have overlooked it. Stashing it here was as safe as anywhere if someone came looking."

"Hidden in plain sight," Carter echoed, her tone dark. "How did we miss this, sir?" she asked, turning to Rievaulx.

Rievaulx shook his head. "I don't think we did," he replied, his expression grim. "Someone put it there. Perhaps, like you," he said, looking at Arden, "they thought they were hiding it in plain sight. But you went looking in his office. What made you suspicious of Atherton?"

"There was something about Atherton's ... confidence," Arden explained. "Just a hunch, really."

Rievaulx studied him for a moment, scrutinizing his expression, before looking away, satisfied that Arden's motives were genuine.

"We must move quickly," Carter added, her voice firm. "If what you're saying is true, they'll soon realize we're onto them."

"Exactly," Rievaulx agreed, the gravity of the situation settling heavily on his shoulders. "But we must tread carefully. One wrong move could put us all in danger."

"Dr. Arden," Rievaulx said, turning to the anxious academic, "thank you for coming forward. But you must understand the risks you're taking."

"I understand," Arden said, determination etched into his features.

"Thank you, Dr. Arden. Constable Carter and I will handle things from here," Rievaulx said, his tone carrying a clear but courteous note of dismissal. Arden's lips tightened briefly in response before he gave a small nod. With a final glance around the room, he cautiously peered around the door, checked both directions, and then quietly slipped out.

As Rievaulx and Carter stood in that hidden room, surrounded by relics of a shadowy past, the atmosphere pressed down on them, heavy and oppressive. The flickering light cast unsettling shadows on the walls, as if the room itself were alive with the secrets it had harbored for so long.

"This place feels like something out of a horror film," Carter murmured, her eyes scanning the room for anything lurking where it shouldn't be. A small shiver ran up her spine; not unpleasant. She loved horror films, a secret vice, not something she advertised on forms. Her brothers used to drag her along to the Saturday matinees whenever a horror flick came to the local cinema. The idea had been to scare the living daylights out of her. Unfortunately for them, and rather satisfyingly for her, she'd sat through the lot without so much as a squeak. Stoicism, as it turned out, had its uses.

Rievaulx chuckled though his heart wasn't in it. "More like a vintage thriller, full of intrigue and danger. They've been operating in the dark, making decisions that shape the future of this College."

Carter picked up a document from the table, her brow furrowing as she read the names listed. One name, in particular, stood out. *Grayson*. "These are some of the most respected academics in Cambridge, not just St Michaels. If they're involved, the corruption runs deeper than we ever imagined."

"Indeed," Rievaulx replied, his expression grim. "It seems we're dealing with a cabal rather than just a secret society. Their influence has been extensive."

"What's the plan?" Carter asked, her voice resolute.

"We confront Grayson," Rievaulx said, the name falling from his lips with certainty. "He's been evasive, and it's time we get some answers."

"And if he refuses to cooperate?" Carter's gaze was steely.

"Then we'll find another way," Rievaulx replied, his tone unwavering. "But one way or another, we will expose *The Fellowship* for what they truly are. The truth must come out."

As they prepared to leave the hidden room, Rievaulx's mind raced with the possibilities that lay ahead. The investigation had led them into the darkest corners of the university's power structure, and the stakes had never been higher.

"Let's get back to the office and go through that journal," Carter suggested, her resolve as firm as ever.

"Agreed," Rievaulx replied. They exited the room, their footsteps echoing in the silent corridors, each step bringing them closer to unravelling the conspiracy that threatened to engulf them.

With the evidence they had gathered and the determination that drove their every move, Rievaulx knew they were on the brink of exposing the truth. A truth that came with danger, and the storm that would follow could be more than they had ever bargained for.

BACK AT THE STATION, THE MUTED glow of a desk lamp cast elongated shadows on the walls of Rievaulx's office. The room was a sanctuary of subdued tones and scattered paperwork, an oasis of calm amid the storm of their ongoing investigation. Rievaulx had just concluded an enlightening phone call with an old school acquaintance, now a prominent neuroscientist at Oxford.

Though their connection had never gone beyond the superficial ties of their boarding school dormitory proximity, Rievaulx had thought it prudent to reach out. His former schoolmate's insights into the field of neuroscience might shed some light on the enigmatic Dr. Grayson. The conversation had indeed proven to be a wellspring of information.

Dr. Grayson was a complicated man. Despite his stellar academic reputation, whispers of unethical practices as a neuroscientist had long trailed behind him like a persistent shadow. There were accusations—troubling ones—of experiments conducted on vulnerable subjects without proper consent. Yet, these serious allegations had done little to tarnish his standing in the scientific community, a testament to his powerful connections and the high regard in which his research was held.

In contrast to his professional acclaim, Grayson's personal life was as barren as the desert, his clinical detachment extending beyond the lab to encompass every aspect of his existence. He was a man singularly devoted to his work, believing emotions to be mere weaknesses that hindered true scientific progress. The portrait that emerged was one of cold professionalism masking a darker, morally ambiguous side; a side that might very well be connected to the unsettling events at St Michael's College.

Rievaulx turned to Carter, determination clear in his expression. "I believe it's time we had another word with Dr. Grayson," he said, feeling certain he now had the measure of the man.

THEY MADE THEIR WAY BACK THROUGH the thinning throng of reporters still clinging to the gates of St Michael's, their presence a lingering reminder of the scandal that had rocked the College. The porter, ever vigilant, stood like a sentinel, his piercing gaze promising swift retribution should anyone dare cross the line he had so clearly drawn. Carter noted with a hint of satisfaction that the press's numbers had dwindled; Dr. Atherton's demise was rapidly becoming yesterday's news, soon to be relegated to the back pages before finally becoming nothing but a wrapper discarded from fish and chips.

As they approached Dr. Grayson's office, the atmosphere shifted. The office itself had the dim lighting casting serpentine shadows that slithered across the room's stark, minimalist furnishings. The space was a shrine to precision, with walls lined by an impressive array of scientific tomes and surfaces meticulously arranged with papers. A solitary teacup sat on a matching saucer, the only hint of domesticity in an otherwise sterile environment.

Dr. Grayson, a gaunt figure with thinning grey hair and icy blue eyes, stood behind a high-backed leather chair, his presence exuding an air of aloof superiority tinged with disdain. He regarded them with a chilling detachment that mirrored the clinical coldness of his surroundings.

"Dr. Grayson," Rievaulx began, striving for composure despite the mounting tension. "We are here to discuss a secret society, *The Fellowship*, and it's possible connection to Dr. Atherton's death." If his aim had been to catch Grayson off guard, he'd missed the mark.

Grayson's cold, calculating eyes flicked up from the papers he was shuffling, his voice dripping with mockery. "A secret society, you say? How quaint. We are, in fact, a fellowship of dedicated academics. Our goal is to preserve the integrity of St Michael's, which means we have a say in who is admitted. Maintaining our reputation is paramount." he gave a cold smile, one that barely left his mouth and made it nowhere near his eyes.

Rievaulx held his gaze, though doubt flickered in his eyes. "And Dr. Atherton? He was a member of this "fellowship," wasn't he? We suspect his involvement might be linked to his murder."

Grayson's lips curled into a sardonic smile. "Dr. Atherton was indeed a valued member. His death was tragic, but not of our doing. His questioning of our methods and subsequent desire to leave is hardly a crime. If anything, it highlights our commitment to rigorous standards."

Carter shifted, and her eyes narrowed. "Rigorous standards, or a means of control and manipulation? Your influence reaches far beyond normal academic procedures."

Grayson's eyes flashed with irritation before he regained his composure. "Control and manipulation? Constable, we ensure that this institution remains at the pinnacle of academic excellence. If you choose to interpret our practices differently, that is your prerogative. But I assure you, our sole concern is the reputation of St Michael's."

Rievaulx sensed a deeper, more sinister undercurrent beneath Grayson's clinical detachment. "We have evidence suggesting that your fellowship may be involved in unethical practices," he pressed. "The journal we found points to a pattern of secrecy and control that extends well beyond ordinary academic boundaries."

Grayson's expression hardened slightly, though his air of calm remained. "A journal? Evidence is only as reliable as its context. If you believe that a few documents can unravel the complexities of a prestigious institution, you are gravely mistaken. Our work—my work—is far more significant than any petty accusations."

Rievaulx felt the weight of Grayson's words, the unspoken threat hanging heavily between them. "And what of Dr. Atherton's research?" Carter interjected, "Was there something in his work that might have made him a threat to your fellowship?"

Grayson's eyes narrowed, his voice dismissive. "Dr. Atherton's research was his own. If he found himself at odds with our principles, that is unfortunate but not unusual. We do what is necessary to maintain our standards, but we do not resort to violence."

Rievaulx scrutinized Grayson closely, trying to pierce through the veneer of academic superiority. The coldness in Grayson's manner spoke volumes about his possible motives.

"We'll be taking this matter further," Rievaulx said. "The truth will come out, Dr. Grayson. One way or another."

Grayson's smile was imperceptible, with a hint of dark satisfaction. "I'm sure you'll do your best. But remember, the truth is often more elusive than one might expect."

As they turned to leave, Carter cast a final, piercing glance at Grayson, her suspicion unwavering. Rievaulx felt the weight of their encounter settle over him. They weren't merely dealing with an academic; Grayson was a man driven by a calculating, almost ruthless disposition. Without concrete proof of his involvement in Atherton's death or more conclusive evidence linking him to any secret society, they were left with little more than a gut feeling and a growing sense of unease.

As they exited the building, the cool air outside was a stark contrast to the stifling tension within. The investigation had taken them down a serpentine path, and each turn revealed more shadows than light. Yet, Rievaulx knew they were drawing closer to the truth.

Chapter 11

The Cambridge University Botanic Garden was a sanctuary of verdant beauty, a serene haven where the frenetic energy of academic life appeared to melt away into nature's tranquil embrace. Rievaulx had always found solace in such places; there was a quiet persistence to nature that mirrored the patient work of a detective, meticulously piecing together clues until the entire picture finally emerged from the shadows.

Today, however, unbeknownst to him, the garden would ultimately serve a greater purpose than mere refuge; it was a potential wellspring of answers. As Rievaulx strolled along the gravel paths, he took in the meticulously tended beds of flowers and shrubs, each bloom, a burst of color against the backdrop of leafy greens. The sun filtered through the branches of towering trees, casting dappled shadows that danced on the ground, while the air was perfumed with the rich scent of damp earth and blooming flora. Birds flitted about, their cheerful trills providing a soothing symphony to accompany his contemplations.

He had ventured here on a hunch, a growing suspicion that had taken root ever since they uncovered the rare orchid at the scene of Atherton's murder, which had been slowly growing in the back of his mind. As he ran his mind across the investigation so far, it was full of dead ends and red herrings, suppositions and possibilities. Perhaps he had, as he'd always cautioned Carter against, allowed himself to be lured into addressing the obvious fragments of information rather than stepping back to examine the full picture ... well as much of the full picture as he could paint in his mind.

This orchid, he reminded himself, had been left for a reason. It was a message to be read by someone clever enough to see the intent behind it, and yet, no one, including himself, had looked further for its meaning and tried to understand why it had been left. The ordinary garden variety orchid he'd found on Matthews's windowsill, he'd dismissed as mere coincidence. The deaths of the librarian and Atherton shared nothing beyond physical proximity and a dispute over the provenance of a manuscript — a detail he now suspected was just a small piece in a much larger scheme.

For that reason, the librarian's death had been handed off to a newly appointed, but by all accounts, capable detective inspector. Walker was a sharp-eyed terrier from Birmingham; he spoke with a nasal twang that often left his southern colleagues nodding blankly, but he had a reputation for persistence and a clear ambition that pointed squarely in the direction of Scotland Yard.

Rievaulx had explained, with as much clarity as he could muster, that the murders of Dr Atherton and Peter Matthews were connected, though not in any straightforward way. To his credit, the young DI hadn't needed it spelled out—and just to keep things balanced, a more seasoned sergeant had been assigned to rein in any overzealous footwork.

"Four pairs of eyes are better than two," Rievaulx had told Carter. "And in any case, we've got more than enough to be getting on with."

Rievaulx focused his mind on the orchid placed so judiciously beside Atherton that was not merely a flower; it was a symbol, a key that could unlock the secrets lurking in the murky depths of the case. Rievaulx felt strongly that the answers he sought could be nestled among the carefully cultivated specimens that had been nurtured by the university's botanists rather than chasing dubious manuscripts and secret societies.

As he wandered deeper into the garden, Rievaulx reflected on the intricacies of human relationships, much like the interconnectedness of the flora surrounding him. Each plant played its role, reliant on the others for survival. Just as the garden thrived on harmony, so too did the dynamics among the people entangled in this investigation weave a delicate tapestry of intrigue. Perhaps it was that very complexity that held the key to understanding the tangled web of events that had unfolded.

The sun's warmth invigorated him, bolstering his resolve as he made his way to the conservatory, a large glass structure filled with exotic plants from far-flung tropical climates. Inside, the air was warm and humid, a stark contrast to the coolness that often permeated the English summer outside. As he stepped through the door, he was greeted by a riot of color; orchids, bromeliads, and ferns flourished in the controlled environment, their vibrant hues and intricate patterns a testament to nature's wondrous artistry.

As he traversed the lush landscape of botanical specimens, a thought struck him: how many secrets did these plants conceal? He chuckled at the whimsical notion of flora as silent keepers of secrets, quietly absorbing the chaos of human emotion and intellect swirling around them. It was a fanciful thought, but it provided a flicker of amusement amidst the weighty burden of his investigation.

It didn't take long for Rievaulx to locate what he was searching for. In a secluded corner of the conservatory, partially obscured by a tall fern, he found a collection of orchids that matched the description of the one discovered at the crime scene. The delicate blossoms were a soft lavender, their intricate veining hinting at their rarity. Kneeling to examine them closely, Rievaulx's mind raced. This orchid was not native to England; it was exceedingly rare even in its natural habitat. Cultivating such a plant required meticulous care, knowledge that only someone well-versed in botany could possess. That realization significantly narrowed down the list of potential suspects.

As he scrutinized the orchids, he sensed a presence nearby. Turning, he saw Dr. Irene Forsyth entering the conservatory. Her sharp, angular features were softened by the vibrant foliage surrounding her. An air of distracted intensity radiated from her, suggesting her thoughts often raced ahead of her physical form. Wearing a lab coat over her attire, her hands bore the earthy stains of her botanical work. Rievaulx wasn't surprised to see her; despite her academic focus on mathematics, he had uncovered during his investigations that she was an exceptionally skilled botanist, often found in the greenhouses of the Botanic Garden rather than grappling with abstract equations in her St Michael's office.

"Chief Inspector Rievaulx," she greeted him, her tone quiet, her manner anxious as she approached. Rievaulx was reminded of the Master's description of her as an "anxious cat". "I wasn't expecting a visit from the police today. What brings you to my corner of the University?"

Rievaulx noted the flicker of unease in her voice but maintained his own tone as neutral as the damp air around them.

"I'm following up on a lead, Dr. Forsyth. The orchid found at the scene of Dr. Atherton's death; it's a rare species, not easily acquired. I've been led to believe you're one of the few individuals in Cambridge with the expertise to cultivate it."

Forsyth's eyes flickered, her arms crossing defensively over her chest. "Orchids are my specialty, yes. But I fail to see what that has to do with Atherton's death. Flowers don't kill people, Chief Inspector." she said.

"No, but people do," Rievaulx replied, calm and steady. "And the presence of that orchid suggests a connection to someone with a deep knowledge of botany. Someone like yourself perhaps."

Her posture stiffened, and a tense silence hung in the air between them. When she answered, her voice was slight and insubstantial, like a flutter on the breeze. He only heard her because it was so silent in the greenhouse.

"Are you accusing me of something, Chief Inspector?"

Rievaulx met her gaze evenly. "I'm simply trying to understand the connection. The orchid wasn't placed at the scene by mere chance. It was positioned there deliberately, as a message. And I believe you're the only one who can help me decipher it."

Forsyth's expression faltered for a moment, perhaps fear or guilt, crossing her features before she quickly glanced away.

"You're mistaken," she replied, jutting her chin and her tone still quivery but firmer now. "I had nothing to do with Atherton's death. My work is in mathematical conundrums; my interest lies in cultivating rare and beautiful plants, not in the lives of people."

Rievaulx took a step closer, his eyes never leaving hers. "You were close to Atherton, weren't you? You worked together on several projects, and you shared interests. But it was more than that, wasn't it? There was a personal history between you, something that transcended the university's walls."

Forsyth's jaw tightened, and she looked away, her gaze fixed on the orchids as if seeking solace in their delicate beauty.

"You have no idea what you're talking about, Chief Inspector," she said, though the tremor in her voice betrayed her.

Rievaulx was letting his instincts lead the way now. He was casting out a line, the lure bright and enticing, concealing its sharp hook, just to see what might bite. He had no real knowledge of any discord between Dr. Atherton and Dr. Forsyth, but some instinct had nudged him to follow this trail.

"Dr. Forsyth, I want you to be honest with me. What happened between you and Atherton? What are you hiding?"

For a fleeting moment, Forsyth appeared on the verge of tears. Then she shook her head, her expression hardening. "You're wasting your time," she stated. "There's nothing for you here."

Forsyth's face had paled, and for a fleeting moment, Rievaulx caught a glimpse of the raw emotion that lay beneath her cool exterior. "I didn't kill him," she whispered, the words barely escaping her lips.

"Then why leave the orchid?" Rievaulx inquired. "Why use it as a symbol?"

"I didn't leave anything!" she snapped, her voice rising. "I wanted him to suffer, yes, but that's not the same as murder. I wanted to see him pay for what he did to my father."

"Your father?" Rievaulx repeated, the name stirring something in the recesses of his memory. Forsyth? There were whispers, weren't there? A scandal long buried but not forgotten. Yes, the name rang a bell, but the details remained elusive. "And what happened to him?" his tone gentle but insistent.

"Nothing that concerns you," Forsyth retorted, the words sharp, though the quiver in her voice gave her away.

Rievaulx could almost see the cracks forming in the stoic facade she'd so carefully constructed. He leaned in slightly, softening his voice.

"Dr. Forsyth, I can see this is difficult, but I need your help. If there's something more-anything-that could bring us closer to the truth, you must tell me."

Her gaze shifted away, focusing intently on the orchids as if they might offer some escape from the weight of her secrets.

"I wish I could," she murmured, the words barely audible. "But I can't."

"Why not?" Rievaulx pressed, his frustration mounting. "You're caught in the web of your own emotions. But it doesn't have to end this way."

With a pained expression, Forsyth met his gaze. "Because it's too late. Atherton had enemies, and I wasn't the only one who wanted him gone. You think I'm the only one with a motive? You're wrong."

"Who else?" Rievaulx asked. "Who else had a reason to harm him?"

Forsyth shook her head, resolute. "I don't know. I can't help you. Not now. Not ever."

Rievaulx studied her, frustration and empathy warring within him. He sensed the turmoil beneath her cool exterior, the years of resentment simmering just below the surface.

"Thank you for your time, Dr. Forsyth," he said, his voice softer. "I'll be in touch."

Forsyth didn't respond, her gaze drifting back to the orchids as he turned to leave.

Rievaulx stepped back into the warm summer air, a feeling of unease settling over him. He was certain that Forsyth was hiding something crucial, a piece of the puzzle that could either lead to the truth or shroud them all in darkness. Rievaulx could sense that he wouldn't glean any more information from her today. Yet, he knew he had seen enough to realize that Forsyth was concealing something; something that could pierce the very heart of the investigation.

THE FAMILIAR SCENT OF DAMP EARTH and the faint fragrance of orchids lingered on Rievaulx as he left the conservatory behind. The garden's serene beauty was in stark contrast to the turmoil within his mind. Sunlight filtered through the canopy, casting dappled shadows on the gravel path; a reflection of the tangled web of secrets and emotions he was trying to unravel.

Rievaulx's thoughts were consumed by the recent encounter with Dr. Forsyth. His fishing expedition had uncovered an unforeseen path, but rather than delivering answers, it had only tossed more questions his way. Her reaction to the mention of her father had been telling, however, a deep, raw wound that had yet to heal. The connection between her and Dr. Atherton was undeniable, but there was something more, something buried beneath layers of professional rivalry and personal vendetta.

He found himself wandering aimlessly through the garden until he came to a weathered bench beneath the ancient oak. The bench, much like the case, bore the weight of years, its surface etched with the marks of time. He sank onto it, closing his eyes, allowing the sounds of rustling leaves and distant birdsong to soothe his racing thoughts. Why had Forsyth reacted so strongly? What was the true nature of her connection to Atherton, and how did it tie into the orchid found at the crime scene?

Determined to dig deeper, Rievaulx's mind began to sift through his memories, not of suspects, but of colleagues whose passions lay in the intricate world of botany. The orchid, rare and exotic, had been a clue from the start, but only now did he begin to see its full significance. A name surfaced from the recesses of his mind, a professor whose expertise in orchids was renowned, and with a newfound sense of urgency, Rievaulx sprang into action.

He mounted his trusted Raleigh bicycle, the wheels spinning as fast as his thoughts. Down Hills Road he raced, his jacket billowing behind him like the sails of a ship caught in a strong wind. He veered along East Road, past the open expanse of Parker's Piece, and on towards the police station, where answers awaited.

Bursting through the station doors, Rievaulx barely paused as Sergeant Pritchard attempted to flag him down.

"I've a message from Miss Carter—" Pritchard began, but Rievaulx brushed past him, focused on his mission.

"Not now," Rievaulx called over his shoulder. "I need to make a telephone call."

In the relative calm of his office, Rievaulx took a deep breath, steadying his thoughts. The adrenaline that had driven him here now gave way to the disciplined focus of a detective on the verge of a breakthrough. His fingers danced over the pages of his address book, searching for the name that had emerged from the depths of his recollection.

The rotary dial clicked with a rhythmic precision as he placed the call. Minutes later, the fog that had clouded his thoughts began to lift. His colleague on the other end of the line was a font of knowledge, meticulously cataloguing a scandal that had unfolded years ago, a scandal that had more layers than an onion.

The pieces began to fall into place. Forsyth's nervous disposition, her deep-seated resentment all traced back to her father, once a prominent botanist whose career had crumbled under allegations of plagiarism brought against him by none other than Dr. Atherton. The scandal had destroyed Forsyth's father, leaving a legacy of bitterness that had festered over the years. This wasn't just about professional rivalry; it was about a family's honor, tarnished and trampled upon.

As Rievaulx digested this information, his colleague promised to deliver the documentation directly to the front desk; a small mercy that spared Rievaulx the inconvenience of yet another errand. His colleague was already pressed for time, with a talk to give and a day filled with appointments. The promise of not being waylaid for a cup of tea was a minor victory in Rievaulx's hectic schedule.

The file arrived quickly, and as Rievaulx sifted through the documents, the story became clearer, yet more complex. Forsyth's father's fall from grace had left scars that were far from healed. The orchid left at the crime scene now took on a new significance. It wasn't just a cryptic message; it was a symbol of deep-seated grievances, a silent accusation that pointed to more than just Forsyth. This rare flower might represent Forsyth's personal vendetta, but it also hinted at a broader spectrum of animosity from those who had suffered at Atherton's hands.

With renewed determination, Rievaulx pieced together the timeline of events. The scandal had carved deep wounds in the botanical world, and Forsyth was not the only one nursing a grudge. Whispers of other disgruntled colleagues—scientists and academics whose careers had been derailed by Atherton's ruthless ambition—began to surface.

The weight of the case lightened as the connections solidified in his mind. The investigation, once disparate and tangled, was now coming together into a coherent tapestry of motive and opportunity. Rievaulx reached for the telephone once more, dialing Carter's number with a sense of urgency.

When she answered, he wasted no time. "What have you found?" he asked, his voice taut with anticipation.

"I've been examining the journal," Carter replied, her tone serious. "The one belonging to *The Fellowship*, the secret society. It's revealed some significant details."

As she explained her findings, Rievaulx felt every part of the investigation sliding into place. It was taking shape, the shadowy figures at the edges of their inquiry coming into sharper focus. The path ahead was still fraught with uncertainty, but for the first time, Rievaulx felt they were on the verge of uncovering the truth.

The case was far from over, but the stage was set for what was to come. The tangled web of secrets, lies, and old wounds was slowly being unraveled, and Rievaulx knew that the answers they sought were within reach. With each step closer to the truth, though, the danger increased, and Rievaulx could only hope that they would uncover the whole story before it was too late, before someone else ended up paying the price for keeping *The Fellowship's* secrets under wraps.

Chapter 12

It was nearing the end of June, nearly four weeks since Atherton's murder, and the College gardens had been transformed into a veritable wonderland of light and sound for the May Ball, as if one had stepped into the pages of an old fairy tale. Lanterns hung from the branches of ancient trees like stars fallen to earth, casting a soft, ethereal glow over the meticulously manicured lawns. The air was thick with the intoxicating scent of blooming roses and fresh-cut grass, mingling with the gentle rustle of silk gowns and the faint clink of champagne glasses. Laughter and music spiraled through the evening, weaving an intricate tapestry of joy that temporarily masked the undercurrents of tension lurking beneath the surface.

Detective Chief Inspector Jonathan Rievaulx stood at the edge of the festivities, his keen gaze scanning the throngs of guests who flowed through the gardens like water through a stream. Clad in a well-tailored black evening suit, he looked every bit the part of a distinguished academic, although the subtle tension in his posture hinted at the weight of the investigation that had brought him to this gala. Beside him, Detective Constable Emily Carter wore a simple yet elegant green gown, her air of quiet confidence lending her an aura of grace that belied the serious purpose of their presence.

"This is quite the spectacle," Carter murmured, her eyes scanning the crowd. Students, faculty, and benefactors moved with an ease born of privilege, their conversations brimming with the casual arrogance of those who believed themselves untouchable, their laughter ringing like chimes on a gentle breeze.

"Indeed," Rievaulx replied, his voice low and measured. "But don't let the glamour fool you. Beneath this veneer of civility, there are darker currents at play."

"Why, exactly, is it called the May Ball when it takes place in June?" Carter mused aloud.

Rievaulx, momentarily diverted from the more pressing matters of the case, allowed himself a faint smile at Carter's question. "Ah, the May Ball conundrum," he said, with a touch of scholarly amusement. "It's one of those endearing quirks of tradition. Despite what the name might suggest, these grand affairs actually occur in the second or third week of June, a period known as May Week. Originally, they were timed to celebrate the rowing victories of the Bumps races held in May. But the name stuck stubbornly, even after the timing of May Week was shifted to June back in 1882. It's one of those charming anachronisms that clings to the past with a sort of nostalgic tenacity."

Carter nodded, her gaze drifting toward a group of academics engaged in animated conversation by a grand marble fountain. She recognized several of them as members of *The Fellowship*, their faces etched with the familiar blend of intelligence and hubris that had become all too commonplace in this investigation. They were the sort of people who believed themselves impervious to scrutiny, shrouded in an aura of respectability that masked their more sinister dealings.

"Do you think they suspect anything?" she asked.

"I doubt it," Rievaulx said, his eyes narrowing. "They're too confident in their own machinations. They think they're untouchable, but tonight, we're going to show them otherwise."

As they moved deeper into the crowd, Rievaulx kept his senses on high alert, attuned to the subtle cues that might reveal something of value. The May Ball was not just a celebration, it was an opportunity for the College's elite to solidify alliances, trade secrets, and perhaps make deals that would ensure their continued dominance. The atmosphere was charged with potential. Beneath the surface, something crackled, tense and electric.

"There's Lang," Carter whispered, her gaze landing on a tall, distinguished-looking man holding court near one of the garden's decorative arches. Professor Robert Lang stood with an air of authority, his charming smile and polished manner belying a more sinister nature. Rievaulx had crossed paths with Lang enough times to recognize the predatory gleam in his eye. The journal Arden had found in Atherton's office had revealed he was a master manipulator, a man whose rise to prominence had been built on the backs of others, and who was now ensnared in the web of deceit spun by *The Fellowship*.

"Keep an eye on him," Rievaulx instructed, his tone grave. "He's the key to all of this."

Carter nodded and began to drift closer to the group, her movements subtle and deliberate. Rievaulx, meanwhile, made his way toward another cluster of guests, his gaze sweeping the area for any sign of Dr. Irene Forsyth. He found her standing alone by a hedge of roses, her face pale and drawn, the festive atmosphere around her seemingly forgotten.

Forsyth looked different tonight; gone was the icy composure she had shown in their previous encounter in the Botanical Garden. Instead, tension radiated from her, her eyes darting nervously as if expecting someone to approach her at any moment. She was dressed for the Ball in something that might have been the height of fashion ten years earlier, perhaps even the very gown she'd worn to her own college ball. A floor-length empire-line number in shimmering taffeta, with a high neckline and sheer sleeves, the sort of thing that had graced the pages of *Vogue* in 1967. Under the soft glow of the garden lights, its bold teal hue all but swallowed her, giving the impression she'd faded into the dress rather than the other way round.

"Dr. Forsyth," Rievaulx greeted, his voice casual but his mind sharp. "I didn't expect to see you here."

Forsyth flinched slightly at his approach, then forced a tight smile. "Chief Inspector Rievaulx. I thought I might find you mingling with the rest of the guests."

"Only doing my job," Rievaulx replied. Although his eyes searched hers for any hint of what lay beneath her surprisingly composed façade and there was no sign tonight of the anxious cat. "But you don't appear to be enjoying the festivities."

Forsyth's eyes flickered with something, fear, perhaps, or guilt. "I'm not much for these kinds of events," she said. "But it's expected of us, isn't it? To show up, to smile, to pretend that everything is fine."

"There's a lot of that going around," Rievaulx said, his voice softening. "But you don't have to pretend with me, Dr. Forsyth. I know you're under a lot of pressure."

Forsyth's composure wavered, and for a fleeting moment, Rievaulx thought she might confide in him. Then her expression hardened, and she shook her head. "I'm fine, Chief Inspector. Just tired. It's been a long few weeks."

"Indeed, it has," Rievaulx agreed, although he knew that there was more at play than mere fatigue. Forsyth was hiding something; something that was gnawing at her and tonight might just be the night it all came spilling out.

As the music swelled and the night deepened, Rievaulx felt the tension in the air intensify. The May Ball was reaching its zenith, but beneath the surface of the celebration, dark currents were swirling.

Rievaulx moved away from Forsyth, giving her space to gather her thoughts, though he remained close enough to observe her. His instincts told him that she was a pivotal figure in this investigation. He watched as she took a deep breath, her eyes scanning the crowd, perhaps looking for an ally or a way out.

As Rievaulx turned his attention back to the larger gathering, he noticed Carter had positioned herself near Lang, who was now engaged in an animated conversation with several other academics. From a distance, it looked like a casual exchange of pleasantries, but Rievaulx knew better. Lang's body language, though relaxed, betrayed a hint of impatience, his gestures too sharp, his smile too fixed.

Rievaulx decided to approach, weaving through the crowd with the practiced ease of a man who had spent years navigating social events like these. He caught snippets of conversation as he passed, most of it idle chatter about the latest academic papers or the outcome of recent exams. But here and there, he detected the undercurrent of gossip, whispers of rumors that hinted at the real power dynamics at play within the College.

When he reached Lang's group, he allowed himself to be drawn into the conversation, exchanging polite nods and smiles with the other academics. Lang acknowledged him with a brief nod, his expression inscrutable.

"Chief Inspector Rievaulx," Lang said, "I didn't expect to see you here tonight. Taking a break from your investigation, I presume?"

"Not quite," Rievaulx replied, keeping his tone light. "Just observing, as always. The May Ball is quite the spectacle, isn't it?"

"Indeed," Lang agreed, his smile widening. "It's one of the highlights of the academic calendar. A chance for everyone to let their hair down after a long year."

"Or to forge new alliances," Rievaulx added. "It's interesting how these events can bring people together, isn't it?"

Lang's smile faltered slightly, but he quickly recovered. "I suppose so. But tonight is about celebration, Chief Inspector. Surely even you can appreciate that."

"Of course," Rievaulx said, returning Lang's smile with one of his own. "But you know, even in the midst of celebration, it's important to remember the responsibilities we carry."

Lang's eyes narrowed, just for a moment, and Rievaulx knew he had struck a nerve. Before he could press further, the conversation was interrupted by the arrival of a waiter bearing a tray of champagne. The group's attention shifted, and Lang seized the opportunity to steer the conversation back to safer territory.

Rievaulx lingered for a few more minutes, but he could tell that Lang was on guard now, careful not to reveal anything that might be used against him later. Satisfied that he had made his presence known, Rievaulx excused himself and moved away, his mind already turning over the implications of the brief exchange.

As he wandered through the gardens, Rievaulx kept an eye on Forsyth, who had retreated to a quieter corner of the festivities. She was standing alone, her back to the crowd, staring out at the darkened lawns beyond the glow of the lanterns. Rievaulx felt a pang of sympathy for her. Whatever secrets she was hiding, it was clear that they weighed heavily on her.

He approached her again, this time more slowly, giving her a chance to collect herself. When she sensed his presence, she turned to face him, her expression guarded.

"Chief Inspector," she said, her voice strained. "Is there something you need?"

"I was just wondering if you're all right, Dr. Forsyth," Rievaulx replied, his tone gentle. "You seem a bit out of sorts tonight."

"I'm fine," she said, though her voice lacked conviction. "It's just . . .there's a lot on my mind."

"I can imagine," Rievaulx said. "You've been through a lot lately. It's only natural to feel overwhelmed."

Forsyth hesitated, her eyes flickering with uncertainty. For a moment, Rievaulx thought she might open up to him, but then she shook her head, as if dismissing the idea.

"I appreciate your concern, Chief Inspector," she said, her tone firming. "But I assure you, I'm fine."

Rievaulx nodded, though he didn't believe her. "If you ever need to talk, you know where to find me."

With that, he took his leave, sensing that any further pressure would only drive her deeper into her shell. But as he walked away, he couldn't shake the feeling that something was about to happen.

As the night wore on, the atmosphere at the May Ball grew increasingly charged. The music swelled to a crescendo, and the laughter of the guests took on an edge. Rievaulx kept a close watch on both Forsyth and Lang, noting the way their paths orbited each other without ever truly intersecting.

It was just after midnight when the first sign of trouble appeared. Rievaulx was standing near the fountain, scanning the crowd, when he noticed a commotion near the entrance to the gardens. Someone screamed, and a group of guests had gathered, their voices rising in alarm. Rievaulx's instincts kicked in, and he pushed his way through the throng, Carter following close behind.

When they reached the source of the disturbance, Rievaulx saw Forsyth standing at the center of the crowd, her face pale and stricken. She was holding something in her hands—a small, delicate object that Rievaulx recognized immediately.

It was an orchid, its soft lavender petals glowing in the light of the lanterns—the same rare orchid that had been found at the scene of Dr. Atherton's murder.

Rievaulx's heart sank as he realized what this meant. The orchid was a message, a warning. And now, it had been delivered to Forsyth.

"Where did you get this?" he asked her quietly.

She shook her head, eyes wide with shock. "It all happened so quickly. Someone bumped into me, I nearly lost my balance, and before I knew it, this was pushed into my hands," Forsyth whispered, her voice unsteady. "Why was this given to me?"

Rievaulx stepped forward, gently taking the orchid from her hands. "I don't know, Dr. Forsyth. But we're going to find out."

He turned to Carter, who was already scanning the crowd for any sign of the person who had left the orchid. "We will get to the bottom of this. Find out if anyone saw someone with this.

I'm heading back to the station, call me there if you turn up anything."

Under normal circumstances, he wouldn't have dreamt of leaving, but these weren't normal circumstances. Pritchard had passed on a message earlier in the day. Lydia had sent a telex from Sydney. She'd be phoning the station at 11 p.m., which, thanks to time zones and international cooperation, translated to 8 a.m. her end. For that, he was prepared to make an exception.

As Carter nodded and scurried away, Rievaulx looked down at the orchid in his hand. It was beautiful, delicate, and utterly out of place in the midst of this unfolding drama; it was the symbol, a reminder that the dark currents they had sensed all evening were real, and that the secrets of St Michael's College were about to be exposed. Rievaulx's mind began piecing together the clues that had led them to this moment. The orchid was more than just a flower, it was the key to unravelling the mystery that had gripped St Michael's, a mystery that was about to reach its dramatic conclusion.

As the evening deepened, the Ball, though alive with music and laughter, began to adopt a different tone, one tinged with an undercurrent of danger. The lanterns cast long shadows across the lawn, their warm glow now inadequate to dispel the encroaching darkness that clung to the edges of the festivities. The air thickened with the scent of flowers and the faint tang of tension, a sharp contrast to the earlier light-heartedness.

Carter had been watching Professor Lang for some time, noting how he glided through the crowd with the ease of a man accustomed to being the center of attention. His conversations were light, his smile disarming, yet there was a guardedness about him that Carter couldn't ignore; a subtle wariness suggesting he was more aware of the stakes than he let on. He was like a predator, carefully sizing up his surroundings while presenting a façade of charm. Each nod, each laugh, was carefully calibrated, hiding the calculating mind that lurked beneath.

As Carter circled closer, she caught sight of Dr. Forsyth standing a few paces away from Lang, her posture stiff and her expression strained. It was abundantly clear that Forsyth was not here by choice. Her discomfort only grew as Lang approached her, his smile a mask that barely concealed his true intentions. The distance between them appeared to shrink, and Carter could almost feel the oppressive weight of the exchange about to unfold.

Why had Dr. Forsyth remained at the Ball? Carter wondered. The arrival of the orchid was clearly a warning—or was it, perhaps, a message urging her to stay and wait for whatever might happen next?

"Dr. Forsyth," Lang greeted, his tone deceptively smooth, sliding into the conversation like a snake through tall grass. "Enjoying the Ball?"

Forsyth barely managed a nod, her voice tight as she replied, "It's . . . lovely."

Lang's smile widened, but it held no warmth. "I've been meaning to speak with you," he said, his voice dropping to a lower, more insidious tone. "About a certain . . . arrangement."

Carter tensed, straining to hear their conversation without revealing her presence. She edged closer, using the cover of the crowd to mask her movements, her heart racing with a mix of anticipation and dread. The words, dripping with menace, hung in the air, laden with implications she could only begin to grasp.

"I don't know what you're talking about," Forsyth replied, her voice wavering, betraying her fear. The facade she had been desperately clinging to was beginning to crack, revealing the vulnerability beneath.

Lang chuckled softly, a sound that sent a chill down Carter's spine. "Come now, Irene. We both know that's not true. You've been rather careless lately, leaving a trail of evidence that could be very damaging if it were to come to light."

Forsyth's face paled, and she glanced around nervously, as if searching for an escape route. "You don't understand," she whispered, her voice trembling. "I didn't mean for any of this to happen."

Lang's smile faded, replaced by a cold, calculating expression. "It doesn't matter what you meant. What matters is how you handle it now. You've put us all at risk, and you know what the consequences will be if this gets out."

Forsyth's eyes filled with tears, her composure crumbling under the weight of Lang's threats. "Please, Robert . . . I didn't want any of this. I just wanted to protect my father's legacy."

Lang's expression softened slightly, but there was no real compassion in his eyes, only the glint of someone who relished their power over another. "I understand, Irene. But you need to understand that you're in too deep now. There's no turning back. You'll do as I say, or . . ."

He let the threat hang in the air, unspoken but all too clear. The implication was obvious: a silent blade held to Forsyth's throat. An imaginary one true, but a blade, nonetheless.

Carter felt her pulse quicken. Lang was blackmailing Forsyth, using her fear and guilt to manipulate her. But for what purpose? What was he trying to keep hidden? The questions multiplied in her mind, but she knew she needed more than just suspicions. She had to catch Lang in the act.

Before she could move closer, Forsyth's expression twisted into one of desperation. "I won't do it, Robert," she said, her voice shaking but resolute. "I won't be part of this anymore."

Lang's eyes darkened, and he stepped closer to her, his voice low and menacing. "You don't have a choice, Irene. You're already part of it, whether you like it or not. And if you don't play your part, you know what will happen."

Forsyth's breath caught, and she looked around as if searching for help. It was then that Carter decided to intervene. She stepped forward, her expression calm but authoritative as she said, "Is everything all right here?"

Lang turned to her, his smile returning as he quickly masked his anger. "Ah, just a friendly conversation between colleagues," he said his voice dripping with insincerity. "Nothing to worry about."

In that moment, Forsyth's eyes met Carter's, and Carter saw the fear and desperation that swirled in her gaze like a tempest. She let Forsyth know that she was there to help, a lifeline in the storm.

"I think it's time we called it a night," Carter said, her tone leaving no room for argument. "Dr. Forsyth, would you like me to walk you back to your rooms?"

Forsyth hesitated for a moment, then said. "Yes, thank you."

Lang's smile tightened, but he made no move to stop them. "Of course," he said, his tone icy. "I'll see you tomorrow, Irene. Remember what I said."

As Carter led Forsyth away from the confrontation, she felt a surge of anger and determination. Lang was clearly the mastermind behind much of the sinister activity, but there was still so much they didn't know. Forsyth, despite her involvement, was more of a victim than a perpetrator, ensnared in a web spun by someone far more calculating and dangerous.

Once they were out of earshot, Carter turned to Forsyth, her voice gentle but firm. "Dr. Forsyth, I can help you, but please tell me everything. What does Lang have on you?"

Forsyth shook her head, tears spilling down her cheeks. "I can't . . . I'm too scared . . ."

"You're not alone in this," Carter said, her voice filled with conviction. "We'll protect you, but we have to know the truth. Whatever Lang is holding over you, it's better if we face it together."

Forsyth hesitated, then finally nodded, her voice trembling as she began to speak. "It's . . . it's about my father. He was involved in something—something that could ruin everything. Lang found out and threatened to expose it unless I helped him. I didn't know what else to do . . ."

Carter placed a reassuring hand on Forsyth's arm, grounding her in that moment. "You did what you thought was right at the time, but now we will make things right. We can bring Lang down if you help us."

Forsyth's resolve strengthened despite the weight of her predicament. "I'll do whatever it takes. I can't let him destroy any more lives."

As they walked back toward the College, Carter knew they had just reached a critical turning point in the investigation. The pieces were finally starting to come together, and with Forsyth's help, they might just have what they would need to expose Lang and *The Fellowship* for the predators they truly were.

As they entered the grand, dimly lit stairwell leading to Forsyth's rooms, the distant echo of the Ball's music barely reached them. Something in the gloom shifted, folding in around them like a curtain, making the passageway feel narrower, more confining. Forsyth's earlier resolve appeared to waver, and Carter could see her hands trembling slightly as she fumbled for her keys.

"I MUST USE YOUR TELEPHONE," CARTER said when they finally entered Forsyth's rooms. The rooms, once a sanctuary of scholarly pursuit, now felt like a place of exile. The familiar scent of old books and dried flowers couldn't mask the undercurrent of fear that hung in the air.

Forsyth merely nodded, sinking heavily into a chair as if the weight of the world had finally caught up with her. She shrank into herself, her earlier defiance giving way to exhaustion. It was as if there was nothing left to sustain her, no more energy to fight the tide that had swept her into this nightmare.

Carter picked up the receiver and dialed Rievaulx's number. As the line connected, she quickly explained the situation, her voice low but urgent. "Sir. Forsyth's ready to talk. She's implicated Lang. He's been blackmailing her, using her father's past against her."

"Good work, Carter," Rievaulx replied, his tone filled with the same mixture of relief and resolve that Carter felt. "I'll be there shortly. Keep her safe until I arrive."

Carter hung up the phone and turned back to Forsyth, who was staring blankly at the floor, her hands clasped tightly in her lap. "Dr. Forsyth," Carter said softly, taking a seat opposite her, "We're going to make sure Lang can't hurt you anymore. But you will have to tell me everything. Start from the beginning."

Forsyth looked up, her eyes red and swollen from crying. She took a deep, shuddering breath and began to speak, her voice barely above a whisper. "My father . . . he was a brilliant botanist. He devoted his life to his research, to discovering new species and cataloguing them. But he was also . . . ambitious. He wanted to make a name for himself, to be remembered as one of the greats."

Carter encouraged her to continue. Forsyth's story was one she had heard before, the tale of a brilliant mind pushed to the brink by the pressures of academic success.

"He made a mistake," Forsyth continued, her voice cracking. "He . . . he falsified some of his findings, claimed credit for work that wasn't his. It was a scandal, and it ruined him. He lost everything, his reputation, his career. It broke him."

Forsyth's hands clenched into fists, her knuckles white. "I was just a child when it happened, but I remember how it destroyed him. And when I grew up, I swore I would clear his name, prove that he was still a great scientist."

"But Lang found out about the scandal," Carter said, piecing the story together. "And he used it to manipulate you."

Dr. Forsyth with tears streaming down her face, said. "He threatened to expose everything, to drag my father's name through the mud again. He said it would ruin me too, that I'd never be able to show my face in the academic world. I didn't know what else to do, so I . . . I did what he asked. I helped him cover up things, falsify documents, anything he wanted. I thought I was protecting my father's legacy, but now I see I was just helping Lang protect his own interests."

Carter reached across the table and took Forsyth's hand, giving it a reassuring squeeze. "You're not to blame for this, Dr. Forsyth.

Lang preyed on your fear and your love for your father and used it against you. But now we have a chance to stop him."

Forsyth wiped her tears away. "I'll help you in any way I can. I just want this to be over."

Carter gave her a small, reassuring smile. "It will be. DCI Rievaulx is on his way, and we'll get to the bottom of this. You're not alone in this anymore."

As they waited for Rievaulx to arrive, Carter found herself thinking of the garden, now far behind them. The beauty of the May Ball, the laughter and music, all felt like a distant memory. The shadows that had lingered at the edges of the festivities had finally closed in, revealing the darkness that had been hiding in plain sight.

With Forsyth's help, they were closer than ever to exposing the truth. When they did, the predators who had been lurking in the shadows would finally be brought into the light.

RIEVAULX MOVED THROUGH THE DIMLY LIT corridor of St Michael's College; the sound of his footsteps barely audible against the ancient stone floor. The dinner jacket he still wore felt oddly out of place in the cold, oppressive atmosphere, where the shadows stretch and shift as if they harbored secrets of their own. Each step brought him closer to the inevitable confrontation, the air thick with the scent of damp stone and a lingering tension that hinted at the gravity of what lay ahead.

When he reached the door to Dr. Irene Forsyth's rooms, he paused, his hand hovering over the wood for a brief moment. The knock he delivered was soft, almost hesitant, but in the stillness of the night, it echoed, as though the entire College were holding its breath. The door creaked open, revealing Carter standing in the threshold. Her expression was tense, her usually sharp eyes softened with concern as she stepped back to let him in.

"She's ready to talk," Carter murmured as Rievaulx entered, the door clicking shut behind them, sealing them off from the world outside. "She's already confessed that Lang manipulated her, using her father's . . . indiscretions to force her into doing his bidding. Do you think she'll be all right?" she added, her brow furrowing with worry. "I mean, after everything that's happened. She's been frantic, but in an oddly controlled way. I didn't stop her; I thought it best to leave her be."

Rievaulx face was a blend of concern and resolve. "We can't afford to dwell on what might be. "We're here for the truth, and the truth doesn't wait for anyone."

The room was suffused with a musty scent of overwatered plants, their drooping leaves like mourners at a funeral. Once a sanctuary of scholarly pursuit, Forsyth's quarters had descended into a chaotic landscape, with books scattered across the floor as if they had been cast aside in a moment of desperation. Papers were strewn haphazardly across every available surface, as though the orderly life she had once led had crumbled into disarray.

"Dr. Forsyth?" Rievaulx ventured, stepping deeper into the room. The sight that met him was jarring; a brilliant academic reduced to a shadow of her former self, sitting amidst the ruins of her once meticulous world. Forsyth was clutching a worn photograph of her father, her hands trembling as she stared at the image with hollow, red-rimmed eyes. It was as if she had been crying for days, and now, she was utterly drained; the light within her dimmed to a faint flicker.

"What do you want?" she whispered, her voice brittle and fragile, as though it might shatter with the slightest provocation.

Rievaulx moved closer, his expression softening, though his purpose remained unwavering. "We will talk, Irene. There are things we must understand about what happened."

Forsyth's gaze drifted back to the photograph, her fingers tracing the edges as if she were trying to hold on to a happier time, a time before everything had gone so terribly wrong. "There's nothing left to say, Chief Inspector," she murmured, the weight of her sorrow heavy in the air, pressing down on them all.

"On the contrary," Rievaulx's voice a quiet but firm anchor in the storm of her emotions. "We know what happened to your father, and how it's been used against you. We would like your side of the story. It's very important."

Forsyth tightened her grip on the photograph, her knuckles whitening as she fought to maintain some semblance of control. "It was supposed to be different," she murmured, her words barely audible. "I thought if I could just make things right, if I could clear his name . . . But it all went so wrong."

Carter, who had been standing quietly by the door, stepped forward, her voice gentle yet insistent. "Irene, you don't have to carry this burden alone. We can help you but tell us what happened."

The words appeared to penetrate the fog of despair that enveloped Forsyth. She closed her eyes, summoning the strength to face the truth she had been avoiding for so long. When she spoke again, her voice trembled, each word heavy with the weight of her memories.

"I didn't mean to kill him," Forsyth confessed, her voice cracking under the strain of her guilt. "I didn't even plan it, it just . . . happened. When I saw him that night, all the anger, all the fear . . . it all came rushing out. And before I knew it, he was dead."

Rievaulx and Carter exchanged a glance, the gravity of the situation settling heavily upon them. They had suspected Forsyth's involvement, but hearing her confession brought a harrowing finality to their suspicions. This wasn't just a theory anymore; this was the cold, hard truth.

"Tell us what happened, Irene," Rievaulx urged softly, his voice steady and calm, coaxing the story from her. "Start from the beginning." From the corner of his eye, he noticed Carter quietly produce her notebook, flipping it open with the practiced ease of someone who never missed a beat. She sat poised, pen at the ready, waiting for whatever Forsyth was about to let slip. How she'd managed to smuggle the thing into an evening dress remained one of life's small mysteries, but he wasn't entirely sure he wanted to know the answer.

Forsyth's throat tightened, and her gaze grew distant as the memories of that night swept over her like a dark tide. "It was late," she began, her voice barely above a whisper, "and I was in my office, buried in papers, trying to make sense of everything. But the walls felt like they were closing in on me, so I stepped outside, hoping the cool night air might clear my head. I never expected to see him out there, Atherton."

She paused, the name lingering in the air like a curse, before continuing, her words trembling with the weight of recollection. "He must have followed me. I didn't hear him approach, but there he was, his face twisted with rage. He was furious about the manuscript, his accusations flying at me like daggers. He claimed I was trying to undermine him, to destroy his career . . . just as he had destroyed my father's."

Rievaulx leaned in slightly, piecing together the elements of the narrative. "The manuscript. Tell us more about it."

Forsyth's voice quivered as she continued, the memories dragging her deeper into the darkness. "It was a rare manuscript, or at least, that's what it was supposed to be. Atherton had been working on it for months, convinced it would cement his place in academic history. But there were . . . discrepancies. I noticed them immediately."

Carter's curiosity piqued asked. "What kind of discrepancies?"

"Errors in the text," Forsyth explained, her voice growing steadier as she focused on the details. "Inconsistencies in the language, the syntax. It didn't match the period it was supposed to have come from. And the botanical illustrations, I knew well, thanks to my father. They were too modern, the techniques too advanced for the supposed age of the manuscript."

"You suspected it was a forgery," Rievaulx said, his tone understanding.

Forsyth concurred the pain of her realization evident in her eyes. "I didn't know for sure, but yes, I suspected. I tried to bring it to Atherton's attention, discreetly. But he wouldn't listen. He was too invested in it; too desperate for the recognition it would bring. He dismissed my concerns, accused me of jealousy, of trying to sabotage him."

She paused, her breath hitching as she recalled the confrontation. "That night, he came to my office, the manuscript in hand. He was livid, more furious than I'd ever seen him. He accused me of spreading rumors, of trying to destroy him. And then he ... he mocked me. He knew about the orchid, you see, how much it meant to me. My father had cultivated it, his life's work, a symbol of everything he'd achieved. And Atherton ... he called it a pathetic attempt to redeem a failure. Said my father was a fraud, and that I was no better."

Forsyth's voice faltered, the memory clearly painful. "Then, when I saw him in the garden, I don't know what came over me. I just ... snapped. All the years of resentment, of guilt, they all came to a head. I grabbed the nearest thing I could find. A hat pin. And I ... I pushed it into his heart. I never thought he had one. But then, he was lying there, lifeless."

The room fell into a heavy silence, the enormity of her confession hanging in the air like a storm cloud. Carter felt a pang of pity for the woman before her, a woman driven to the edge by forces beyond her control. Forsyth, once a brilliant academic with a promising future, had been pushed to the brink by a toxic combination of professional betrayal and personal anguish.

Rievaulx, ever the detective, was already considering the broader implications of what Forsyth had revealed. The manuscript, now known to be a forgery, was after all a key piece, but not in the way they'd imagined. Atherton's obsession with it, his willingness to overlook the obvious flaws, spoke volumes about the pressures and ambitions that had driven him and ultimately led to his downfall.

Rievaulx leaned back slightly, thinking through the ramifications. The manuscript was more than just a forged document; it was a symbol of the rot that had set in at the very heart of Cambridge's academic world. The pressure to succeed, to be recognized, had driven one man to madness and another to his death. Now, the web of deceit, manipulation, and ambition was beginning to unravel, with Forsyth's confession.

The manuscript, and its possible connection to *The Fellowship*, was one such factor. Then there was the matter of *The Curator*, the shadowy figure who had been lurking in the background, orchestrating events. Could Atherton's death have been nothing more than a footnote? The consequence of a strained mind snapping under the weight of a lingering personal grudge? Unrelated to *The Fellowship* and all that shadowy society stood for?

As Rievaulx contemplated these questions, he couldn't help but feel a sense of foreboding. No, he told himself. There was more beneath the surface here. Lang's involvement raised the stakes considerably. Dr. Forsyth was simply a pawn in a game played by unseen, nameless figures. She might have had her motives for wanting Atherton gone, but he knew she wasn't the only one. The case was far from over, and while Forsyth's confession had provided some clarity, it had also opened a door to the investigation, one that promised to be just as dark and dangerous as the one they had just traversed.

"What about the orchid?" Rievaulx asked gently. "Why did you leave it at the scene?"

Forsyth's eyes filled with tears, and she looked down at the photograph in her hands. "It was my father's. After everything that happened, it was the only piece of him I had left. I thought . . . I thought if I left it with Atherton, it would be like . . . like closing the chapter on everything that had happened. A final act of defiance, of revenge."

Rievaulx nodded, understanding dawning. The orchid had been more than just a flower; it had been a symbol, a way for Forsyth to reclaim some semblance of control over a life that had spiraled beyond her grasp.

"And Lang?" Rievaulx asked, his tone still calm but insistent. "Where does he fit into all of this?"

Forsyth flinched at the mention of Lang's name, a fresh wave of fear washing over her. "He found out what I'd done. I don't know how, but he knew. He's been blackmailing me, threatening to expose everything unless I did what he wanted. He kept telling me that Atherton knew everything and when it came out about the manuscript, Lang had told me Atherton would destroy me like he'd done to my father. He'd spill the beans. I'd never be able to hold my head up. It felt as if the destruction of my father wasn't finished with until I had been destroyed."

"What did Lang know about your father?" Rievaulx asked, sensing that there was more to the story.

Forsyth averted her gaze, her voice barely a whisper as she murmured, "Plagiarism . . . in academic circles, it's the kiss of death. Once that accusation sticks, you're finished. No one trusts a word you say, no one dares to publish your work. The journals, especially the reputable ones, won't touch you. And in academia, being published is everything. Without it, you might as well pack up and leave; your career, your reputation, it all crumbles."

She paused, the weight of her words hanging in the air like a heavy fog. "My poor father became a pariah. The accusation destroyed him. And my mother . . . the shame of it all, it was more than she could bear. It broke her."

Carter stepped closer. "And what did Lang want?"

Forsyth shook her head; her expression was one of despair. "To keep it all quiet, to protect *The Fellowship* and his own position. I don't really know. II think Dr. Atherton knew too much about him, and he feared being exposed. The man was a gambler, always drowning in debt. He didn't care about me or my father, he just wanted to make sure nothing could jeopardize his career. He used me, played on my fears, my guilt . . ."

Her voice trailed off, and she began to sob quietly, the weight of everything she had been holding inside finally breaking free.

Rievaulx placed a hand on her shoulder, his touch gentle but firm. "Irene, you did something terrible, but you're not beyond redemption. We can help you, but you have to help us bring Lang to justice. He's manipulated you, just as he's manipulated so many others. It's time to stop him."

Forsyth looked up at Rievaulx through her tears, her expression a mixture of anguish and determination. "I'll do whatever it takes," she said. "I can't keep living like this."

Rievaulx's own resolve hardened. "Then we'll do it together. Lang's reign of terror ends now."

THE COLD, STERILE ATMOSPHERE OF THE police station provided a stark contrast to the emotional tumult that had filled Dr. Irene Forsyth's College rooms just hours earlier. The antiseptic scent of the station clung to the air, mingling with the faint odor of stale coffee and the ever-present haze of cigarette smoke. The fluorescent lights above cast harsh, unforgiving shadows on the walls, turning the small, dimly lit office into a place of tension and unease.

Rievaulx and Carter sat at a narrow desk, its surface cluttered with files and documents, the remnants of their ongoing investigation. The rustling of papers was the only sound that broke the heavy silence as they pored over the evidence spread before them, the weight of Forsyth's confession hanging over them like a storm cloud ready to burst.

Carter's thoughts drifted to Forsyth, now confined to the secure environment of Fulbourn Mental Hospital. She stared out the window into the inky night beyond, her mind grappling with the fragmented pieces of the case. Poor Dr. Forsyth, she thought. The woman had been so fragile, teetering on the edge of sanity, her mind fractured by guilt and fear. Fulbourn might be the only place where she could find any semblance of safety, sheltered from the storm that raged within her and the one that brewed outside, where Professor Robert Lang's shadow loomed large and menacing.

Lang was a dangerous man, a master manipulator who had used Forsyth's vulnerabilities to his advantage. What troubled Carter more was the knowledge that Lang was not acting alone.

There were others, shadowy figures who orbited around him, each as perilous as the man himself. Fulbourn might have been a sanctuary for Forsyth, but Carter couldn't shake the feeling that nowhere was truly safe, not while Lang and his associates still roamed free.

"Lang is blackmailing Forsyth, using her father's past to control her," Rievaulx mused, breaking the silence. His fingers drummed lightly on the arm of his chair, a subconscious rhythm that echoed his restless thoughts. "And Forsyth, out of fear and desperation, has been complicit in whatever scheme Lang is running."

Carter nodded; her brow furrowed in concentration as she traced the connections in her mind. "But why? What does Lang hope to achieve by manipulating Forsyth and the others in *The Fellowship*?"

Rievaulx leaned forward, his eyes narrowing as he considered the question. "Power, control, perhaps even revenge. Lang is a man who thrives on manipulation, who enjoys having the upper hand. He's used *The Fellowship* as his personal tool for advancing his career, and now he's willing to destroy anyone who threatens that."

"But why give her an orchid tonight? The manuscript? What's the connection?" Carter asked. She rubbed her temples, trying to stave off the impending headache that always accompanied a dead-end.

Rievaulx ran his hand through his hair, the gesture was one of fatigue and determination. "The orchid is a symbol, perhaps sending her a message. Reminding her that he knew what she'd done. The manuscript . . . it could be a key to something bigger, something that ties all of this together."

"And Matthews, the librarian?" Carter pressed. "Where does he fit into all this?"

Rievaulx paused, gazing into the distance before giving a slight shake of his head. "He fits," he replied, "but not here. Not with the schemes of *The Fellowship*. His link was solely to the manuscript. For the moment, we focus on Lang and *The Fellowship*."

He stood and began pacing the room, his mind working. The sound of his footsteps on the worn linoleum floor added to the tension in the room, each step a reminder of the urgency that drove them. "We will focus on the connections between Lang, Forsyth, the manuscript, and *The Fellowship*. There's a pattern here, something that we're not seeing yet."

Carter watched him, her own thoughts racing to keep pace with his. "Forsyth said that Lang uncovered something about her father, something that could destroy everything. It must be worse than plagiarism. That's damaging enough in academic circles, but would it be worth killing over? If we could work out what it is, we might just have an advantage against him."

Rievaulx paused, turning to Carter with a determined look. "That's our next move. We dig deeper into Forsyth's father's past, find out what Lang is holding over her. And we keep the pressure on Lang. He's starting to crack. Tonight's confrontation proves that."

Carter felt a renewed sense of purpose as she met Rievaulx's gaze. The stakes had never been higher, but she knew they were on the right path. With each piece of evidence they uncovered, they were closer to bringing down *The Fellowship* and exposing the truth.

As the first light of dawn began to filter through the windows, casting a pale glow across the desk, Rievaulx and Carter continued to work, their determination unwavering. The night had been long, and the road ahead was still uncertain, but they were ready for whatever lay ahead. The time for secrets was ending, and the truth to brought out in the open.

Carter broke the silence. "We know Lang was holding something over her, something involving her father, and it's more serious than just the issue of plagiarism. Why target Atherton? What did Lang stand to gain from his death?"

Rievaulx, who had been flipping through Forsyth's file, paused to consider the question. "Control," he said finally, his voice grim. "Atherton was a threat to Lang; someone who knew too much, who could have exposed *The Fellowship's* activities. By eliminating him, Lang not only protected himself but also strengthened his hold over *The Fellowship* and the University."

"But that's not all, is it?" Carter asked as she studied the files spread before her. "Lang wasn't just protecting his position—he was using *The Fellowship* to line his own pockets. The art thefts, the forgeries ... he's a gambler. Perhaps it all ties back to him."

Rievaulx said. "I suspect Lang has been orchestrating the thefts to fund his lifestyle, using *The Fellowship's* influence to cover his tracks."

Rievaulx leaned forward, his eyes narrowing as a plan began to take shape in his mind. "We will take this to the next level. Forsyth's confession is crucial, but it's not enough on its own. There is more evidence; something that directly ties Lang to the thefts and ..." he stopped and froze. "And murder ..."

"Atherton's," Carter began.

"No," he cut in. "Forsyth was behind that one. Matthews."

"But, I thought ..."

"So did I," he interrupted her again, "but maybe there's more linking them than simple proximity. Why did Lang go to Matthews to verify the manuscript's authenticity?"

"Well, he's an expert," Carter replied, frowning. "He knows his field."

"Yes, but why Matthews specifically? Cambridge is full of paleographers he could have consulted. I'm not saying Matthews was unqualified—he certainly knew his subject—but why choose him?"

Carter nodded slowly, following his line of thought. Matthews, once dismissed as a minor figure, had just stepped into the main story. It was beginning to make sense. "I'll speak to Walker. He needs bringing up to speed," Rievaulx said.

"Are we combining the investigations?" Carter asked, a little too hopefully. It wasn't that she disliked DI Walker—far from it—but something about him reminded her of her eldest brother, and that always brought out her competitive streak.

To her dismay, Rievaulx shook his head. "Not for the moment," he said, delivering it in the tone of a man who had already decided that was quite enough discussion on the matter.

"What's our next step, sir?" she asked, hiding her disappointment.

"We'll look through Forsyth's records, as well as Atherton's and Lang's. We're looking for anything that shows a direct connection; letters, financial transactions, correspondence, anything that links Lang to the crimes. If Lang gets wind that we're onto him, he could destroy the evidence before we have a chance to act."

Carter's eyes narrowed as she considered the magnitude of the task ahead. "And if we find what we're looking for?"

Rievaulx's voice was steely with resolve. "Then we set a trap. We use Forsyth's confession to pressure Lang, make him believe that he's about to be exposed. With any luck, he'll make a mistake, something we can use to nail him."

The weight of their mission settled on them both, but neither was willing to back down. The web of deceit and corruption that Lang had woven was complex.

As they continued to sift through the evidence, a sense of anticipation began to build. The endgame was in sight, and with each step forward, the stakes grew higher. Lang was not a man to be underestimated, and they knew that the final confrontation would be fraught with danger for them both.

THE SECLUDED TEAROOMS IN THE HEART of Cambridge were a far cry from the opulence of the May Ball or the austere atmosphere of the police station. It was a small, unassuming place, tucked away in a quiet corner of the city where the noise and bustle of university life appeared to fade into the background. The smell of freshly brewed coffee mingled with the sound of the Bee Gees' latest hit, *How Deep Is Your Love*, creating an atmosphere of calm—a brief respite from the storm that was about to break.

Rievaulx and Carter sat at a corner table, their faces tense with the weight of their discussion. The café was nearly empty, the few patrons scattered around the room paying little attention to the two detectives who spoke in low, measured tones.

"Forsyth's confession is a start," Rievaulx said, his voice steady as he laid out their plan. "But it's not enough to bring Lang down. We have to make him believe that his carefully constructed world is about to collapse."

Carter nodded, her expression, one of focused determination. "How do we do that without tipping him off? Lang's smart: he'll see through any obvious attempts to corner him."

Rievaulx considered this for a moment. "We use Forsyth's confession as a bargaining chip. We tell him that she's ready to talk, that she's going to expose everything, including his role in the art thefts. It's a bluff, but if we play it right, it could force him to act."

Carter frowned, her concern evident. "And if he calls our bluff? If he decides to cut his losses and run?"

Rievaulx said. "Then we make sure he has nowhere to run to. We'll have to monitor his movements, tap his communications, and make sure he doesn't have the opportunity to destroy any evidence. If he tries to bolt, we'll be ready."

"What's our timeline?" Carter asked.

"Soon," Rievaulx replied. "We'll give Forsyth a little time to recover, and then we'll move."

The plan was settling into place in her mind. "I'll start investigating into Lang's financial situation and correspondence, see if there's anything we've missed. And I'll keep a close eye on Forsyth; make sure she's ready when the time comes."

"Good," Rievaulx said. "And I'll reach out to our contacts in the force, make sure we have everything in place for when we move on Lang. This has to be airtight, Carter, there's no room for error."

As they sat in the quiet of the café, the weight of their mission pressing down on them, they both knew that the final confrontation with Lang was fast approaching. The trap was being set.

As they finished their coffee and prepared to leave, both Rievaulx and Carter were acutely aware of the danger that lay ahead. Lang was a man who had built his life on secrets, lies, and manipulation, and he would fight.

Chapter 13

A FEW DAYS LATER, DC EMILY CARTER found herself fully immersed in the murky depths of Professor Robert Lang's past. Every piece of information she unearthed painted a more unpleasant picture, revealing a tangled web of deception and greed. It had taken her a while to find the first clue, but once she had it the rest began to crumble. Lang's life was interwoven with art thefts, forgeries, and a fellowship corrupted to serve his insatiable ambition. His professorship was the first real indication that something questionable was afoot. His academic career had been, to put it mildly, uninspiring, certainly not deserving of such a distinguished position. There had been doubts about the authenticity of his research dating back as far as his doctoral thesis. Gambling?

As she investigated further, Carter realized that Dr. Atherton had known far more than was safe, knowledge that had ultimately led to his death. Lang had found in Irene Forsyth the perfect pawn, her fragile state of mind easily bent to his will. How convenient for him, Carter thought bitterly, that Irene had been so vulnerable, so desperate to protect her father's tarnished legacy.

The next day, Carter and Rievaulx made the journey to Fulbourn Mental Hospital, where Irene was now confined, hidden away from the world that had driven her to the brink. They hadn't expected much from the visit, perhaps just a few confirmations of what they already suspected. Instead, Irene, in her confused and fragile state, had delivered something more. In her halting, tremulous way, she had confirmed that she had not been alone in the garden that fateful night when Dr. Atherton had met his end.

There had been no trace of the hat pin in Irene's rooms, despite their thorough search, and more intriguingly, Irene had no memory of ever owning such a thing. True, she was a woman untouched by modern fashion, but even so, she was no wearer of hats. The pin, then, was most likely not hers. But whose was it?

As they left the hospital, the question lingered in the air between them, heavy with implications. Rievaulx and Carter exchanged knowing glances as they pieced together the possibilities. If the hat pin wasn't Irene's, it could very well have been something Lang had access to; perhaps even something from his own household. The suggestion hung in the air, unsettling in its plausibility. Lang's wife, perhaps? It was a connection that was as dangerous as it was likely.

The picture was beginning to take shape, each piece falling into place. Lang had found Irene Forsyth malleable, her fragile state making her the perfect tool in his twisted game. In his arrogance, however, had he overlooked the simplest of details? The hat pin, an innocuous object on the surface, might just be the key to unravelling his carefully constructed lies.

Armed with this new knowledge, Rievaulx and Carter approached Professor Lang's rooms at St Michael's College with a deliberate calm, their steps measured and purposeful. They were not there to confront but to unsettle; to plant seeds of doubt and stir the pot just enough to see what might bubble to the surface. Lang's arrogance was well-known, but even the most self-assured could be shaken, and today, they intended to do just that.

Lang was seated in his leather armchair, a picture of academic distinction. The room was as meticulously organized as the man himself, books lined up in perfect rows, papers neatly stacked on the desk. He barely acknowledged their presence, his gaze fixed on the papers before him, as though their interruption was little more than a trivial nuisance.

"Ah, Chief Inspector Rievaulx, Detective Constable Carter," Lang drawled, finally glancing up with a faint, dismissive smile. "To what do I owe this unexpected visit? Surely, you've concluded your little investigation by now?"

Rievaulx returned the smile. "Oh, we're just tying up a few loose ends, Professor. You know how it is—never quite done until everything is in place."

Lang arched an eyebrow; his expression was one of mild amusement. "I see. And what might that be? I do hope you're not here to waste my time with baseless accusations."

Carter, standing just behind Rievaulx, caught Lang's eye, her gaze steady, unwavering. "We wouldn't dream of wasting your time, Professor. we're more interested in making sure everything is properly accounted for."

Lang leaned back in his chair, exuding confidence. "Accounted for? What exactly are you implying, Detective?"

Rievaulx took a seat across from Lang, crossing one leg over the other, the picture of relaxed authority. "Let's talk about Irene Forsyth, shall we? She's been quite forthcoming lately. Ready to, shall we say, set the record straight."

For a split second, Lang's composure faltered. It was barely perceptible—a tightening of the jaw, a flicker in his eyes—but Rievaulx saw it.

"Dr. Forsyth?" Lang recovered, his tone dismissive. "A troubled woman with a vivid imagination. I wouldn't put too much stock in anything she has to say. She's been through a lot, poor thing."

"Indeed," Rievaulx agreed, his voice smooth. "She has been through a great deal. The pressure of academic life, the weight of her father's disgrace . . . it's enough to push anyone to the brink, wouldn't you say, Professor?"

Lang's lips curled into a condescending smile. "Precisely. The poor woman is barely holding herself together. Her mind, I'm afraid, is not what it once was. It's a tragic situation, but I fail to see how it concerns me."

Rievaulx leaned forward, just enough to invade Lang's personal space. "Oh, but it does concern you, Professor. You see, Forsyth's mind may be fragile, but her memory is remarkably sharp when it comes to certain details. Details about her dealings with you, for instance."

Lang's smile wavered, but he held his ground. "I've done nothing but try to help Miss Forsyth. Any suggestion otherwise is absurd."

"Help?" Carter's voice was almost sympathetic. "Is that what you call it, Professor? Because from where we stand, it looks an awful lot like manipulation."

Lang's eyes narrowed, a flash of irritation breaking through his polished veneer. "I don't care for your insinuations, Detective. I've been nothing but a mentor to Miss Forsyth, guiding her through difficult times."

"Guidance," Rievaulx echoed, as though tasting the word. "Is that what you were offering when you threatened to expose her father's past? When you held her fears over her like a sword, ready to drop at the slightest provocation?"

Lang's composure cracked, if only for a moment. "You have no proof of any such thing. This is nothing but speculation, an attempt to tarnish my reputation based on the ramblings of a disturbed woman."

Rievaulx's smile didn't waver. "You're right, Professor. We don't have proof. Yet. But Forsyth is ready to talk, and when she does, I'm sure we'll find the necessary information. You know how thorough we can be."

Lang's face tightened, the arrogance beginning to bleed into something closer to panic. "She's a liability, that's all. A liability that has to be handled delicately, not fed with wild accusations and paranoia."

"And yet," Carter interjected, her tone thoughtful, "it looks to me that it's you who's grown increasingly paranoid, Professor. Always looking over your shoulder, wondering if this is the moment when everything unravels."

Lang's fingers tapped restlessly on the arm of his chair, his once smooth exterior now visibly fraying. "You're wasting your time. Forsyth's words will hold no weight, she's been discredited, dismissed. No one will believe her."

Rievaulx stood, his movement slow and deliberate, as though to emphasize the power dynamics at play. "That's where you're wrong, Professor. People will listen because it's not just Forsyth, is it? There are others who've suffered under your thumb, who've been forced to dance to your tune."

Lang's eyes darted to the door, the first true sign of anxiety creeping into his eyes. "You think you can come here, throw around baseless accusations, and force a confession out of me? You're barking up the wrong tree, Chief Inspector."

"Confession?" Rievaulx's voice was light, almost amused. "No, Professor. We don't need a confession. We just want you to know that we're watching—every step, every move you make. *The Fellowship*, Atherton, Forsyth; it's all connected, and we're not going to stop until we've laid it all bare."

Lang's mask of confidence had slipped entirely now, his eyes betraying the fear he'd tried so hard to keep hidden. "You think you've won, but you're mistaken. This isn't over."

Rievaulx said. "No, it's not. But the end is in sight, and we'll see it through no matter what you throw in our path."

With that, Rievaulx turned and made his way to the door, Carter following close behind. As they left Lang's rooms, the door clicking shut behind them, Rievaulx couldn't help but feel a twinge of satisfaction. Lang might have clung to his arrogance, but the cracks were showing, and it was only a matter of time before the whole facade came crashing down.

CAMBRIDGE, THAT VENERABLE TAPESTRY OF HISTORY and academia, lay under the heavy mantle of night, the city seemingly holding its breath as darkness draped its ancient buildings. The cobblestones, which usually thrummed with the soft rustle of scholars' gowns and the low murmur of intellectual discourse, were now unnervingly still. The occasional chime of a distant bicycle bell or the faint echo of laughter from unseen revelers felt out of place in the thick, almost oppressive silence. Streetlamps flickered uncertainly, their glow casting long, anxious shadows that skittered along the old College walls, as if the buildings themselves were unsettled by the presence of modern law enforcers treading on their hallowed ground.

Rievaulx stood at the edge of King's Parade, his breath a foggy whisper in the crisp night air. The mist that clung to the city like a spectral veil appeared to absorb all sound, magnifying the tension he and Carter felt. She fidgeted with her watch as though trying to measure the passing time against her mounting anticipation. They had been on this stakeout for what felt like an eternity, their senses heightened by the knowledge that Professor Lang could make his move at any moment. The shadows that clung to the stone facades around them were not empty; they concealed uniformed officers crouched low, truncheons ready, whistles clutched in expectant hands. The surrounding streets, appearing deserted, were in fact under siege, panda cars discreetly parked under trees and behind walls, their engines idling, poised to spring into action should Lang attempt an escape by motor vehicle.

"Lang's not the type to just stroll into our arms," Carter murmured, her voice a threadbare whisper against the backdrop of the still night. "After our visit, he's sure to know, or at least suspect, that we're watching him. The man's as sharp as they come."

Rievaulx gaze was fixed on the entrance of Trinity College, where Lang had been spotted just hours earlier. "Smart, yes. But desperation has a way of turning the cunning into fools. If we're fortunate, he'll try to flee tonight."

Carter frowned, her thoughts mirroring the intensity of the situation. "And if he does? The city's practically locked down. Where could he possibly go?"

"Given the choice," Rievaulx replied, "I'd wager he'll head for the river. The Backs are shadowy and quiet at this hour, and if he can commandeer a punt, he might think he can slip away into the darkness."

Carter's breath caught as realization dawned. "The River Cam," she whispered. "He could indeed simply vanish into the night..."

Before she could finish, a sudden burst of footsteps shattered the stillness. Both officers turned sharply, their muscles tensing as a shadowy figure emerged from the darkness, moving with the kind of urgency that spoke of fear and flight. The man's hurried gait and the way the moonlight glinted off his dark hair as he glanced anxiously over his shoulder left no doubt in their minds.

"It's him," Rievaulx said, his voice low but resolute. "Let's move."

Without a moment's hesitation, they sprinted across the cobblestones, their footsteps a rapid tattoo against the ancient stones. The distant shrill of a police whistle echoed through the night as Lang, realizing he was being pursued, quickened his pace, darting down a narrow alleyway that wound toward the river.

Rievaulx's heart pounded in his chest, adrenaline surging as they closed the gap. Lang was a slippery character, and he knew these streets with the familiarity of a man who had walked them countless times. If they lost him now, the chase could easily turn into a prolonged game of cat and mouse through the maze of Cambridge alleys.

As they rounded a corner, the beam of a police torch briefly illuminated Lang's figure before he disappeared into the shadows of the Backs, where the Cam's dark waters gleamed like polished onyx. The gentle lapping of the river became more distinct as they neared, their eyes straining to keep him in sight amidst the dim light. Somewhere behind them, another whistle sounded, joined by the distant growl of a panda car's engine.

"He's headed for the punts," Carter hissed, her breath coming in quick bursts.

"Not if I can help it," Rievaulx muttered, his determination hardening into resolve. They closed in on Lang, whose panic was now palpable. Reaching the riverbank, he faltered, his eyes darting to the line of punts tied securely to the shore. A moment of indecision flickered across his face. Should he fight or flee? But the sound of Rievaulx and Carter's approach spurred him into action. He leapt into the nearest punt, his hands fumbling with the mooring rope in his desperation.

"Stop!" Rievaulx shouted, his voice cutting through the night like a knife. But Lang, too far gone in his flight, ignored the command. With a final, frantic effort, he shoved off from the bank, the punt gliding into the water as he gripped the pole and began pushing downstream.

Carter skidded to a halt at the river's edge, her eyes wide with frustration as she watched Lang slip further away. "He's getting away."

Without wasting a breath on curses, Rievaulx grabbed the pole from a nearby punt and vaulted into the boat, beckoning for Carter to follow. "Get in. We can't let him slip away."

The punt wobbled dangerously as Carter clambered aboard, but Rievaulx steadied it with practiced ease. Moments later, they were pushing off from the bank, their punt slicing through the water in pursuit of their quarry. The tension crackled in the air, the night's silence now broken only by the rhythmic splashes of the poles and the distant, eerie notes of police whistles echoing across the water.

Lang's punt wove erratically as he struggled to keep his balance, the pole slipping from his grasp with a loud splash. Panic etched itself into his features as he frantically tried to regain control. It was the opening Rievaulx had been waiting for. They closed the gap quickly, soon gliding alongside Lang's floundering punt.

"Give it up, Lang," Rievaulx commanded, his voice firm, brooking no argument. "There's nowhere left to run."

Lang's face, pale and glistening with sweat, reflected the hopelessness of his situation. He weighed his options for a torturous moment, then, with a resigned sigh, slumped to his knees in the punt. The pole that had slipped from his fingers was drifting away on the current, leaving him powerless and defeated.

Rievaulx maneuvered their punt alongside Lang's. Carter steadied herself, her heart racing with the thrill of the chase, tempered by the gravity of what they had just accomplished.

"Let's get him back to shore," Rievaulx said quietly, his voice a mix of triumph and exhaustion. "This is over."

As they guided the punts back to the embankment, the distant sounds of another college's May Ball continued, a stark contrast to the solemnity of the moment. Curious onlookers had gathered along the riverbanks, a blend of students and locals, drawn by the spectacle, their expressions a mixture of astonishment and intrigue.

Lang's capture was a victory, but still Rievaulx had a gnawing suspicion that this was merely the beginning. As they reached the shore, uniformed officers stepped forward to escort the defeated professor away. Lang's eyes darted to Rievaulx, filled with a mix of defiance and something else, something darker, more dangerous.

"Do you think you've won?" Lang hissed as they hauled him up the embankment. "This is just the start. You have no idea what you're dealing with."

Rievaulx met his gaze evenly, the weight of the moment settling on his shoulders. "Maybe. But tonight, you're finished."

Lang was led away, but his words lingered in the cold night air, echoing in Rievaulx's mind as he and Carter stood by the river, watching the last of the police cars pull away. The university, that ancient bastion of knowledge and tradition, had been shaken to its core, but Rievaulx felt sure that further inspection would find the roots of the rot ran deeper than they had imagined.

"This is far from over," Carter murmured, echoing his thoughts as she gazed out across the water.

Rievaulx nodded, his eyes narrowing as he contemplated the web of deceit and power that had been slowly unravelling over the past weeks. "Lang was right about one thing," he said, his voice grim. "We have no idea what we're dealing with. But we're going to find out."

The night's victory was a hollow one, overshadowed by the realization that their battle had just begun. Lang's downfall would be the first thread pulled in a tapestry of corruption that threatened to engulf everything they held dear.

As they walked back toward the waiting cars, Rievaulx cast one last glance at the river, its dark waters flowing silently under the bridge. Somewhere in the shadows of Cambridge's storied halls, more secrets lay waiting to be uncovered, more truths hidden behind the veneer of respectability.

They would find them. No matter how deep they had to dig, no matter what dangers lay ahead. The truth would come to light, and those who had used the university's traditions as a shield for their misdeeds would be brought to justice.

The night was quiet once more, but the silence was not one of peace. It was the calm before the storm, and Rievaulx knew they were heading straight into its heart.

As the car door slammed shut, the finality of it echoed in the night air. Rievaulx and Carter exchanged a glance, the reality of the night settling over them like a heavy fog. They had captured Lang, the mastermind behind so much suffering, but they both knew that their work was far from complete. There were loose ends to tie up, questions that demanded answers.

"Back to the station," Rievaulx said, his voice firm with resolve. "We have a long night ahead of us."

Carter's mind was already racing ahead. "We must make sure we have everything we need to nail him down. One thing's for certain Lang's not going to go down without a fight."

Rievaulx's face hardened. "We'll be ready for him. But for now, let's take a moment to breathe. We've earned that much."

As the police car wound its way through the still streets of Cambridge, the significance of what they had accomplished began to crystallize in Rievaulx's mind. They had captured Lang, the architect of so much chaos and misery, but he knew the ripples from this night would extend far beyond the man now shackled in the back seat of a police car.

Cambridge, with all its ancient traditions and hidden secrets, will be shaken to its core. The arrest of a prominent professor would send shockwaves through the university, and the repercussions would be felt for some time to come. There would be enquiries, meetings behind closed doors, reputations at stake, and more than a few sleepless nights for those who had played their parts in this dark drama.

For now, though, Rievaulx allowed himself a moment of quiet reflection. They had taken a significant step towards justice, but he knew better than to believe the battle was won. Lang's capture was a victory, yes, but it was only the beginning of a much larger struggle; a struggle that would require every ounce of their determination and cunning.

As they approached the station, the familiar façade looming ahead, Rievaulx steeled himself for what lay ahead. They would interrogate Lang, sift through the evidence, and continue to untangle the web of deceit that had ensnared so many. The road ahead was fraught with challenges, but they were ready.

The car came to a halt, and as they watched Lang being led inside, Rievaulx couldn't resist a final glance across the vast expanse of Parker's Piece, its two main paths cutting diagonally across the green. At their intersection stood the lone lamp-post, known locally as Reality Checkpoint, a solitary beacon casting light into the darkness. The city had seen its share of scandal and intrigue over the centuries, but this . . . this felt different. There was something deeper, more insidious at work here, and Rievaulx knew they had only just begun to scratch the surface.

As they stepped into the harsh, sterile light of the station,

Rievaulx felt the weight of the night's events settle heavily on his shoulders. There was no time to dwell on that now. There were reports to file, evidence to review, and a man who needed to answer for his crimes.

"Let's get to work," he said, his voice steady and resolute.

Carter nodded, her expression mirroring his determination. "No rest for the wicked," she murmured, a hint of a smile playing at the corners of her lips.

"No," Rievaulx agreed with a grim smile, "and no rest for us either."

They moved forward, ready to face whatever came next.

Chapter 14

THE POLICE STATION, STARK AND UNYIELDING in its utilitarian design, its cold, clinical glow from the fluorescent lights stripped away any semblance of comfort or warmth, leaving only the hard edges of reality. The hum of activity—officers at their posts, the clatter of keyboards, the occasional ring of a telephone—created a low, rhythmic undertone that emphasized the gravity of what had just transpired.

In a small, sparsely furnished interview room, Rievaulx and Carter sat across from Professor Robert Lang. The room, devoid of any personal touches, mirrored the impersonal and unforgiving nature of the confrontation that was about to unfold. Lang, who had once carried himself with the arrogance of a man accustomed to power and influence, now sat slumped in his chair, his wrists encircled by the cold steel of handcuffs. The defiance that had characterized his earlier attempt to escape had evaporated, replaced by a weary resignation that drained the very life from his eyes.

Rievaulx, ever the embodiment of calm authority, opened the file that lay before him on the table. He spoke with a quiet firmness that brooked no argument. "Let's get started," he said, his tone measured and controlled. "We've been pursuing this for too long, Professor Lang. It's time to lay everything on the table."

For a long moment, Lang said nothing. His gaze remained fixed on the table, his bloodshot eyes downcast, as though he were trying to find the words in the grain of the wood. When he finally looked up, there was a hollowness in his voice, an echo of the man he once was. "What's the point?" he mumbled, his words barely more than a whisper. "It's over. You've won."

Rievaulx leaned forward slightly, his gaze unwavering, his voice as sharp as a scalpel. "This isn't a game, Lang. This is about the truth. You're going to tell us everything about *The Fellowship*, about Forsyth, about the art thefts. You'll explain how you manipulated the lives of those around you for your own gain."

Lang's lips curled into a bitter smile, one that held no humor, only a deep, abiding cynicism. "You think you understand," he said, his voice tinged with a mixture of bitterness and exhaustion. "But you don't. You'll never grasp what it's like, the pressure, the expectations. I'm not the villain here. I was just trying to survive in a system that chews you up and spits you out."

Carter, who had been silent until now, leaned forward, her eyes narrowed with intensity. "Surviving doesn't justify what you've done," she said, her voice cold and unyielding. "You've ruined lives, manipulated those who trusted you, all for what? Money? Power? Murder even. Matthews. What about Matthews? Why kill him?"

At the mention of Matthews, Lang's manner shifted slightly, his posture straightening as if to distance himself from the accusation. "Matthews?" he repeated, his tone tinged with a faint note of indignation. "Now wait a minute. I never killed anyone. Matthews . . . well, all I know is he was getting too close. Someone else, I don't know who . . . I don't."

Rievaulx's mind raced, piecing together the fragments of information they had gathered. *The Curator*? He ventured, his tone probing.

Lang's reaction was subtle but telling. He turned his head away, his shoulders slumping once more under the weight of whatever secrets he was carrying. "Maybe," he murmured, his voice barely audible. A flicker of something, regret, perhaps, or the last remnants of pride, crossed his features. "I didn't have a choice," he whispered, his voice breaking as he spoke. "*The Fellowship* . . . it's not what you think. It's a machine, a system designed to maintain control and keep the university at the top, no matter the cost."

Rievaulx's regard gaze hardened. "And you used that system for your own advantage," he said each word deliberately. "You exploited it, manipulated it, and when Atherton became a threat, you orchestrated his murder. You used Forsyth as your pawn, didn't you?"

Lang's shoulders sagged further, as though the weight of his deceit was finally too much to bear. He looked diminished, a man who had always relied on his arrogance to shield him from the consequences of his actions, now facing the reality of his own downfall.

"I didn't kill him," he murmured, his voice barely more than a whisper. "But I admit, I did nothing to stop it. I knew what Forsyth was going through, how close she was to the edge. I pushed her, exploited her fears . . . but I never thought she'd actually do it. You have to believe me. I was as astonished as anyone."

"Astonished?" Rievaulx echoed, his voice thick with disgust. What did it say about Lang's character that a man's murder could stir nothing more than mere "astonishment"? "Astonished, but not appalled?"

Carter's voice sliced through the tension in the room, cold and unforgiving. "But she did," she said, her tone devoid of sympathy. "And you let her take the fall to protect yourself."

There was a moment of silence, the weight of what had been said hanging heavily in the air. But Rievaulx wasn't finished. He leaned in slightly, his voice dropping to a near whisper, his words laden with the suspicion that had been growing ever since their visit to Irene Forsyth. "You see, Lang, we're not entirely convinced you weren't in that garden yourself when Irene plunged that hat pin—one she didn't own—into Atherton's heart. A hat pin that just might have come from your own home."

Lang's eyes flickered with something; panic, perhaps, or the final realization that his carefully spun web of lies was unravelling faster than he could control. He had counted on Irene's fragile state to deflect suspicion, but now, with the detectives closing in, the cracks in his armor were becoming all too apparent.

Rievaulx continued, his voice still low but carrying the full weight of his accusation. "It's one thing to manipulate a vulnerable woman, Lang, but it's quite another to get your own hands dirty. Were you there that night, guiding her hand? Or did you simply watch from the shadows, making sure she carried out your plan?"

Lang opened his mouth as if to protest, but no words came out. The defiance that had once characterized him had crumbled, leaving behind a man who, for the first time, grasped the gravity of his situation.

Carter leaned forward; her gaze fixed on Lang's increasingly pale face. "You may not have plunged the pin yourself, but you were there, weren't you? Right there in the garden, ensuring that Atherton was silenced once and for all."

Lang's silence spoke volumes. The confidence that had once cloaked him like an impenetrable shield had crumbled, revealing a man who was no longer in control of the situation. The cracks in his composure had widened into deep fissures, and the once unflappable professor was now visibly shaken. He nodded slowly, the fight drained from him, leaving only a hollow shell of the man who had believed himself untouchable.

"I didn't anticipate it spiraling so far out of control," Lang admitted, his voice, a weary resignation that suggested he had finally accepted the inevitable. "I thought I could manage it."

Rievaulx's eyes narrowed, his mind working quickly to piece together the remaining fragments of the puzzle. "And what," he asked, his tone sharp and probing, "did you have over her? It was more than her father's alleged plagiarism. That wouldn't have been enough to manipulate her. It was common knowledge."

Carter, caught off guard by this shift in questioning, cast a curious glance in Rievaulx's direction. This was a new angle, and it piqued her interest.

For a moment, it was as though Lang might refuse to answer, his gaze fixed stubbornly on the floor. Then, as if the weight of his secrets had finally become too much to bear, he slumped in his chair, the last remnants of his arrogance evaporating.

Lang's voice was barely more than a whisper, the weight of what he was about to say hanging heavily in the air. "I don't suppose it makes much difference now," he murmured, almost to himself, as if speaking aloud would somehow lessen the impact of the truth he was about to reveal. "Irene has no career left to protect. Her father . . ."

He hesitated, the words caught in his throat, as though even now, after everything, he was reluctant to bring the dark truth into the light. The room felt smaller all of a sudden, as if it had taken a breath and held it, the silence stretching, thick with anticipation. Finally, Lang said with a sound filled with resignation and the weariness of a man who had carried a terrible secret for far too long.

"Her father was . . . a *Nazi*."

The revelation struck Carter with the force of a physical blow. Her eyes widened in shock, and she instinctively recoiled, as if the very word had leapt from Lang's lips to slap her across the face. In the world they inhabited, even thirty years after the war, the mere mention of Nazism still sent a chill through the bones. The dark days of that era had left scars that time could not erase; the atrocities committed under that vile ideology were wounds that had barely begun to heal in the collective consciousness.

The horrors of the Holocaust, the systematic destruction of entire nations, and the unimaginable suffering inflicted on millions had left an indelible mark on humanity. To be a Nazi was to be the personification of all that was monstrous and inhuman. For Carter, the echoes of the war were more than just history; they were woven into the fabric of her upbringing. She had grown up in the shadow of a generation that had been irrevocably scarred by the conflict. Her own father, a man who had endured three years in a POW camp, had returned home a changed man, his spirit damaged beyond repair, his sanity hanging by a thread.

The war had ended before she was born, but its legacy was a burden her generation still carried. They lived with the knowledge of what had happened, with the stories of loss and sacrifice, and with the understanding that the world could never truly return to what it had been before. *Nazi* was more than just a word; it was a symbol of everything evil in the world, a reminder of the darkness that had once threatened to consume it.

Now, to hear that Irene's father had been one of them . . .

Carter shook her head, struggling to process the enormity of what Lang had just revealed. Disbelief and confusion warred within her, each thought clashing violently against the other. How could it be true? How could a man who had walked among them, lived an ordinary life, harbor such a dark and terrible secret? It defied comprehension.

As Carter grappled with the revelation, she felt the walls of her understanding begin to crumble, the secure foundations of her world shaking under the impact. What did it mean for Irene? What did it mean for them all? Carter shook her head, disbelief and confusion warring in her expression. "But . . . wasn't he English?" she asked, her voice trembling with the effort to make sense of what Lang was telling her. "How . . . ?"

Lang nodded, and the motion was heavy with the burden of his revelation. "Which makes him a traitor," he said, his voice heavy with a bitter finality. The word hung in the air like a noose, tightening around them.

In the years after the war, the concept of treachery had taken on an almost mythic quality in England. To be a traitor during the time of the Nazis was to betray not just your country, but the very essence of humanity. The word conjured images of collaboration, of men and women who had sold their souls to the enemy, who had embraced an ideology that sought to annihilate all that was good and just in the world. It was the ultimate betrayal, a sin that could never be washed away, no matter how much time passed.

For Irene Forsyth, the discovery that her father had been such a man—an Englishman who had aligned himself with the Nazis—cast a haunting light on the deep well of anguish she had borne for so long. The secrecy, the burden she had carried with such quiet desperation, made sense in a way that nothing else could. It wasn't merely the shame of being the daughter of a plagiarist, though that alone would have been enough to cripple any academic's spirit. This . . . this was something darker, something that transcended the petty scandals of academia.

Rievaulx had been right all along. This was never just about the stain of plagiarism, a blight on any scholar's name but not one that typically drove a person to murder. No, the shadows that haunted Irene were cast by something far more insidious, a legacy of betrayal that went beyond the bounds of the university and into the darkest chapters of history.

The weight of that truth must have been unbearable. To carry such a secret, to live in the constant fear that it might be exposed, to know that your very existence was tainted by the actions of someone you loved; actions that were not merely unethical, but monstrous in their implications. It explained the depths of her isolation, the walls she had built around herself, the way she had clung so desperately to the fragile threads of her father's tarnished reputation.

Lang's face was etched with a deep weariness, the years of keeping this secret clearly taking their toll. "He was seduced by the ideology," Lang explained, his voice flat, devoid of emotion. "He believed in it, the rhetoric, the promises of a new world order. He wasn't just a sympathizer, he was an active participant, a collaborator. He provided them with information, helped to spread their propaganda. He was instrumental in some of their operations . . .

and when the war was over, he fled. Changed his name, tried to start over. But the past . . . it has a way of catching up with you."

Carter felt a cold dread settle in her stomach. She had known this investigation would lead to dark places, but this . . . this was beyond anything she had imagined. The realization that they were dealing not just with murder, blackmail, or academic deceit, but with the ghost of Nazism itself, was almost too much to bear.

"And Irene," she whispered, barely able to form the words, "she knew?"

Lang nodded, the motion slow and deliberate. "She found out later, when she was old enough to understand. She's spent her entire life trying to atone for his sins, trying to find some way to cleanse her family name. But you can't erase something like that, no matter how hard you try."

And there it was. As Rievaulx absorbed Lang's confession, the final pieces of the twisted puzzle that had haunted them for so long began to fall into place. *The Fellowship*, Lang's manipulation of Forsyth, the art thefts—it all pointed to a deep-seated corruption festering within the hallowed halls of Cambridge. A corruption that had reached into the very heart of the university's power structure, where secrets and lies had been carefully cultivated for decades, waiting for the right moment to be uncovered.

Rievaulx exchanged a glance with Carter, the unspoken understanding between them, clear. They had unearthed something far darker and more insidious than they had initially imagined. The battle was not over, but now they knew the true nature of the enemy they faced.

As Lang was led away by a uniformed officer, his head bowed in defeat, Rievaulx and Carter remained in the interview room, the weight of victory overshadowed by the knowledge of what it had cost. The cold, clinical environment of the station felt oppressive, the air thick with the ghosts of those who had been caught in Lang's web.

"It's over," Carter murmured, her voice tinged with relief but also exhaustion. The night had been long, and the toll it had taken on them was evident in the lines of fatigue that etched her face.

"For now," Rievaulx replied, his gaze distant as he contemplated the far-reaching implications of their discovery. "But the fallout is only beginning. There are still questions that must be answered, still those who will seek to bury the truth."

Carter met his gaze with a fierce determination that had not dimmed despite the long hours and the emotional strain of the case. "Then we'll ensure they don't," she said, her voice resolute. "We've come too far to let this slip away now."

Rievaulx allowed a weary smile to break through the seriousness of the moment. "Agreed," he said, his tone softening. "But for tonight, let's take a moment to breathe. We've earned it."

As they stepped out of the interview room and into the corridor, the first rays of dawn began to filter through the small, barred windows, casting a faint, golden light over the ancient spires and cobblestones of Cambridge. The night had been long and fraught with tension, but they had emerged victorious. The quiet hum of the station continued around them, a reminder that, while one chapter had closed, the world outside carried on, indifferent to the dramas that had unfolded within these walls.

As they made their way through the station, the cool morning air greeted them with a freshness that was almost invigorating. The city of Cambridge, with its blend of ancient history and modern life, was just beginning to stir, the first signs of life emerging as the sun slowly climbed over the horizon.

Rievaulx and Carter paused for a moment outside the station, breathing in the crisp morning air. The cobbled streets were still largely deserted, save for the occasional cyclist or early-morning worker. The city, bathed in the soft light of dawn, felt almost peaceful, a stark contrast to the turmoil that had consumed their lives over the past few months.

"It's strange, isn't it?" Carter said quietly, breaking the silence. "To think that all of this has been going on, hidden beneath the surface, while life here just carries on as if nothing has happened."

Rievaulx's eyes swept over the familiar skyline of the city he had called home for so many years. "Cambridge has always had its secrets," he replied, his voice thoughtful. "But secrets have a way of coming to light, no matter how deeply they're buried."

Carter glanced at him, her expression serious. "And what about *The Fellowship*?" she asked. "Do you really think this is the end? Or just the beginning of something else?"

Rievaulx considered her question for a moment, his mind turning over the possibilities. "*The Fellowship* has been dealt a serious blow," he said finally. "But organizations like that don't just disappear overnight. There will be others who will try to step into the void, who will try to carry on where Lang left off. But we'll be watching, and we'll be ready."

Carter's resolve mirrored in his words. "Then we'll make sure they don't get the chance," she said firmly.

"As for Matthews's murder," Rievaulx continued, sounding every bit as tired as he felt, "we'll have to find another loose thread in the tapestry to tug at. We'll get there. Not today, probably not tomorrow. But it's tied to *The Fellowship*, I'm certain of that. The trick is working out how."

As they turned a corner and disappeared into the bustling streets of Cambridge, the city began to come alive with the sounds and sights of a new day. The ancient spires, the cobbled lanes, the ivy-clad walls—all bore witness to the passage of time, and the endless cycle of life that continued, indifferent to the secrets that lay hidden within its heart.

It was in that moment, as the sun rose higher in the sky, casting its warm light over the city, Rievaulx and Carter knew that no matter what lay ahead, they would be ready.

Chapter 15

Detective Constable Emily Carter sat alone in the stillness of the police station; the usual bustle of the day reduced to a muted hum. The fluorescent lights overhead flickered intermittently, casting a harsh glow that did little to dispel the fatigue weighing her down. The large wooden desk before her was cluttered with a chaotic array of files, notes, and half-empty cups of tea, remnants of a case that had consumed her every waking moment for weeks. The clutter mirrored the turmoil in her mind, each item a reminder of the long hours, the adrenaline-fueled chase, the grim capture, and the harrowing final interview. Now, as the station around her settled into the quiet of the night, the exhaustion she had pushed aside finally caught up with her.

Carter rubbed her temples, trying to ease the tension that had lodged itself there like a stubborn knot. She knew it wasn't truly over, not yet. Matthews's murder was still unresolved, a dark cloud that hung over the otherwise successful conclusion of their investigation. She flipped through the pages of her well-worn notebook, each page a testament to the intricate steps they had taken, the interviews they had conducted, and the evidence painstakingly pieced together. The weight of it all pressed down on her, but beneath the exhaustion, there was a flicker of satisfaction, a quiet pride in having seen the investigation through to its bitter end.

The journey had not been without its trials. Carter had always understood that the road to becoming a respected detective would be fraught with challenges. The Equal Pay Act and the Sex Discrimination Act had opened doors, but the shadows of old prejudices lingered, making every success feel hard-won. In her early days on the force, she had often doubted herself, second-guessed her instincts because the men around her did. But this case, this tangled web of deceit, corruption, and murder, had forced her to trust those very instincts—and they had not failed her.

She thought back to her first days on the force: the sidelong glances from her male colleagues, the casual dismissals of her ideas, the subtle but unmistakable signals that she didn't belong. Even Rievaulx, with his calm, assured manner, had taken time to recognize her abilities, yet the events of the past few weeks had brought a shift, an unspoken acknowledgment of her strength. She had felt it in the way he listened to her, in the moments he relied on her judgement during the most critical phases of the investigation.

Flipping to a blank page in her notebook, Carter began to jot down her thoughts, a habit she had developed early in her career, a way to process the chaos and find clarity in a world that often felt overwhelming. The words flowed easily, the act of writing a comfort as she reflected on the case, on what they had uncovered, and on what it all meant for her.

The case was more than just about solving a murder, she wrote, the pen gliding smoothly across the paper. *It was about understanding the dynamics of power, of privilege, and how they shape the world we live in. The Town vs. Gown conflict, so often dismissed as nothing more than a quaint rivalry, revealed itself to be something much deeper, much darker. It's a conflict born of resentment, of inequalities that have festered beneath the surface for far too long.*

She paused, the pen hovering above the page as she thought about the students she had interviewed, the locals she had spoken to. The resentment was palpable, a simmering tension that had erupted in the most tragic of ways, yet it occurred to her that it wasn't merely about the University's power over the town, it was about the insidious way that power corrupted, the way it protected those who wielded it, no matter the cost.

Carter's thoughts drifted to Forsyth, to the woman who had been so easily manipulated, so deeply broken by the system that had failed her. She had seen in Forsyth a reflection of her own struggles, her own battles against a world that so often appeared determined to undermine her. Where Forsyth had succumbed to that pressure, Carter had found strength. It was a sobering reminder of the fine line she walked every day.

I've grown as a detective, she continued writing. *Not just in skill, but in understanding. Understanding the complexities of the world we operate in, the human frailties that drive people to commit unspeakable acts. And perhaps most importantly, I've learnt to trust myself, to trust my instincts, even when others might doubt them.*

She set the pen down and leaned back in her chair, a small, satisfied smile playing on her lips. The case was officially over; the paperwork would soon be filed away, and life would move on. She knew, though, that the lessons she had learnt, the confidence she had gained, would remain with her long after the echoes of the case faded.

There was still much to do, still battles to fight, but for the first time in a long while, Emily Carter felt ready. Ready to face whatever challenges came her way, ready to prove to herself and to the world that she belonged here, that she was more than capable of holding her own.

With a final glance at her notes, she closed the notebook and stood, a sense of closure washing over her. As she left the station, the cool night air greeted her, invigorating and refreshing. She allowed herself a moment to breathe, to appreciate the journey she had been on.

As she walked home through the quiet streets of Cambridge, the pavement glistening under the moonlight, she felt a renewed sense of purpose. Whatever lay ahead, she would meet it with the strength and determination that had carried her this far. And perhaps, she thought, she would inspire others along the way.

THE CAMBRIDGE UNIVERSITY BOTANIC GARDEN WAS a haven of tranquility, a refuge from the relentless pace of life outside its gates. Rievaulx often found himself drawn to its serene paths and lush greenery, especially after the conclusion of particularly taxing cases. Today was no different. The soft rustle of leaves, the gentle hum of insects, and the distant sound of water trickling through a nearby fountain provided a soothing backdrop as he wandered the garden's winding trails, seeking solace in nature's embrace.

Rievaulx had always been a man of contemplation, a thinker who valued solitude and reflection. As he ambled through the garden, his thoughts returned to the events of the past few weeks, the grim discovery of Atherton's body, the unravelling of the clandestine secret society, and Lang's desperate flight into the night. Yet, more than the individual components of the case, his mind lingered on the broader implications of what they had unearthed. The corruption festering within the university, the abuse of power by those charged with its stewardship, was a betrayal of everything Cambridge was supposed to stand for.

He paused by a bed of orchids, their delicate petals swaying gently in the breeze, a vivid contrast to the dark undercurrents he had just navigated. The orchid had been central to their investigation, a symbol of both beauty and tragedy, of the twisted way in which Forsyth had tried to reclaim her father's legacy. Rievaulx's gaze softened as he recalled Forsyth's confession, the pain in her voice as she recounted the events that had led to Atherton's demise.

Rievaulx's thoughts drifted back to Lang, the man who had orchestrated so much pain and suffering all in the name of self-preservation. Lang was not the first, and he would certainly not be the last, to exploit the system for his own gain. The secret society that had protected him, that had allowed his transgressions to go unchecked for so long, was a testament to the rot that had taken hold at the heart of the institution.

Yet, despite everything, Rievaulx still harbored a deep love for Cambridge. He cherished its history, its traditions, and the sense of intellectual pursuit that permeated its very air. But that love was now tinged with a profound sadness; a recognition that the place he held in such high regard was not immune to the same flaws that plagued the rest of the world.

"Perhaps that's the real lesson," Rievaulx mused, his voice tinged with melancholy. "Even the most revered institutions are vulnerable to corruption. It's up to us to hold them accountable, to ensure that they live up to the ideals they claim to represent."

As he continued his stroll, his steps slow and deliberate, he grappled with the complexities of what lay ahead. The case was closed, yet the issues it had unearthed were far from resolved. The secret society, *The Fellowship*, was still out there, its members likely regrouping, plotting ways to shield themselves from the impending fallout.

Rievaulx knew that his work was not finished. There were still questions that required answers, still shadows that needed illumination. While he valued the peace and solitude of the garden, he understood that he could not retreat from the challenges ahead.

THE POLICE STATION BUZZED WITH THE low hum of activity as Rievaulx and Carter returned to tie up the final loose ends of the case. The frenetic urgency that had driven them for weeks had now settled into a more measured, deliberate pace. Officers moved through the corridors with a sense of relief tempered by the knowledge that another case was likely just around the corner. The air was thick with the familiar scents of old paper and strong coffee, grounding them in the reality of their work even as they prepared to put this chapter behind them.

In a small, cluttered office at the back of the station, Rievaulx and Carter sat across from each other, the final paperwork laid out between them. The room, cramped and filled with the detritus of past investigations, was alive with the sound of pens scratching against paper and the occasional rustle of a file being opened and closed. It was a routine task, yet it held a significance that both detectives felt deeply. The end of an investigation always carried with it a sense of closure, but also the faintest whisper of uncertainty about what might come next.

Carter glanced up from her report, her brow furrowed in thought. "There are still loose ends, sir," she said, her voice betraying the concern that had been simmering in her mind. "The secret society, *The Fellowship*. Lang may be out of the picture, but they're still out there. And we don't know how deep their influence goes."

Rievaulx nodded, his expression thoughtful as he considered her words. "You're right, Carter. Lang was just one part of a much larger puzzle. *The Fellowship* has been operating in the shadows for years, and its reach extends far beyond what we've uncovered so far."

He leaned back in his chair, his gaze distant as he contemplated the implications. "But we've dealt them a serious blow. With Lang's arrest and Forsyth's confession, we've exposed their activities to the light of day. They won't be able to operate with the same impunity they once did."

Carter set her pen down, her expression serious. "But what if they regroup? What if they find a way to cover their tracks, to protect themselves from the fallout?"

Rievaulx met her gaze, his eyes steady and resolute. "We'll be watching. We'll keep an eye on the members we've identified, continue to gather evidence, and make sure they know that we're not going to let this go."

A small smile crept onto his face, one tinged with camaraderie and appreciation. "Besides, you've proven yourself more than capable of handling this, Carter. If anyone can keep them in check, it's you."

Carter felt a flush of pride at his words, but she quickly pushed it aside, focusing on the task at hand. "Thank you, sir. But I couldn't have done it without you. Your guidance, your experience, it's made all the difference."

Rievaulx waved off the compliment, his expression turning serious once more. "This isn't about me, Carter. It's about doing what's right, about ensuring that the truth comes out, no matter how powerful the people trying to suppress it might be."

He glanced down at the final report, the words blurring slightly as he considered the broader implications of the case. "The University, the town, the people who live and work here, they deserve better than what they've been given. It's our job to make sure that those in power are held accountable, that they can't continue to exploit the system for their own gain."

Carter nodded, her determination mirroring his. "And we will, sir. We'll keep digging until we've exposed every last one of them."

Aunties Tea Shop in St Mary's Passage was a haven of quiet amidst the bustling city. Its old wooden beams and low ceilings, the waitresses in their black dresses and white aprons like maids from a bygone era, gave it a comforting atmosphere. The scent of freshly brewed tea mingled with the subtle aroma of freshly baked scones, creating a space that felt timeless.

Rievaulx settled into a corner table at the back, his hands wrapped around a steaming cup of Earl Grey. Across from him, Lydia sipped her tea, her gaze steady as she studied him over the rim of her cup. She had, to his quiet relief, returned not just to London but to him too. There was a comfort in their shared silence, but it was the kind of comfort that hinted at unspoken thoughts, things left unsaid for too long, like dust settling on forgotten shelves.

"Jonathan," Lydia began, her voice measured, breaking the

silence with the precision of a well-aimed dart. "I think we've reached a point where we need to be more deliberate about our decisions."

Rievaulx nodded, his expression unreadable as he set his cup down with a soft clatter. "I've been thinking the same," he replied. "We've been moving along without much consideration for the long-term, living in the moment, as it were. But that can only take us so far."

Lydia placed her cup on the saucer with a soft clink, her fingers tracing the rim thoughtfully, as if trying to draw out the essence of their conversation. "It's a fine approach for a while, but life isn't just a series of moments strung together. We have to consider what those moments add up to, don't we?"

Rievaulx leaned back, his gaze drifting to the rain-speckled window, where droplets traced erratic paths down the glass. Outside, the world carried on; students cycling past in academic gowns, tourists wandering the cobblestone streets with maps in hand, oblivious to the gravity of the conversation taking place within. "You're right, of course. But the difficulty lies in reconciling our individual paths, doesn't it?"

Lydia arched an eyebrow, a faint smile playing on her lips, the kind of smile that suggested she had just caught him in a moment of vulnerability. "You've always been adept at intellectualizing things, Jonathan. But we're not just dealing with abstractions here. We're talking about our lives, about whether we can merge two very different worlds into something cohesive."

He took a breath. "Are you talking about marriage? Children?" The words emerged awkwardly, as if they'd been filed under "In Case of Emergency" and were now seeing daylight for the first time. They hung there, uncertain, like party guests who'd turned up on the wrong night.

He faltered. If this was the direction they were heading—*if*. A word doing a lot of heavy lifting.

To his quiet relief, Lydia shook her head. A faint smile touched her lips, not unkind, but clearly amused by the effort it had cost him to say it.

"Not yet, Jonathan," she said. "But that might change."

She glanced down, fiddling absently with the cuff of her jacket. "It's easy to think you've made a decision when time's on your side. But one day, it won't be. Then it stops being a decision and starts being . . . a fact."

She looked up again, voice calm but final. "But for the moment?" She gave a small, definitive shake of her head. "Not yet. I mean now. London or Cambridge?"

Rievaulx met her gaze, his expression thoughtful. "Cambridge has been my world for so long, Lydia. It's not just a place, it's a way of life, an intellectual pursuit that's ingrained in every aspect of who I am. The thought of leaving it behind, even partially, is . . . unsettling."

Lydia nodded, her manner calm and measured. "I understand that, and I respect it. But we have to ask ourselves what we're willing to compromise on. You've built a life here, but I've built one in London. We've been balancing on this tightrope for some time now, and it's starting to fray."

Rievaulx tapped his fingers on the table, the rhythm echoing the thoughts racing through his mind. "Compromise is necessary, but it's also fraught with difficulty. If I'm being honest, I've never been entirely comfortable with the idea of splitting my time between two places. It's not just about geography, it's about where I feel most intellectually alive."

Lydia tilted her head slightly, her expression softening. "So, you're saying Cambridge fulfils that need for you in a way that London can't?"

"Precisely," Rievaulx replied, his tone reflective. "Cambridge isn't just my home; it's where my mind is most engaged, where I feel connected to something greater than myself. The intellectual tradition here . . . it's hard to replicate that anywhere else."

Lydia's fingers drummed lightly on the table, the sound a steady beat against the backdrop of their conversation. "And yet, you must admit that the world is broader than this city. London has its own vibrancy, its own intellectual currents. The idea of being confined to one place, especially one so insular, seems limiting."

Rievaulx acknowledged her point. "True. And I'm not blind to the fact that Cambridge can be insular. The academic world here can sometimes feel like an echo chamber, where ideas are discussed endlessly but rarely put into practice. London, on the other hand, is where those ideas are tested against the realities of the world."

Lydia smiled, appreciating his willingness to engage with her perspective.

"So, where does that leave us?"

Rievaulx took a deep breath, considering the question carefully. "Perhaps it leaves us with the understanding that we don't have to decide everything at once. We can explore the possibility of living in both worlds, finding a rhythm that allows us to engage with both Cambridge and London without feeling torn between them."

Lydia considered this, her expression thoughtful. "A dual existence, then? It's not the easiest path, but it's a start. And it gives us time to see how things unfold, without forcing a premature decision."

Rievaulx nodded, his manner more relaxed now that they had outlined a potential way forward. "We can take it one step at a time. There's no need to rush into anything definitive. After all, life has a way of surprising us, doesn't it?"

Lydia's eyes sparkled with a hint of amusement. "That it does. And perhaps we can find a way to surprise ourselves along the way, see where this path takes us without feeling the need to control every aspect of it."

Rievaulx smiled, the tension in his posture easing. "I think that's the most sensible approach. We'll navigate this as we've navigated everything else, with a clear mind and a willingness to adapt."

Lydia raised her cup in a mock toast, a glint of humor in her eyes. "To intellectual rigor and open-mindedness, then."

Rievaulx clinked his cup against hers, a smile tugging at the corners of his mouth. "To the journey ahead."

As THE FIRST LIGHT OF DAWN broke over Cambridge, the city was bathed in a soft, ethereal glow. Delicate shades of pink and gold painted the sky, and the ancient architecture looked almost otherworldly, softened by the early morning mist that clung to the edges of the River Cam. The iconic spires and towers of the Colleges emerged through the haze like sentinels of history, their reflections shimmering faintly in the water below, creating a mirror image that blurred the line between reality and reverie.

Rievaulx cycled through the deserted streets, the steady rhythm of his peddling matching the calm that had settled over the city. The cool air touched his face, carrying with it the gentle sounds of birds beginning to stir in the trees. It was a far cry from the tension and urgency that had gripped him in recent weeks, and he found himself savoring the peacefulness, letting it wash over him like a balm for his weary soul.

As he rode along the paths that wound through the heart of Cambridge, his thoughts inevitably drifted back to the case that had consumed his life. The secret society, the twisted motives, the lives that had been shattered, it all felt like a distant memory now, something neatly tied up and put away. And yet, Rievaulx knew better than to believe that anything in Cambridge was ever truly resolved. The city, with all its layers of history and tradition, had a way of holding onto its secrets, burying them deep beneath its tranquil surface, only to have them resurface when least expected.

He turned onto the Backs, the narrow path that ran alongside the river, offering a view of the majestic Colleges with their manicured lawns and ivy-covered walls. The mist hung thick here, hovering just above the water like a ghostly veil. As Rievaulx cycled along, he felt a strange sense of timelessness, as if he were moving through a landscape that had remained unchanged for centuries.

The familiar comfort of his flat greeted him as he stepped through the door, the scent of old books and polished wood enveloping him in a sense of calm. The city outside was just beginning to stir, but already the day felt different, filled with a quiet energy that hinted at new beginnings.

He set his bicycle against the wall and walked into the living room, his thoughts still lingering on the case, on the threads that had been tied up and those that had been left hanging. *The Fellowship*, for all the damage it had caused, was still a shadowy presence in his mind, a reminder that some secrets were never fully revealed, that some mysteries persisted despite their best efforts.

As he moved toward the window, the telephone on the side table rang, cutting through the silence with a sharp, insistent tone. Rievaulx hesitated for a moment before picking it up; the receiver cool against his ear.

"Rievaulx here," he said, his tone as steady as ever, though his mind was already sharpening to a fine edge.

On the other end, Carter's voice cut through the line, cool but with an undercurrent that Rievaulx had come to recognize. "Sir, it's Carter." There was a slight tremor, almost imperceptible, but it was there, a signal that something had shifted. "I've been going over the case files again, and I've found something . . . something that might indicate, that as we suspected, *The Fellowship* is still very active."

Rievaulx's fingers tightened around the receiver, the shift in gears almost palpable as his mind began to churn through possibilities. "Go on," he urged, his voice a model of composure, though the intensity beneath it was unmistakable.

"There are references in some of the older documents, bits I initially overlooked, thinking they were insignificant. But when you piece them together, they start to form a different picture. It suggests *The Fellowship* hasn't disbanded at all. They're still out there, still pulling strings, but quietly, in the background." Carter's voice dipped slightly, as if she were holding back, and then she added,

"And there's something about Grayson. I almost missed it, hidden, seemingly inconsequential."

Rievaulx waited, the silence between them thick with anticipation. "Grayson's involvement," Carter continued, "it's deeper than we anticipated."

Of course, it was. A familiar tingling sensation crept up Rievaulx's spine, a mix of excitement and a gnawing unease. The case had been declared wrapped up, all the loose ends neatly tied, or so they had thought, but this . . . this was a thread that suggested otherwise, something unfinished, something still lurking in the shadows. *The Fellowship* wasn't content to fade into obscurity. They were still playing their clandestine games, and that meant the danger hadn't passed. There were secrets yet to be unearthed.

"How deep?" Rievaulx asked, his tone deceptively mild, though the question was loaded.

Carter hesitated, as if weighing her words. "Well," she said cautiously, "we never did establish who *The Curator* was."

"Ahh," Rievaulx exhaled slowly, the sound more a contemplative sigh than anything else. It was the kind of breath that signaled both understanding and the knowledge that what lay ahead was going to be far from simple. The mention of *The Curator*, the shadowy figure who had danced around the edges of their investigation, was a reminder that *The Fellowship's* web was more intricate than they'd dared to imagine.

This deadly game was very much afoot, and Rievaulx knew that exposing *The Fellowship* would be a long, grueling, and dangerous business. He reminded himself that this wasn't chess. There were no rules. Just consequences.

"Good work, Carter," he said, his voice firm with resolve. "We'll investigate this—discreetly, of course. The last thing we want is to alert them that we're onto them."

"Understood, sir," Carter replied. "I'll start investigating the connections, see if I can find anything that links them to current events."

"Keep me updated," Rievaulx said. "And Carter—be careful. We're dealing with something that goes deep, and we can't afford any mistake or to put ourselves in danger."

"Will do, sir," she replied, her tone steady with determination.

As he hung up the phone, Rievaulx felt the familiar stirrings of purpose. The case had been closed, but the story was far from over. There were still shadows lurking in the corners of Cambridge, secrets to be brought into the light; as long as there was work to be done, Rievaulx knew he would be there, ready to face whatever challenges lay ahead.

Nancy L. Mangan holds a master's degree in medieval history and spent several years working within the Department of Zoology at Cambridge University. Originally from New Zealand, she later became the proprietor of the beloved Black Cat Café in Cambridge, a haven for students, academics, artists and eccentrics alike. Her connection to the city continues to inform her fiction, which draws on the intricate processes of historical research: following faint trails, uncovering obscured truths, and piecing together hidden narratives. For Nancy, crafting a mystery is not unlike studying the past as both require patience, curiosity, and an eye for the significance of what others overlook.

She now divides her time between Ely, in the heart of Cambridgeshire, and Ullapool in the Scottish Highlands. When she's not writing, Nancy house- and pet-sits in evocative locations across the UK and Europe, most recently aboard a catamaran in Cartagena, Spain. Each new place adds a layer of inspiration and atmosphere to her work, as she continues to explore the human stories, both imagined and historical, that lie beneath the surface.

www.ingramcontent.com/pod-product-compliance
Lightning Source LLC
LaVergne TN
LVHW031539060526
838200LV00056B/4575